Shake
Hands
or
Die

2 December 2023

To Lyn,
With best wishes
Michael

Shake Hands or Die

Michael Northey

Michael Northey

Matador
9 Priory Business Park,
Wistow Road, Kibworth Beauchamp,
Leicestershire. LE8 0RX
Tel: 0116 279 2299
Email: books@troubador.co.uk
Web: www.troubador.co.uk/matador
Twitter: @matadorbooks

ISBN 978 1785898 372

British Library Cataloguing in Publication Data.
A catalogue record for this book is available from the British Library.

Printed and bound in the UK by TJ International, Padstow, Cornwall
Typeset in 11pt Bembo by Troubador Publishing Ltd, Leicester, UK

Matador is an imprint of Troubador Publishing Ltd

To Margaret

Chapter 1

He was very good at washing feet. 'Best foot-wash in town,' he said, 'pity it's only once a year. It's a pity,' he said. 'If we could do it even once a month, we'd fill the church, grow the congregation and cash all year round.'

He did such a good foot-wash just before Easter that people flocked in from half the county. Giggling teenagers told their friends. Middle-aged mums nervous of those little nibbling fish that eat dead skin did not hesitate. Tired professionals dropped in on the way from work.

Maisy Dwyerson was always first in the queue. It was the custom at St Martha's Parish Church, Hillford, that anyone could come to the front, sit down and have their turn. He accepted all-comers and was proud he was not so pedantic as to stick rigidly at twelve people. That's not the way we do things at St Martha's, he told the clients.

It was a rolling system. There were twelve chairs, one each for the Disciples for he had to keep some symbolism, but once you had your foot done, you moved away and the next person sat. He made a grand picture of humility, cassock hitched high, large towel round his waist. His lay reader poured the water, while he both washed and wiped.

However long it took, each person got their foot washed. One foot only, mind. If one foot were washed, there was no need for the other, as the person was now wholly clean. Maisy loved it and always insisted on the two. 'Vicar,' she said, 'why did He Above give us two feet if he wanted you to wash only one?'

Every year he explained. It was no good. Maisy simply smiled. 'Very good, Vicar, now can I have the two? You do it so well.' She did not tell him that she looked forward all winter to the sensations from his manly and sensitive hands.

'Father John,' he sighed. 'Don't call me Vicar. Call me Father, or John, or Father John. I don't mind.'

'Just as you say, Vicar,' she smiled.

He sighed and washed both her feet. Just hers, just the one parishioner.

He was effective and well-liked. He preached a good sermon, not too long. His services moved along briskly. He had most of the gifts of a successful pastor. He lacked one thing.

He flatly refused to stand by the door after service and shake hands.

The inevitable complaints came to a crisis two years into his ministry. During his first few weeks he was given the benefit of the doubt. Everyone expected the new vicar to make some changes, have his funny little ways. 'He'll get used to us,' said Old Harry, 'once he settles and sees how things are done.'

He did not. The first three weeks people excused him for not being at the porch to say goodbye. Old Harry said, 'He's busy counting all the extra collection in the vestry, with all these people come to see what he's like,' and laughed into his wise old beard.

From the fourth week, people began to be offended. He doesn't care for us, some people concluded. The first exodus occurred; ten people transferred to St Calida's, and were not seen again. Four others went over to Rome and three joined the Salvation Army. Otherwise things settled. New people came along from the new housing, mainly single, professional people and young families with their one or two children. The congregation and Father John got along quite well during the first year of novelties.

Father John was friendly during the services. He had no problem in greeting people during the Peace, where people wander about mid-service saying hello, peace, waving, some greeting others with a chaste hug, in general recognition of being one big family. He had a nice smile. Only he never stood at the church door after service to shake hands or say goodbye.

The year of novelties made up for this at first. He was good at washing feet. At Pentecost – which at St Martha's was known as Whit Sunday, and Father John soon put them right about that one – he laid on a special treat. To illustrate the gift of tongues, he did not speak in tongues – that was done in other places. Rather, he acted in papal fashion. He learnt "The Lord be with you" in the forty most widely spoken languages. He spoke them all in a faultless accent from memory. At the astonished applause which greeted this feat, he smiled, nodded, and raised his hand for silence. 'You see, dear sisters and brothers, how our faith is one for the whole world.'

That gained him a few more weeks. The rumbling currents of discontent over his unpastoral lack of handshaking after the service had not really gone away.

St Martha's was waiting.

At every season he excelled. He allowed Harvest Festival. He recognised that the old tableau displays of fruit and vegetables, such as in an old-fashioned market, or a new-fashioned farmer's market, were not the modern thing. These days most people trundled down to supermarkets and bought as many tins and packaged goods as they did fresh fruit and veg.

He made things modern. He asked everyone to bring a tin. He called it "Bring a Tin Sunday." During the service everyone was invited to stand at the back of church. People then walked down the aisle and placed their tin on the front table. However, anyone who wanted was dared to play a special game, to show their joy at the Lord's goodness. The servers and choir led the way.

They rolled their tins down the aisle. Old Harry was scandalised for the moment, then joined in with enthusiasm. Maisy rolled two tins of baked beans. Three noisy boys tried to knock each other's tins off course. About one third of the people rolled their tins. Some guided them along, curling fashion, some used tenpin bowling techniques, some did the roll in stages along the pews. Most people walked with their tin to the front. Some people in wheelchairs rolled their tins and chased after them.

It was universally agreed it was the most fun Harvest Festival for years. Father John said it was one more example of the Lord wishing people to take joy in creation.

Only he never stood at the church door after service to shake hands or say goodbye.

On Advent Sunday, he got everyone to light one candle and wave it, and he gave everyone sweets. On Christmas

Eve, at Midnight Mass, he gave everyone a small wrapped present. The church aflame with candles and coloured wraps was like a Russian palace. Everyone fluttered lit sparklers in the air.

At Epiphany he shocked everyone by bringing a llama into church. It was under the supervision of a friend of his, a keeper at the local wildlife park. Father John apologised that it wasn't a proper camel, and that there were not three of them, one each for the Wise Kings, although it was not certain there were three Wise Kings, even though there probably were, judging from the Three Gifts. He wanted to bring alive the mustiness and difficulties faced by the kings, and the sacrifices they had made, and we should too. The children loved the beast's raw smell.

And so it went on; at every festival, he livened it up with unusual, effective and doctrinally correct illustrations. He was attracting a new, young and lively congregation. Well into his second year, Father John was feeling at home. Only he never stood at the church door after service to shake hands or say goodbye. The core of the congregation did not like it. The majority of those who attended week after week and not just the special times began to feel left out. Trouble was brewing into crisis.

It blew up quite suddenly. A regular family had a barbecue and some of their friends asked about the new vicar. It came pouring out: OK; weird; tries too hard; does funny things but ignores the basics; unfriendly, neglects people; no respect; too busy getting in new people, no time for the existing ones. True he was good when Ben got ill;

always smiles at you in the street; does a good sermon; nice speaking voice; always very polite when he does speak to you.

But he doesn't shake hands after service. He's not there for you. He doesn't really love us.

Several families and long-standing members of the church were having similar conversations. They decided to ask the churchwardens to have a word with the vicar.

The catalyst was visitors from Vermont. Every two or three years a couple came over to England for summer vacation and always attended a morning service at St Martha's. They gazed in pride at the great sculptured plaque on the wall, commemorating their puritan ancestor Thomas Cheesewright Esq., who had fled in the time of James II.

They loved the old service and the friendly old vicar, who always asked the same questions about snowy Vermont. He welcomed them after service at the church door, as part of his congregation, with hearty handshakes all round, and when he was free then walked them round the church, always adding a new little fact about Thomas, or the flaking plaster in the vestry, or a new discovery made about the old brickwork, and then led them to join everyone in the church hall for coffee. The visitors made sure to leave a wadge of dollars.

They returned after a three-year gap and found the new vicar did a fine modern service. He was young; Ethel thought around thirty-seven, with a fine head of blond hair, good-looking in a quaint English way, medium height, neat figure. Yet after the service, he was invisible.

The family from Vermont missed their ritual. They

were told the new man did not welcome people at the door.

'Henry,' said Ethel, 'we come all this way and the minister won't talk to us.'

'Seems so, honey,' said Henry. 'Let's go get coffee.'

They took themselves to the hall, met old friends, were warmly greeted and met the new vicar. He was most interested in their story.

'Nice to meet you, sir,' said Henry.

'Guess you don't shake hands no more, though,' said Ethel. 'It's got to be the new liturgy – makes the minister too busy to meet folks at the church door. Guess that's it.'

'Father John,' he said. 'Please call me John. It is lovely to see you. Thank you for coming, what a great custom you have.' He gave them a friendly smile.

'But don't get no tour. Don't get no handshake,' said Ethel, later in the hotel. 'I guess he's one of those ministers who thinks church is only about religion.'

They decided to tell the churchwardens. It wasn't right for visitors to come from right round the world and the minister won't even wait at the door to say hello. Does he not know how much that means to ordinary folk? There's got to be hundreds of people come round the world to see this fine old church and no welcome and handshake from the minister. It just ain't right.

Faced with four families, upset Americans and five or six other complainants, the churchwardens had a consultation. As senior lay administrators it was their job to keep the show on the road.

'Can't have mutiny among the troops,' said Major

Blake. He had left the army ten years ago and now ran a small horticultural company. 'If the punters are unhappy, it's down to the officers. No such thing –'

'– as bad soldiers, only bad officers,' said Polly. She grinned.

'Took the words right off me.' He laughed. 'You know me too well.'

'I love it when you put on the military act. You're sweet when you do that. We both know you're really into flower power these days, Bernard.'

'Time for tactical withdrawal,' he said. 'Now, what do we do about Father John? He's upsetting the troops. Can't have it, can't have it.'

'Why don't we just tell him there's a problem and ask him nicely to do what they want?'

'Dammit, Polly, just tell him his duty. When I was in the army, if I told a man to go, he just went.'

'… and if I tell a man to come he always does.' Polly giggled.

'Behave.'

'Let's invite him to my best coffee and cake and I'll use my charms, eh?'

'Polly, put the kettle on.'

Three days later, Father John, Polly and Major Blake formed a triumvirate in her cottage. The major and Polly worked at strategy and some tactics in advance. The major admired her hollyhocks and asked for seeds for his business.

'Everyone loves your ministry, they really do, John,' said Polly, as John wolfed down her home-made chocolate cake. He was a vicar who truly liked tea. Polly gave him Earl Grey and not her best Brazilian coffee.

'How kind,' he said, and waited for the "but".

'But, dear chap, they were just wondering why you don't say goodbye to the troops at end of service, with a firm handshake, that sort of thing, eh? They want that.'

'It's nothing to do with health issues, is it?' asked Polly. She ran a little alternative health business on a part-time consultancy basis. 'Did you, for example, get norovirus on a cruise and it's frightened you from human contact?'

'No,' said John.

The silence rumbled on for a full half minute.

The major rushed in. 'Can we help you, dear man? Not everyone's cup of tea, admitted. But the troops expect. Duty calls. Part of job. In my day…'

'What is the problem, Father?' It was hard to resist Polly's direct gaze.

'That is something I will not discuss. There is no problem. I choose to run the church in my own way.'

'But, John—'

'I'm sorry. I have to go now. Thank you for a lovely tea, Polly. I love your chocolate cake, I really do.' He dusted the crumbs from his cardigan on to her carpet. He stood up to go. A dark shadow stirred in the corner of the room. It stood, bounded across and blocked the priest's way. It growled.

'Oh dear, he doesn't like tension.' Polly was close to tears. The large black cross-bred Labrador reared up.

'Down, Caesar!' yelled Polly. 'It's only the vicar and he's going now.'

'See you, Father,' said the major.

'Go now, John, see you later.'

Father John left in one piece.

The churchwardens let it be known they had tried and failed. For the next five weeks the congregation was down. Professor Tavistock applied his powers of logic to the situation. He advised everyone to calm down. 'That whereof nothing can be done, thereof we must remain inactive,' he said.

It was no good. Pressure mounted on the churchwardens to do something, or what's the point of them, people grumbled. Polly and the major referred the matter to the archdeacon. 'That'll sort it,' said the major. 'Nobody disobeys the archdeacon.'

Archdeacon Barbara had fought hard to get where she was. She was a veteran of the battles to gain women their rightful place in church authority. Very few people went against her wishes. She had a secret weapon. She was a thoroughly loveable person, with great understanding of people and their foibles, and knew how to laugh at herself. Her charm was legendary.

She did not summon John to her office in the cathedral precincts. She did not ask him out to coffee at Costa's or anywhere they might be overheard and he embarrassed. She invited herself for morning coffee at his house at eleven on a hot Tuesday.

He made an exception to his rule of tea and drank coffee with her. He offered her some German biscuits with chocolate on them.

'Oh, how nice, John,' she said. 'Splendid place you've got here. Not bad at all for a man.'

'How kind,' he murmured.

'Sorry, John, a girl can't help teasing. For a man who lives alone, and no housekeeper, you really have got this place neat. Meant as a compliment, Father.' She laughed, and patted him on the arm. 'It's really good.'

'Thank you. You didn't come here to admire my furnishings.'

'True.' She took a demure sip of coffee. 'Mind if I dunk my biscuit?' she said and did it anyway.

The silence stretched.

'OK, John, let's talk ministry.'

'If you insist.'

She leant over and patted his other arm. 'Such modesty,' she laughed. 'You know you're a damn fine priest.'

'If you say so.'

'Come on, John, not so defensive. We're friends.'

'I'm waiting for the "but". Look, Archdeacon, it's a pleasure to see you, but you don't invite yourself to my house just for coffee, cakes and compliments.'

She flicked back her hair, as she did in her student days. 'When did a woman last invite herself to your place, John? Do you think I'm attractive?'

'Archdeacon!'

She laughed. 'Gave you a shock, didn't I? Forgive my private parable. Two can play at being unorthodox. We love your modern, wacky methods, John, yes we do – but just sometimes they can frighten and shock people; like I did you, just now.'

He looked thunderous.

'Oh, John, I'm sorry. Really sorry – forgive me any abuse of power.' She looked like a little girl walking to the naughty step.

He laughed. 'Me too; take myself too seriously. Tell me, Barbara, did you ever get, do you ever get called Babs?'

'Frequently: sometimes Babe; by best friends, by a boyfriend long ago, and my worst enemies. When I was fighting for women in the church, my enemies called me that to pull me down. No, sorry, my opponents. In the church we have no enemies – just people entitled to their own principled opinions. Room for everyone, John, room for all.'

She brushed imaginary crumbs from her lips, and tidied her dress. She curled her legs under her. She was not wearing clerical costume.

'You're doing it again.'

'Yes, John, I am.' She made no attempt to charm him. 'Yes, John. You see how it upsets people when one persists. When one sticks with unusual behaviour but refuses to do what is normal and comfortable.'

'Me and my gimmicks in church. And I won't stand in line and shake hands with people. And I won't change my ways.'

'No one wants you to change, John, please do keep your wonderful wacky services, yes do. Only I beg, please also, and as well, give people what they need; the cosy greeting at the end of service, the comforting handshake, to show them, and make them feel their pastor cares. John, love, it's not either or, it's both and.'

She leant over as if to pat his arm again, but he brushed her off.

12

She stared at him. It was like a light slowly dawning in a dark room. She looked at him. 'Oh, I see. Oh, John, I see, I see. Did you love her very much?'

The next port of call was the bishop. He was astonished when the archdeacon told him she had failed in her mission. 'Babs,' he said, 'if you can't persuade him, what chance have I got?' He put his fist to his forehead in exasperation. 'Babs, what can I do that you can't?'

'Exert a little manly episcopal authority?'

'Babs, stop it. When you get to be bishop – and believe it, you will – you'll find it doesn't work that way.'

She smiled and patted his arm. 'I'll say one for you.' She swished round in her black robes and opened the old oak door. 'Best of luck.' She was gone.

The following Friday, Bishop Edward called Father John in for a warm weekend chat.

'Come in, dear fellow, come in,' gushed the bishop.

Father John looked round at the rose-rich lounge with its warm red carpet. The view outside was glorious. It was early July and the sun was hot.

Was this fellow's sniff caused by hay fever, wondered the bishop. Or was he unable to disguise his disapproval of this lovely room, being a puritan at heart? That might explain this handshake nonsense.

Father John accepted a cup of coffee, one milk, no sugar. The bishop did not think to offer tea. No, thank you, very kind, Bishop, no shortbread but Father John would accept a plain Rich Tea biscuit. Bishop Edward took two chunks of shortbread. He was a big man who had played rugby for the England B team. He was a hearty no-nonsense sort of guy who said he liked the gargoyles on his cathedral. They were the only thing that made him feel handsome, he told his wife.

She informed him that she had not chosen him for his looks. She had discerned rare spiritual qualities in him, she said. It had taken him their whole first year to realise that she was teasing.

'Right, John, tell me about this handshake business. You're a fine priest, John, but dammit why don't you seal things with a handshake? Say hello to people at end of service, send the team home happy, like everyone else does?' He crunched off a slab of shortbread. 'I'm getting a lot of complaints, John. Don't like to hear it of such a fine chap.'

Father John sighed. 'You too, Bishop.' His voice implied it was the hundredth time this week he had been reminded that the sun rises in the east.

'Your choice, John, your choice. Let's talk about it, shall we? It's all very odd, very odd. Here you go on the one hand improving the congregation – '

'Increasing, Bishop, increasing. Who am I to say if they are improving in their life and faith?'

The bishop was irritated. He was beginning to understand why nobody had got anywhere with this pedantic fellow. He pressed on. 'Very good, John, very good. So why won't you do the decent thing and shake hands with people? Might help improve their spiritual qualities, eh?' He raised his paw. 'Tell you what, John, let me guess. I'll go through some reasons, you tell me if I'm right, then we'll talk through and see what we can do to break out of the scrum. What do you say?'

Father John said nothing.

'One: they're not here in church to see you. They go to meet God. You don't want a cult of celebrity. So you leave 'em at the end to think of God, not you. Let 'em leave after service with their mind on higher things than you.'

'If you say so, Bishop.'

'But damn it man – you're standing in for God in church – they meet you, they meet God. You're his sales representative – as good as they're going to get. But you won't do the after-sales service, after service, if you get my drift.'

'All very theological, Bishop.'

Bishop Edward put his great fist to his head. He looked as if he could do with a double whisky.

'Let's try again. Very well. You do wonderful services. People like them. They like you – except they think you are aloof. You're so busy giving your little shows that you haven't got time for people. It's just what you say you don't want, John, a cult of celebrity. Here's the famous showman, star of pew and pulpit, full of his act – and I'm afraid, John, some would say, so busy showing off, making himself the centre of attention, he has no time for people. It's all very self-willed, I am afraid, Father.'

'Who exactly are my accusers, Bishop?'

'Just talking generally, John, talking generally.'

'I am sorry, Bishop, if the impression given is what you describe. Please believe me that is not my intention. I am just a small cog in God's machine.'

'That's good, John, and a very good image. I must use it myself. Thank you.'

'You're welcome.' John smiled.

'OK, John, OK. You're not a celebrity show-off. I will give you my third and final point.'

'Somehow I thought there would be three.' John smiled again.

'You do a brilliant foot-wash. Once a year. You wash more feet than the whole of St Barnabas, St James the Greater, St Mary's and Saints Crispin and Crispinian put together. Very good, John, very good. The foot-washing is a brilliant example given to us of serving other people.

But can't you see it, man, can't you see it? In those days foot-washing was the ordinary way of looking after people. Nothing better than a good foot-wash after coming in from the sweaty streets of dust. It was chosen precisely because it was so normal, exactly what people needed. We don't do that now. Don't need to. Did then; just the thing then. Often. Normal. Everyday. We don't do that, John, we don't do that in our normal life, don't need it. For us the everyday expression of friendship, ready to serve people, is your normal, boring, commonplace handshake. Even sometimes through gritted teeth with people you don't like very much.

So, John, why just do the showy and frankly – unnatural – thing once a year when you would much better express your love every week with an ordinary smile and handshake after church?'

The bishop sank back exhausted. He rarely gave such a long speech in private. His pugilistic nose was redder than usual.

'I hear you, Bishop. I think I express all that during the service.'

'Then dammit, man, why not give 'em a handshake

too at the end? You're living in the past, man. Look, John, if you don't shake hands, people think you're unfriendly. They won't come again. Church will die, John. Shake hands or die.'

'But Bishop, I am accused of methods which are only too modern.'

The bishop angrily crammed another piece of shortbread into his mouth. 'We're getting nowhere. We'll have to end it here, John – I implore you, go away and have a think. Tell me, John, why are you so stubborn? Exactly what is it that makes you so unable to do this normal pastoral duty?'

For the first time, Father John looked uncomfortable. 'I wish I could tell you, Bishop. But forgive me, I cannot. I cannot.'

After the meeting Bishop Edward did some hard thinking. He was not a man easily deflected. He was determined to sort things out. Father John was a good man, as fine a minister as any the bishop had known in twenty years, but like the rich young man in the scriptures, he seemed to lack one thing. Was it that basically he didn't like people?

Bishop Edward decided on a bold course of action. By pure good fortune, he was free that last Sunday of July. Perfect. It was nearest to St Martha's feast day. He would pay an official patronal visit to the church and take the service alongside John. He would learn a lot, Father John wouldn't mind, the congregation would love it.

And what is more, he the bishop would give an example of true humility and service by shaking hands with all and sundry at the end.

It was a very nice, safe service. Word had got around that the bishop was on his way. The congregation was a very decent size for the start of the school holidays. Father John put on a special show of swinging incense, specially flavoured with cedar of Lebanon. Five choirpersons processed in scarlet robes. The organist played his best anthems and the Psalm for once was sung. It was High Church Anglican at its best.

Father John was good as gold. There were no gimmicks. People remembered last year when he had brought in a microwave oven. He plugged it in and heated up a pre-prepared cup of soup. Remember, he said, how St Martha had to work so hard in the kitchen to look after her guests only to be told that her sister Mary was wiser to sit in the lounge listening to stories. Yet Martha too would have had the chance to sit and listen if only modern methods had been available then. He had always felt a soft spot for Martha, who he suspected had a raw deal. In some ways we now lived in happier times, but the lesson of serving others was still relevant. He then drank the cup of soup.

There were no such gimmicks today. The hymns were modern and regular, the readings were relevant and the bishop was entrusted with the sermon. It was sensible and it was long. The bishop said he felt a soft spot for St Martha who did all the hard work, only for her sister Mary to get the credit for sitting and being a good listener. However, Martha was so busy getting Jesus his supper that she had no time to enjoy his company and hear his liberating message. So it is with us. Are we not in danger sometimes of being so busy with our smartphones, our apps, our computers, our iPads and all the range of gadgetry and gimmicks that we don't actually have time for either God or other people? We must set ourselves free. We need to avoid too many modern fads and settle for solid things. Father John gave the bishop an old-fashioned stare at this point. So it went on. Maisy got through half a packet of fruit pastilles, nodding vigorously. Several people dozed half-listening in the hot sun, which flung colours through the stained glass saints.

It all came to a nice end, perfectly regular, all present and correct, team playing well. As the last hymn played, the little procession moved off. Halfway down the central aisle they turned right towards the north porch door and then right again towards the vestry.

Then it happened. The bishop and Father John were at the end. At the last moment before their final turn, Bishop Edward seized Father John's arm in a firm rugby grip. He was certain that the man would now see sense and join him at the door to finally – finally meet people and shake hands. He would give John no choice. The bishop would guide his man into position.

You do not defy a bishop in church.

The bishop's grip was implacable. He moved John inexorably to the dark recesses of the north door, like a New Zealand winger in all-black strip heading for the try line. It was the old muscular Christianity.

John struggled but he was trapped. He hissed at the bishop, who smiled like an avenging angel. John was being driven to a rocky shore with no escape. He had no wish to make a scene in church and the bishop knew it. John had not the strength to steer against the bishop's strong body and the bishop knew it.

Bishop Edward was smiling in quiet triumph. There

was always a way to bring recalcitrant clergy to heel. Once at the door, squashed next to a beaming bishop, there would be no way that Father John could refuse to meet and shake hands with the happy, excited crowds thronging round the bishop. People would line up first with the bishop for a cheery word, then Edward taking good care to block off John's escape would shunt each one along to John. He could hardly then refuse the hand of friendship.

John would soon accept the logic of the situation, and find he liked meeting people in this way after all. Whatever the blockage was would be healed and removed. It would be like a pastoral exorcism. People would love it and praise and thank the bishop for putting everything right. Happiness all round.

Father John did the unthinkable. He stamped hard on the bishop's left foot. Really hard. The bishop yelped but gripped all the harder. A few faces turned round. The choir procession had already disappeared into the vestry.

The people were moving out of their seats. The hymn book gatherers were braced all ready.

Finding that his struggle was unavailing, Father John stamped hard again. Really viciously. The bishop's grip weakened. He yelled, 'Stop it, man!' He regained his grip.

The congregation took real interest. What was going on? Father John had had enough. He gave the bishop a good kick in the leg. The bishop let go and shouted, 'For God's sake, man!' The father and the bishop began to scuffle and struggle.

Now this really was interesting. Maybe it was one of Father John's gimmicks which he had practised with the bishop. It was clearly designed to keep people's interest after the formal service was over. It must have a religious message in it. (The bishop had said something about God.)

The bishop and father appeared to be fighting. The people surged forward and the major interposed his body between the two protagonists. 'Come along, you two,' he commanded. 'I'll get you both a sherry and whatever it is, come along with me and make up.' The two clerics trotted along meekly.

The congregation cheered. Yes, of course. It had obviously all been staged as a practical demonstration of brotherly love; how even the most intractable quarrels were overcome and healed by the Gospel. What a clever vicar: what a lovely bishop.

No one got their hand shaken that day. But everyone felt very much better. It had been the best service for years.

After that they left him alone. The bishop went nowhere near this mad priest who kicked people in church. If he had to deal with him, the bishop would use Babs. She was sympathetic and felt it best to let Father John be in peace. He could sort himself out in the unlikely event he might think he needed sorting. She would be around if he needed her. Archdeacon Babs was surprised how much she wanted that.

For the churchwardens it was business as usual. They did their duties in the normal round. Sometimes Polly thought Father John looked pale, and consulted the major. He told her briskly he could see nothing wrong with the man, beyond tiring his brain with too much reading; nothing that a quick four-mile walk every morning wouldn't cure.

So the autumn weeks drifted by. The first shock was that

Father John did a strictly traditional harvest service. There was a fine display of potatoes, swedes and marrows on a table at the front, with tomatoes, apples, pears and tins of exotic fruits which could not be grown locally. After traditional hymns, a traditional sermon, traditional church lunch, traditional giving of produce to the local food bank, everyone was reassured and disappointed. Father John had lost his zest.

The weeks passed into late October and there was no school half-term special event. Nothing for Halloween or Bonfire Night. All was faultlessly regular, splendidly dull. The traditional congregation held up well and the modern newcomers with or without children stayed away.

There was no concert on 22 November for St Cecilia's Day. There was no more talk of modern music. He frowned on any ideas of replacing the pews with chairs. It was as if the church had reverted to its old ways — minus the handshake of course. Nobody dared to broach the subject. No one thought there was any point.

Father John was becoming listless and depressed. Late November is a time when traditionally many people are weary. It has been a long time since the summer sun and Christmas is nowhere in sight. No one personified this bone tiredness as much as Father John.

People began to whisper, then to chatter and then to wonder how long he would last as their vicar. He'll be gone by Easter, intoned Old Harry. Maisy told Harry she would hear no such nonsense, the vicar was a lovely man and she must ask him round for a proper Sunday roast. Professor Tavistock said he had nothing to say on the subject. He could see no logic in it.

A few people tried to cheer the vicar up but it was no

good. He seemed to have lost heart. Some people started to pray for a miracle.

On the last Sunday in November before Advent, Father John showed a tiny spark of his old flame. He made a point of reading the famous "Stir Up" prayer right at the start of the service. That made people smile. Good man, he still knew how to please people – stir them, even. Traditionalists naturally thought of stirring up the ingredients for Christmas pudding.

It was promising. It had been a long time since one of the vicar's specials. Perhaps he would do one today.

They were disappointed. It was back to basics. The congregation was quite large, but a number of people wondered about sloping off to St Calida's. It was just as traditional there but at least you got a warm handshake and the vicar wasn't depressed.

Everything was normal. Father John clambered into the pulpit to preach. He had done this now since the summer. It was a bad sign – his little talks at the front steps had been so entertaining and so full of message. Now he seemed merely to repeat the Gospel reading in his own words.

Halfway through a tired sermon the north door opened and two women walked in. They sat down discreetly near that door. People turned to see who had come in. One was the archdeacon. The other was an attractive person in her thirties. No one had the slightest idea who she was.

Father John noticed. He sailed on serenely for a couple more sentences and took note of his extra listeners. A few more paragraphs, he stared intently at the two. His engine started to splutter and he nearly ground to a halt. He recovered, struggled on and resumed. His voice was close to breaking. People, chiefly Maisy and Old Harry, who sat near the front, saw the vicar was deathly pale and his face was in deep sweat. He managed to finish and sat down in his seat.

It was also his turn to say the intercessions. When he came to pray for the lonely and dispossessed, his voice broke. He recovered again and all was well.

Father John went through the motions and galloped through the rest of the service at high speed. He kept staring at the congregation. People noticed that today as well as no handshake as per usual, he wasn't even mixing with them for the Peace. He must be seriously ill or depressed. This could not go on.

They noticed his agitation as he constantly stared down the church. What was wrong?

Perhaps he was worried at the archdeacon's sudden appearance. Maybe the vicar was in serious trouble and was about to be sacked. They hoped it wouldn't be in public. That would not be right. He was a good man who had just for the moment lost his way. The service ended, the blessing given, choir left, last hymn, one line left to sing. The vicar had remained motionless in his chair. For a few seconds all was still.

The miracle was swift. Father John seemed to come to a decision. He sprang from his seat and raced like a greyhound down the aisle, skidded right and stood inescapable, alone, at the church door.

Babs smiled and nudged the woman.

She rose and went to Father John.

To everyone's astonishment, in full view of eighty people, John shyly held out his hand. She shook hands with him and would not let go.

The congregation next saw a thing more amazing than any of the previous shows. It was the vicar and this strange woman in a close embrace. Tears were flaming down his cheeks and she was sobbing uncontrollably.

'My love,' she said. 'Forgive me. So, so sorry.'

They clung and swayed together oblivious to the fact they were in church.

'She must have liked his sermon,' said the major.

Laughter eased the tension. The couple broke up, but John would not let go of her hand.

Babs beamed. 'Don't worry, John,' she said, 'she's not going anywhere.'

The congregation mulled round. Father John shook hands with every one of them.

The next morning Father John woke up and was surprised to find a head on the pillow, which had not been there before.

He remembered. A blissful smile broke out on his face. 'Oh, it's you,' he said. 'Would you like me to shake your hand – again?' He roared with laughter.

'Don't,' she said. There were tears on her pillow. 'We will stay together this time? Won't we?'

They sat up without talking. Then John sprang out of bed. He said, 'I'll bring us some tea.'

'No, love,' she said. 'I will.'

'I'm already out of bed. Let me.'

'John,' she said. 'Do as your woman says. Secret of

happiness.' She pulled back the sheets. 'You'll learn.' She was wearing nothing but a vest. As she left the room, she grinned at him over her shoulder. 'You're a very naughty vicar.'

His heart broke then and there with happiness. He was still weeping when she returned with two steaming mugs of tea and three broken biscuits. On a tray. She put them down on the floor and held him tight.

'My tea's not that bad,' she said.

'I know. Sorry. I can't believe you're back.'

She clung on. 'Oh I'm back, my love, my love. If you'll have me that is. You'll never get rid of me now.' She retrieved the tray. 'Here. Tea. And biscuit bits.'

They supped their tea. He said, 'Katie, we've got to talk.'

'Yes,' she whispered. 'We have. That's the bit I'm dreading.'

'You first,' he said.

'No, you. Remember what I said about the secret of happiness.' He remembered that submissive-defiant turn of her lip, which he had adored. He had not expected to see it again. Do as your woman says.

They sipped their tea.

'Katie,' he began. He hesitated. He tried again. 'When we spoke last night…'

She interrupted. 'You said you had forgiven me. It was wonderful to have me back again. That's what worried me.'

'What's to dislike?'

'There was no anger. We should have had a blazing row, lots of tears and only then the forgiveness and welcome.'

'I'm a vicar.'

'You're a man. Look, John, I'm serious. I did you wrong, then I turn up out of nowhere, ask for forgiveness just like that and please take me back, and you do and it's wonderful. But we need to sort out what happened.'

'Why? It won't happen again; will it?'

'No, love, no, not if I live to a thousand years.'

'Well then.'

'It's not that simple. I'm afraid it will poison things. I will always be the errant woman and you will always be the wronged lover and gracious forgiver. It won't work that way. We've got to start again clean, things all settled.'

'OK. Then tell me.'

'First tell me how it was for you.'

'OK. Five years ago, to the week, we got engaged. We celebrated, special dinner, fabulous night. I broke my usual rule – never on Saturday, get full night's sleep, fresh for busy Sunday, on best form for the people in church—'

'Such a puritan, Father John.' She laughed. 'Lots of men sleep better after—'

'You an expert on many men?'

She thumped him on his shoulder.

'That night was wonderful. We were going to float through Sunday, you in the congregation, keep our little secret, special smile as I gave you Communion. We were going to tell everyone on the Monday.'

'Good plan.'

'I never suspected a thing. Everything like a dream. There was a bigger than average attendance, my sermon went well, I was full of energy—'

'—see what I mean?'

'—shook hands with all and sundry left, right and

centre, even that 'orrible old woman who kept telling me I was wrong all the time. Then it was you – the star at the very end of the queue.'

'I was the last?'

'You were the last person I shook hands with in church that day. You went off to your flat. I thought we'd be meeting for supper. I never saw you again.'

'So the last time we touched was a formal handshake in church.'

'Yes.'

'I walked out on you. I was too much of a coward to tell you face to face.'

'I still have the note you sent me.' He quoted it from memory. '*My darling, please forgive me. I love you, I do. But I can't go through with this. I am not ready. I've got to find my own vocation. Please don't try to find me. I have gone to nurse in Africa. They need me even more. You will heal, John, you will, and you will find someone better than me, more worthy. I may fail as a nurse in Africa, but I must try. Why is life so full of conflict? Forgive me. Katie.*'

She winced. 'I did go. I did help for several months. Then I realised it wouldn't work. I came back, trained as a teacher, began a new life, hid up north and was ashamed and decided you would hate me too much for me to make any contact.'

'Katie, Katie, how little you knew me. There's never been any other woman since you.'

'Your archdeacon somehow pieced the story together. She knew both you and your work were suffering. She rooted around in your previous parish. More people had understood what was between us than we realised. I had left more of a trail than I realised. She never gives up, your Babs. Eventually she got at the whole story. One day she turned up in my house after school. She more or less ordered me back.'

'In my interview with Babs I said nothing about a lost love.'

'Oh, she read all that.'

'So,' he said, 'she understood – the last handshake I ever gave in church was to you. If I clung to that as the last handshake I would ever do, it was my only way to cling to your memory. I could not bear to shake hands at the end of service again. I vowed I would never do it.'

'You really mean – any handshake might result in betrayal?'

He was silent.

'I am sorry, John.'

'So much harm has religion done,' he whispered. 'Or in this case, so much harm has a nursing vocation done.'

'That's not fair.'

And then the two of them embarked on the most blazing row either of them had ever known. And the sparks flew, and the wounds were probed, and hard things were said and voices were raised, and the storm came, and the winds blew, and the lightning flashed, and the tears raged. And they knew each other as never before, and they wept and laughed and were healed, and they knew they loved each other for ever, and they would make that silly old bishop and the marvellous Babs marry them at once.

'In the meantime, love,' said Katie, 'will you wash my feet? Both of them?'

'I shall wash you all over. Get in the bath, girl.'

She giggled.

Chapter 2

Fred Vestal wished he could find a good scandal. Circulation was badly down as people got more of their news online. The editor was muttering about staff cuts. That was the biggest scandal; that a man of Fred's ability should even be in the frame for such a thing. His London editor had been instructed by his bosses to send Fred down to Hillford for six months to shake up their sleepy provincial rag. He had six months to get the circulation up. If not, then Fred would have shown he was not worthy of a great London tabloid. He would be out. If the catastrophe should occur, then Fred Vestal would have to go back to teaching. Which would be the scandal of all scandals. Such a waste of talent.

If he could stir up the locals, then it was back to London in glory, perhaps an editorship and appearances on TV press reviews. He would have the career he deserved.

He must start writing for American papers – then he would qualify for the Pulitzer Prize. He wished at times he were a young blonde woman; it would be so easy to seduce a juicy story from a man of power. His only chance of a local scandal was to try his charms on a local head teacher and make her his headmistress. She would reveal all.

He smiled at his wit. He would have to content himself for now, just as a temporary measure, with the dull local round of dull, dull council news, local fetes, noisy students who were not a tenth trouble enough, a restaurant serving dodgy food, a supermarket flooded in the recent rains, traffic chaos on the ring road, hospital incompetence if you could find it. Dull, dull, dull.

It was all so unworthy. Here he was, intrepid Fred, Vestal but no virgin, fearless fighter for truth and there was nothing to be intrepid about. Couldn't he even find a naughty vicar story?

There was that vicar at St Martha's. Fred kicked himself he had not taken his chance – the vicar used to pull crazy stunts: llamas in church, throwing tins of beans down the aisle, dangerous fireworks in church at Christmas. Congregation split and the vicar wouldn't even shake hands with people – Fred could have made a "brings the church into disrepute" story out of that and stirred up the bishop into disowning the mad priest, got some good quotes, maybe with a bit of luck hit the tabloids. Fred would have been noticed. Too late. He had gone quiet before Fred got the chance to quieten him.

Apparently the mad vicar was now living with a strange woman who had turned up one day in church. Nah – "Vicar living in sin" – did not have the same ring as it used to. Not worth a peal of bells. Even vicars lived with people these days.

Rumour had it, since the woman had moved in, the vicar had perked up. His tricks were starting again. Pity he wasn't fiddling with the choir girls – it was even less likely now. That would have sold a few papers. Still, there must be something good there somewhere. Fred would find it now the vicar was starting up again.

Nothing for it. Fred sighed. He would have to go to church next Sunday.

Fred got off to a bad start. He was never late; he had to be known as reliable, as well as maverick and fearless. He generally got better quotes when people were off guard before and after the main event. Who wanted the pompous words of some council boss droning about his successful strategy? What people wanted was the same worthy person falling down a pothole.

He arrived ten minutes late and crept to the third row from the back. Maisy beamed at him and rushed up with service sheet and hymn book. They were all singing from the same hymn sheet, Fred observed, just like the local politicians. He looked round. He had a perfect view.

Fred could not believe his luck.

There was a comely woman with shoulder-length hair, dressed in a one-piece white nightie. It reminded him of those medieval pictures of penitent sinners. She was standing at the front of the choir steps, near the pulpit, and everyone could see her. Fred looked closer. He could not believe his eyes.

She was tied by thick ropes to the reading desk – what was it called? – the lectern. It was something out of a bondage novel. What the…? Was this the vicar's woman?

Fred started taking notes.

The action began. A pantomime dragon appeared and danced about and around the woman. Two children's voices from inside the apparatus hissed in solemn intonation, 'You are going to die. I shall eat you. With my fiery breath I shall cook you. I shall eat you for dinner. Maiden and chips for dinner tonight.' They said this three times.

Other children gathered round imploring the dragon to show mercy and to be kind. They were the local villagers. They promised to feed the dragon a basket of biscuits every day and fish and chips on Fridays if only it would let the woman go.

The dragon stamped its foot and chased the children away. Fred began, against his wishes, to enjoy this. He wondered if the dragon would breathe fire.

No, apparently not. No fire came. It was presumably not beyond the wit of the vicar but was beyond the pale of fire regulations.

Right, where was St George?

He entered right on cue. Up rode the vicar in full garb, robes flowing, fighting for the right, with a great big England football team red cross on his shield, prancing on his makeshift theatrical horse. The audience went wild. St George turned his horse's head right, left, and ahead as the dragon turned.

The people cheered. They clapped, applauded, gave wolf whistles. 'Go for it, Georgie boy,' called out Maisy. The major admired St George's tactics. Cause a diversionary movement, catch the enemy by surprise and up and at 'im. There was an excellent fight. It took quite a time but the result was not in doubt.

St George pierced his lance with great care in the back of the dragon. 'Die, wicked dragon,' shouted Father John. The audience watched in raptures as the beast struggled and staggered round the woman. It died with a great deal of leg waggling from the child actors.

The dragon was dead. The woman gave a radiant smile. St George kissed the woman. The audience stamped and hooted. Even Fred joined in. He had thoroughly enjoyed it. There was a great story here. He had come to scoff and remained for the play.

So this is how vicars got at people these days. This one was clearly very good at it. Fred knew he must get an interview. Then he would know how to spin it. He might even manage a happy wacky story. Happy wacky stories sold nearly as well as shock at other people's sins. There were at least two angles. "Our little city shows the nation how it's done. Church revival starts here. We change the nation for ever." Or: "Charming local custom cheers the nation." Yes, he could sell this story to the red-top tabloids.

Fred was on his way. Thanks, Vicar. Choose the quotes carefully, get some audience colour, and this might be Fred's Big Break-Out Story.

Who would have thought it? It would be a happy wacky story that did it. This was against Fred's deepest convictions. He was sure he would get on by exposing Scandal In The Highest. As a journalist that is what he liked and it was his duty to expose it.

The children bowed. They waved. The mums and dads wiped tears away. The children were led away to other rooms, no doubt to resume their religious studies.

All settled down. The fun was over and the serious Bible readings were due to begin. Fred knew this from his service sheet. It was going to be deadly dull for the next fifty minutes. He would sit through it patiently, for the sake of the goodies at the end.

All that remained was for the woman to be unroped

by St George. (Unroped but not unrobed, thought Fred, amused at his wit. Could he get that in somewhere?) She would go into another room, change her clothes, slip into some demure dress and resume her place in church.

After all, the lectern to which she was tied was needed for the Bible readings. One could hardly stand behind her to read holy messages, while her white negligee revealed her woman's contours so deliciously. Wherever would one look – at the holy reader or at the woman's heavenly blessings?

That was better. Fred smiled. He was himself again.

Absolutely nothing happened. The woman did not move. St George disappeared. The vicar came back in full clerical garb. He sat in his special chair. Nothing happened. There was silence for a whole two minutes.

The audience became restless. Fred was puzzled, then worried. Whatever was this guy playing at? The charming St George scene was becoming sinister. This was not playing by the rules.

Nothing continued to happen. Finally the vicar rose to his feet. He made no reference to the bound woman. He opened his Bible and began to read. It was something about sin. Normally Fred would have been interested as sin was very much his speciality, and sold papers. This time he could not concentrate. Neither could the audience. Something was badly wrong. How could the vicar just drivel on like this? Didn't he know there was a tied up woman just feet away from him?

She was clearly the vicar's girlfriend. Had he really forgotten her in the heat of the religious moment?

The vicar sat on his chair. He looked down deep in

contemplation. He was as still as a cold philosopher's statue. Some people began to cough. The carved angels on the beams looked down impassively. Professor Tavistock gazed round uneasily. This was not normal: it was not logical. The organist wondered if he should strike up a chord. Two butterflies began flapping at the great east window. They stopped and fell on the altar.

Still nothing happened. At the back someone began to cry. The woman bound to the lectern stood still in her bonds. Fred wanted to make notes but the mood held him gripped.

The vicar rose suddenly. He took no notice of the people. As if far away, he produced a Bible from under the chair. As if to himself he read a thunderous passage from one of the fiery prophets. He read a passage from St Paul at his grimmest. He finally chanted a savage passage from a Gospel book denouncing sin. He looked neither at the people nor the stained glass windows nor the pulpit, nor the woman at the lectern nor the hammer beam ceiling nor the whitewashed walls.

The people stood obediently for the reading. At the end the vicar stared at them and waved them to sit. They sat.

There then followed the most thunderous denunciation of wrong, iniquity, moral turpitude, sin and general moral decay heard in that diocese for over twenty years. It would have frightened Moses. The people heard it all in total silence. Their unpredictable vicar had surprised them again. They did not expect this sort of thing in the Church of England.

Fred was impressed. It was all he could do not to

applaud. It was glorious. None of it applied to him of course – but what splendid oratory. No wonder people enjoyed that sort of thing.

Then Fred got angry. It was a vicar's job to be nice. How dare this vicar usurp Fred? It was Fred's job to expose people, name and shame and generally hold people up to ridicule. What was this vicar doing denouncing sin so much? Did he have special knowledge of it? He was going on about the vile, disgusting deeds of nasty terrorists, then on a sort of sliding scale through to robbery with violence, then stealing food from supermarkets and our selfishness in making people so desperate as to make them do that and creating the need for food banks, to being rude to bus drivers, to cutting up people dangerously in traffic. It was utterly weird, this mixing up of things that had nothing to do with each other.

The vicar might think that. Fred, for one, was not buying it. Nobody else did. There was a hell of a difference between what terrorists did and someone losing it with a crazy driver. The vicar was talking a load of taurine effluvia. What was all this stuff about hating sin but loving sinners – we are all in need of mercy, blah, blah? In Fred's book, sinners deserved all they got and it was his job to make sure they got it.

In that instant, Fred conceived a violent hatred of Father John. Fred put aside his plans for a cute story about a nutty vicar and St George. Fred would spin a much better and darker story. He could more than match this man.

Fred could hardly believe what happened next. Suddenly the vicar gave his audience a radiant smile and a big broad wink.

'Scared you there, didn't I?' he said.

Maisy beamed back at him. Trust the vicar to know best. Professor Tavistock reminded himself that whereof we do not understand, thereof we cannot seek comprehension. No, that can't be right – we often seek to understand what we do not at present comprehend. He busied himself in seeking the logical flaw in his thought process. The major wondered about the next prong in the vicar's strategy. It came at once.

Father John sprang to the bound woman, and in three deft steps uncoiled the ropes. She stepped out of them, like Aphrodite from her bath. He kissed her. They both smiled at the congregation. The couple laughed and waved.

'I'm free,' she called. 'Praise be, I'm free,' she sang. It was as lyrical as sudden sunshine on a dark lake. The spell was broken. People laughed and applauded. It was wonderful. A few teenagers did high-fives.

'You see?' said the vicar. 'God's mercy sets us free. All the darkness is forgotten. However bad we have been or awful we feel – it's over, folks, we can be happy, those dark days of sin – yes, awful, never underestimate the badness of things – we must constantly fight wrong, but God sets us free, to be happy and to stay happy. Are we happy now?'

'Yes, we are,' roared, whispered, said, murmured, shouted the audience. Professor Tavistock nodded his head vigorously.

'Here she is then, the woman – who stands for us all today – newly liberated, once tied by the ropes of wrong – now free by the power of the Gospel.'

The audience assented to his proposition. Father John squeezed Katie's hand, gave her a peck on the cheek, and she skipped away into another room. She came back in proper clothes to join the congregation.

The rest of the service proceeded normally. Fred sat it out. He could not believe his luck. He would get a few quotes from the audience. He would seek an interview with the vicar, and maybe the vicar's girlfriend.

It was going to be the most glorious story of Fred's career. It would make his career and get him back to London. It was a fabulous story of a vicar and sex and bondage in public, in church.

Chapter 3

The vicar was most agreeable to an interview. Fred arrived at ten o'clock on the Tuesday morning. He was shown into the main lounge. This was a large room full of light and dancing shadows. It was on a hillside overlooking the city. In the far distance could be seen the cathedral turrets twinkling in the sunlight.

Fred could not help himself. He went over to the window. 'Nice view you've got here,' he remarked.

They shook hands. 'Yes, thank you,' said Father John. 'It's inspiring – nice mixture of nature, city and cathedral. It's lovely to see the changing seasons. Yes, I'm very lucky.'

Katie came in. She smiled. 'Make yourself at home,' she said. 'I won't stay. I'm sure you men have a lot to talk about and don't need me.' She liked the look of the young journalist. Medium tall, trim figure starting to fill out, pale in his face, he was smart in a grey suit, though it was a little crumpled. His burgundy tie matched his lovely dark brown hair. Katie reckoned he was making an effort for the vicar. He even spoke with a really nice Lancaster accent. Though a daughter of York herself, she could forgive him that.

Fred liked her spirit. They shook hands.

She went out, and almost before the vicar and the journalist had time to size each other up, she returned. She banged the door open. She was carrying a tray with real fresh coffee, hot milk, cream and a plate of Belgian chocolate biscuits. 'Have fun.' She grinned and was gone.

'It's very good of you to see me, Vicar, and I'm really grateful. My readers have heard such a lot about the great work you are doing, and would be glad to hear more. In this day and age, it's wonderful to see the church doing so well. They say it has a lot to do with your exciting modern style. I'm impressed.'

'One does one's modest best,' said Father John.

Fred asked permission which was readily granted, to use his recording machine – "for the sake of the record, Vicar, so there'll be no misunderstanding." Then Fred snapped open his notebook. He was a gifted writer of shorthand and missed very little. The vicar agreed that everything was now on the record. He knew it always had been since the minute Fred set eyes on the vicarage.

'Father John, I do hope you won't mind if I include some difficult questions, so you can tell everybody exactly what you are doing.'

'Not at all,' said Father John. He took a large bite of biscuit.

'Since you arrived around three years ago, you've caused quite a stir in your church by your unusual methods. Attendance has gone up. Do you think these unusual methods are needed because the church is so generally dull and outdated and can't attract people?'

'Oh no,' replied the vicar, 'the church's message is never dull. We just have to package it, to make it more attractive, or in such a way that modern people can take it. We must be "all things to all men" as St Paul says.'

'What, Vicar? Your message is only for men?'

John smiled. 'Sorry,' he said. 'I was quoting the old translation. I should have said, "all things to all people"; a perfect example of needing to modernise our message.'

'I'm glad to hear it. Your message is for everyone after all then, Father,' said Fred with a grin. He was well-read though he tried to hide that fact. He was perfectly aware of the old language. He made a note in his book.

'So, basically, the old traditions are dull and you have to liven things up, otherwise people won't come.'

'No, no, that's not what I'm saying.'

'Even so, Father, that's what you've just done. Tell me about your methods. How do you think up your next stunt?'

'They are not stunts.'

'I do apologise, Father, wrong choice of words. Where do you get your ideas for presenting the unchanging message in modern ways?'

Father John nodded in approval. This was better. There was promise in this young man. 'Well,' he began. He told himself not to preach. 'Most church services are seen as dull, and way out of touch. So my job is to be modern. I have to show that our message is for today's people.'

'You're good at that, Father, aren't you?'

'I try. Hence what you call my stunts. People seem to like what we do. Church attendance has increased by 69.3 per cent.'

'Very impressive. Isn't there a risk of going too far?'

'I'm sorry? Do you mean we can have too many people in church?'

'Your bondage session on Sunday; don't you think, Father, it is highly dangerous and simply wrong to expose children to what is – forgive me, Father – a bondage scene? You are playing with fire, Father.'

The vicar said nothing. Fred persisted.

'Father, can't you see, in these times, the enormous risk you are taking? A bondage scene, Father, a bondage scene in public, in church, in front of children, held up as a parable, how can you possibly justify that? Is there no risk of sexualisation of children?'

'Serious questions indeed,' said the vicar. He poured Fred and himself a second cup of coffee, and pushed the biscuits over to Fred. 'Katie got them in Paris last week. You're lucky there are any left.' He smiled.

Then he said: 'What was the date on Sunday?'

'I don't get you, Father.' Damn, the slippery fish was not going to get away after all this trouble. Stop him now. 'I really do not see—'

'Sunday 23 April. Does that date ring a bell?'

The fish was now asking questions.

'Can we get back to the bondage question, Father? Please?' Fred was proud of the civil tone he put into the question.

'Sunday 23 April. Does that date mean anything to you?'

No it didn't, actually. Better not to admit it. 'Yes, of course. Now, Vicar, if you don't mind, can we get back to the question?'

'The twenty-third of April; St George's Day.'

Damn, damn. St George and the Dragon. They were acting out the story on the right day. The vicar was amusing the kids, he was entertaining the adults and worse, had made some religious point or other out of the whole thing.

'I was,' said Father John mildly, 'getting the children to act out a well-known Christian legend. They loved it, as you undoubtedly saw. The adults were fascinated. I was able to draw out some theological truths.'

'That is not how most people would—'

'And, one might add, is it not appropriate to make reference to the national saint of England, on his own day, in the Church of England as by law established? If not there, then where? The church is not just about religion you know. Also,' the vicar warmed to his theme, 'whose flag do people wave when supporting England?'

It was impossible to read the gentle smile on his face.

Damn and thrice damn, thought Fred. He was the more determined to use the story. No journalist likes to be made a fool of by a vicar. A thought occurred to Fred. Down the labyrinth of his mind, he remembered. 'Ah,' he said, 'that story bears a considerable similarity to the old Perseus rescuing Andromeda story when she was chained stark naked to the rock. He saved her from some horrible monster.'

'Precisely,' beamed the vicar. 'Aren't you glad our church maiden wasn't naked?'

'I bet you thought of it, Vicar.' No harm in humouring the old boy. Wasn't this woman the vicar's mistress or something?

Father John blushed. 'I thought of it for no more than half a minute.' Let's get a little humour into this encounter. Perhaps I've been a little hard on the boy. 'Sadly, we can't do that sort of thing in church.' He smiled like a schoolmaster. 'Yes, there is a certain resemblance to the old pagan myth. Symbolic truth is found everywhere.'

'Aren't you training up the children in very wrong attitudes? And isn't it even worse that you are doing this in an attractive, fun way, so they like this weird stuff you are teaching them?'

Father John held up his hand. 'Fred, there is more. You will, I am sure, not be aware of the old Provençal legend, in which St Martha herself tamed a dragon at Tarascon. She sprinkled holy water on him and tied her scarf around his neck. Then she led him off to be killed. How's that for your abused woman angle, Fred? It was the dragon led in bondage, not her. Answer that, Fred. She was the strong one. Why can't we show a dragon being killed in St Martha's church?'

'You're having me on.'

'No, I assure you.' There was a little smile on the vicar's face.

'If St Martha is really the strong woman you say she was – why show a play in her church showing a woman as victim who needs a man to save her? Wrong play, Vicar. You should have shown St Martha, not St George, killing a dragon. It seems you are using modern methods to reinforce traditional gender stereotyping. You're using modern methods to indoctrinate a religion of dead myths.' He sank back in his chair and took a sip of coffee.

By George, the boy's good, thought the vicar. He doesn't let up. Then Father John got weary of the young fool. He stood up. 'I'm sorry you feel that way,' he said. 'However, I don't have time now to enter upon a long, detailed doctrinal discussion. Please forgive me, I have to visit some parishioners.'

'Father, aren't you worried about the bondage? About

teaching that and pagan myths in church? Your female actor was in very skimpy clothes. She was tied up tight in real ropes. You got awfully close when you released her. She ran off half naked in front of children. Are social services aware of what you are doing?'

Father John stood up.

Fred then used his disarming little boy's smile. 'Forgive me, Father. I'm so sorry. I've been acting as devil's advocate. Forgive me, I was flattering you with imitation – the way you frightened people on Sunday with your fierce sermon on sin – then you smiled and made it all right. Father, you're doing wonderful work. Your exciting methods are just what people need. You've explained about the children's play very well. Thank you so much for humouring me and I do hope I wasn't too rough. You've given me some excellent answers. I'll be able to write a very nice article.'

There was suddenly a woman in the room. 'Let me show you out,' said Katie.

'That's very kind of you,' he said. 'And thank you, Father John, so much for your time and patience.'

Katie saw Fred to the door. When she returned, John gave her a radiant smile. 'Well, that went pretty well, don't you think? Charming fellow.'

She patted his hand. 'My poor, naïve darling. He's a reptile. He's out to destroy you.'

The story broke eight days later. *The Weekly Bugle* ("We Make a Noise for the County") was published every Wednesday. Fred, his editor and the senior team had worked on this story for several days. They agreed Fred

46

should have the byline. They took advice, they consulted the proprietors. They went ahead.

It was one of their best editions. On page one, there was a large picture of John in clerical robes and in a smaller frame appeared Katie. The flaming headline read: "VICAR IN SEX-BONDAGE SCANDAL". There was an idyllic picture of a church in winter snow. The caption was *"St Martha's in the Field."*

The front paragraph was in bold screeching print. The byline read:

By Fred Vestal, Award Winning Journalist.

Questions are being urgently asked how the Rev John Newman was allowed to enact an act of extreme sexual impropriety in church, involving children. This happened in full view of a shocked congregation at the main mass of the Sunday morning. Horrified parents told me: "We had no idea. This man is a menace with his attempts to draw people into church. It's disgusting. We won't be coming back."

For full story see pages 3, 4, 5 and 6, and the editorial on page 14. Read Humphrey Dumpty on page 10.

With a heavy heart, Katie brought a copy into John's study. Together they read it all.

Page three had a screaming headline: *Vicar and the Bondage Girl.*

The article calmed down and settled to business. It read:

All Hillford and the parish of St Martha's are reeling over recent revelations. By pure chance I was there in church to witness the most disturbing scenes to shake our city and church in decades. Even now I can scarcely credit what I saw last Sunday with my own eyes.

In what can only be described as a desperate stunt to enlarge his sleepy congregation, the vicar put on a public enactment of bondage. It certainly woke up his flock. One churchgoer told me: "It's disgusting. I'm never going to that church again. My children have been traumatised."

To put it as decently as we can – a woman was left standing in her flimsy nightie, which was not full length, at the front of the church. She was tied by real ropes to the reading lectern. She pretended to moan and wriggle.

A group of children entered. They gaped at the woman. They screamed and ran away. Along came a pantomime dragon – the costume was quite skilled. We give credit where it is due. This was a convincing theatrical creature.

It became clear that it was children in disguise. The dragon pranced about for a bit and leered at the woman.

Vicar to the rescue. He came in thinly disguised as St George. He frightened the children, made them cry and pretend to die. It is a miracle he did not hurt one of them very badly as he poked his lance at the dragon.

Vicar then untied Bondage Girl and they kissed. Her nightie rucked high above her knees, she ran off half-naked to change.

The vicar then tried to justify this performance by some theological reference to sin.

Members of his flock were visibly shocked. I looked

round and saw people go pale. Some were crying, some even shaking.

He then tried to cheer them up by saying it was all a joke. It was a theological lesson about stopping sin.

We do not pretend to be professional in matters of religion. It looked to me more like an exercise in sin than in trying to stop it. We do say it is a very dangerous game to play at a time when we are so rightly concerned with the protection of children.

This vicar has laid himself open to questions regarding child abuse. The matter has been referred to the bishop. We expect it will also go to the police.

When we asked the bishop for comment, he refused to speak with us.

Enquiries are ongoing. You can keep up to the minute on our Bugle website.

Now see pages 4, 5 and 6 for our Exclusive Interview with the vicar.

There was more in similar vein. Quotations from parishioners were included:

Churchwarden Polly Radstock said, "Our new vicar has certainly shaken things up." Churchwarden Major Blake said, "Damn unorthodox fellow. But he knows how to rally the troops. Needs to tighten his personal discipline."

Other comments included: "I have nothing to say, so will not speak of it"; "Shocking. The vicar has no right to frighten people by talk of sin"; "I'm not surprised he's so keen on sin, as he's living in it"; "I blame that woman"; "It's disgusting. I phoned the bishop's office to complain";

"You'd have thought he would be more careful with all this child abuse in the church. It's horrible"; "He should be arrested".

John and Katie finished reading at the same time. She squeezed his hand. His eyes were closed as if in prayer.

'Horrible man,' she said, 'after we were so nice to him, in our own house.'

'No chocolate biscuits for him next time, eh love?'

He looked pale. She was worried.

'There's still the editorial; then the interview; then Humphrey Dumpty. Let's crack on.'

The view of the city nestled round the cathedral had never looked so lovely.

'Let's do the editorial,' said Katie. 'They may tone it down. They may hint the lad is being dramatic.'

'And I am the King of Bulgaria.'

She smiled. 'Such cynicism.'

They read the editorial:

This newspaper applauds the attempt by the church, which has so often shown itself to be fuddy-duddy, dreamy and out of touch, to engage with modern people in a modern way. But there are limits.

Today's truly shocking revelations by our brilliant young reporter Fred Vestal on loan from London need thorough investigation. Is the bishop really aware of what is going on in his patch? How long has it been happening? Our readers deserve answers.

We like the church. We like the bishop, even if at times he seems remote. Now is the time for him to act.

There are serious questions to be asked.

It may be there is serious action to be taken. This newspaper is not puritan. We are realistic. What happens in the privacy of their own bedrooms between fully consenting adults is their business.

A public performance of a scantily-clothed woman tied up in bondage, involving children, in church, is quite another matter. We look to the bishop for action.

We make no secret that our London proprietors have long thought Hillford to be a sleepy sort of place. They felt that your local newspaper which has served you since 1783 was dreamy. They have lent us Fred for six months to shake us up. Thank you, Fred, you have certainly done that.

Katie giggled. 'What do they sound like?' Then she scrunched the paper and flung it across the room. 'It's even worse than Fred.'

They were hooked, like someone who dreads the next round of abuse on social media, but cannot help being drawn to watch in horrified fascination.

'OK, the interview,' said John. He picked up the paper. He smoothed it down. 'Fred might find something nice to say. He might show a glimmer of understanding what we are really trying to do. Don't you think the last bit is the editor's way of an apology, he saying he's been forced by London to do what he doesn't want?'

'And I am the Queen of Bulgaria.'

Chapter 4

Katie and John held hands as they read:

John Newman is in some ways a modern priest, an effective communicator, just the sort of vicar the church is crying out for. In three years since his arrival, St Martha's has certainly been shaken up. The congregation has increased by an impressive 70 per cent.

His style, however, is controversial. After the events witnessed in church by myself, I decided to seek an interview. He was only too pleased, perhaps jumping at the chance to justify his methods.

The modern, four-bedroom, three quarter million pound vicarage is set in a charming location on the northern slopes of Hillford. It looks down over the leafy parklands across the ancient city to the misty cathedral in the distance.

It was a lovely, early summer day. One in which it was very easy to believe in goodness, and God, and the message of the church.

I was shown in by the charming Katie, 33, the partner of Father John, who has been living with him for the past few months. As a modern vicar, he feels no need to marry his partner. She is a nurse recently returned from heroic work in Africa. She brought in coffee and lovely chocolate biscuits. She then tactfully withdrew.

I began by asking Father John about his methods. He said the message was timeless but needed modern packaging. He aimed like St Paul to be all things to all men.

This sexist bias did not seem to trouble Father John. With just a touch of irritation, he corrected himself. "All people, of course. I was using the old translation — which you wouldn't know of course." He was equally touchy about my describing his methods as "stunts".

He agreed that most church services are dull. It was his mission to modernise without losing the message. It was difficult for me to get a word in as he warmed to his theme, and cited previous events — not "stunts". He was not a little proud to say it seemed to be working. Attendance had gone up by 69.3 per cent. He was curiously pedantic on this point. It is 69.3 per cent, not 70 per cent.

I asked him about the highly disturbing service I witnessed.

"Aren't you in grave danger, Father, of endangering children by such methods? By what some people would call a scene of sexual bondage, the woman as victim, needing a strong man to save her? Aren't you — far from modernising the message — taking it back to the Dark Ages, by all this old-fashioned talk of scary dragons, ladies chained up in flimsy nightwear, knight in shining armour stuff?"

As a hardened journalist, I am not easily shocked. However, what he said next gave me pause for thought. He admitted he had thought of having the lady naked, but "Aren't you glad our church maiden wasn't naked? Sadly we can't do that in church."

I hope I am right in thinking this was a feeble vicar attempt at humour. You never know, however. He is, after all, trying to modernise the methods.

"Father, can't you see, in these sensitive times, the enormous risk you are taking? Don't you agree that some will see that morning as tantamount to sexualisation of children, even potentially leading to child abuse? A bondage scene, Father, in church, in front of children, held up as a parable, how can you possibly justify that? At the very least, an indoctrination in old gender stereotyping which we have only recently started to challenge and root out?"

He poured me and himself a second cup of coffee, and pushed the chocolate biscuits my way. "Just in from Paris," he said. "Katie went over last week and brought them back. You're lucky there are any left." He smiled, in his rather boyish way. I can see why the ladies flock into his church.

I duly smiled at this vision of the vicar allowing his partner freedom to come and go as a modern woman. It was clear he was using this pause to prepare his answer.

He went on to the attack. "You deserve direct answers," he said. He was bold enough to remind me that the date of that service was 23 April, St George's Day, England's saint. I played along as ignorant journalist, although well aware that the flag of England, the cross of St George is frequently flown at church masts of the dear old Church of England.

With a sigh, he proceeded to put me right. This had

been a simple re-enactment of the myth of St George and the Dragon, on St George's Day. He had drawn out orthodox Christian teaching on morality from it. Where was the harm in any of that? He did not buy my dramatic interpretations.

I felt, in my humble non-churchgoing way, that the good vicar just did not get it. You cannot do this sort of thing in the modern age. The Sunday school methods of fifty years ago simply cannot be used in our much more knowing age. For all his talk of modernising, this good man seemed curiously unaware of how he was playing with fire in today's tinderbox.

The vicar then produced what he imagined was his ace. He told me of some medieval French legend where St Martha sprinkled holy water on a dragon, tied her scarf round him and led him off to be killed. I asked in that case why he chose not to show a strong independent woman as hero, but chose instead the other dragon legend to act out, with a weak female victim? Father John elects to put on a play about bondage. Even the old folks of the Middle Ages knew a lot better than that.

I fear that Father John is at root an old-fashioned clergyman, earnest, trying oh-so-hard, and totally out of touch, while fondly imagining himself to be as up to date as can be. This can be very endearing, but this sort of complacency is dangerous. The protection of children is paramount.

I put to him the dangers of appearing sexist, old-fashioned and patriarchal, while at the same time, however unwittingly, exposing children to the wrong sort of liberal over-sexualised imagery and behaviour; in other

*words, the very worst of old and new in an unholy mix.
I asked him how he would react if people were to think
that.*

*At this point this saintly man seemed to lose
patience. As if on cue, his girlfriend, the charming Katie,
rushed in and invited me to leave.*

*As I left I noticed the lovely new grandfather clock
in the hall.*

Katie and John said nothing. Then John gave a sort of groan.
'That man will get me unfrocked,' he said. 'You know what
the bishop's like. He gets his opinions from the press.'

'Oh, don't be so wet, love,' she said. 'I'm sure he'll stick
up for you. Surely even the bishop can't be that naïve.'

'Let's see if Humphrey Dumpty is any better,' said John.
'In for a penny, in for a national debt.'

They turned to what was usually, after the letters page,
the most readable part of the paper.

HUMPHREY DUMPTY
The hard-boiled writer who cannot be broken

*I see the city ghost tours are ceasing during the winter.
Pardon me, but I thought the winter months are the best
to wander round our ancient streets at night, looking for
the ghoulies, the ghosties and frighties. Whooo – it's quite
scary to think it's too cold to chase the spooks from their
nooks.*

*Or is this another case of 'elf and safety? Perhaps
we'll get sued if the poor spirits slip on the ice.*

You can't help feeling sorry for the dear old C of E. That by the way, stands for Church of England, whose churches we all love to give a miss to mass to on Sunday, but scream blue murder if one might just close. Whatever they do, they seem to get it wrong.

Enter Father John Newman, priest extraordinaire, part of the new dynamic workforce. He's like a top manager, parachuted in to save an ailing club from relegation. He uses funny methods, but it works.

And by heavens, how it works. Any business would be proud to grow by 70 per cent in three years. That's Father John. With his sparkly new stunts, he pulls in the punters. Seventy per cent more parishioners in the pews; what's not to like?

Well it seems my old mate Fred doesn't like it. Don't get me wrong. Of course Humphrey does not justify any and all means. Of course we have to protect children. What's to disagree?

So what if the vicar does a wacky play about St George? After all, it was his own girlfriend he planned to expose to the dragon. Of course it was the vicar to the rescue. Maybe that old story is just a myth and a legend. Maybe it is just like the old Greek yarn of Perseus. Maybe the vicar is a bit muddled in mixing them. Maybe he isn't quite so sure about what he believes. But hey, it charms the congregation.

Come off it, Fred. I see how you choose to spin the story. No doubt the vicar has a different spin. Doubtless he'll let us know after reading our special edition.

Humphrey wonders what the bishop thinks. More important — what do our readers think? Is this a

marvellous vicar modernising the church? Is he a weird
creep going to the very edge or beyond – in trying to keep
the church alive?

Let us know, good people. See our website and our
Twitter feed. Email me at the usual address.

We look forward to the verdict of Hillford.

They put the paper down, as if it smelt.

'Rat, rat, rat, king of the rats.' Katie tore the paper into strips. 'Toad, weasel, cow, bitch, dunk-head, dung-stool, journalistic pervert.'

'I don't get it,' said John.

'You dear, sweet, naïve man,' she said. She put her arms round his neck and squeezed hard. 'You see the good in everyone. Don't you get it? Humphrey and Fred are the same person.'

'How?'

'Vicar, think,' she said. 'A small paper like that hasn't got many staff. They have to stretch and pretend they're someone else. Fred's trying to have it both ways – both nasty and vicious, the old crusading journo stunt, while making the paper seem to be so reasonable, fair and objective. Do you really think the paper would allow real dissension on this one? Rat, toad, swine, skunk, cobra, shark—' She repeated a list of unfortunate animals, some on the endangered register.

'I can't believe that.'

She was angry. 'OK, Mr Naïve. How does Humphrey know about the Perseus and St George connection? Fred's interview makes no mention of any Greek myth. Do you actually need evidence? Isn't that enough?'

'Oh. I see. I can't believe anyone would stoop that low.'

'Fred is a rat. He doesn't care what spin he puts on things, or how he hurts people. So long as he makes his name, pleases his editor, and sells newspapers. In that order, with the stress very much on Number One.'

'So this nonsense about my being a child molester – he doesn't believe it?' John felt a little lighter.

'Course not, you baboon. If it served his purpose, he would have made you out as a male St Theresa, a saviour and doctor of the church.'

'So it's going to be all right.'

Her face scowled. 'Sorry. I'm afraid not, my darling. He's dropped you in it. The fan has well and truly splattered the excreta.'

The phone rang. She ran and took it before he could. 'So, it's you,' she said. 'I'm surprised you've got the insolence after your massacre in today's paper, and betrayal of our hospitality and a good man. What are you playing at? Don't try to explain. You don't get it, do you?'

She turned to John and arched her eyebrows. 'No, he doesn't want to speak to you. Goodbye.' She put the phone down as if it were a soiled nappy.

She sat next to John. She got up and put a glass of whisky in his hand. 'Fred. He said he hoped you were all right and would understand and won't take it personally. Rat, rat.'

The phone rang again. 'Persistent,' she said. John stirred but she strode across the room. She picked up the phone and yelled. 'No, he doesn't want to speak to you. Didn't I – oh sorry, Bishop, I'll pass on your message. No, he's too upset to come to the phone.'

She came back. 'He wants to see you.'

'I wonder why.' John attempted to smile. 'Must be serious, he's acting direct for once. Not using Babs to do his work for him.'

'He'll get his secretary to ring you.'

The meeting was arranged for ten the next morning.

The couple discussed at length the feebleness of the bishop who ignored his clergy but took the media as his guide to public morality, and what he should do next. They asked why the press could do as it liked. It was getting quite heavy.

The doorbell rang. 'Oh no, it's starting,' said Katie. She rushed out.

She came back. 'It's someone called William. He wants us to vote for him in tomorrow's election.'

They both laughed. 'Tell him to go and vote for himself,' said the vicar.

'Now, now,' said Katie, and disappeared.

Chapter 5

John had no time to brood on his problems. It was the evening of the annual parish meeting, Wednesday, 3 May. He had to prepare and chair.

All-comers from the parish and beyond could turn up and discuss the church's performance. People voted for the two churchwardens, secretary, treasurer and parochial council members. These elections usually did not take long as commonly, few people wanted those jobs. It was quite normal to have one candidate per post.

At St Martha's before this vicar's arrival, around a dozen people would turn up. Now it was around twenty-five.

That afternoon, John thought there would be a few more, following the excitement of his scandal. He was ready for all eventualities, and expected a lot of support as well as some hostile mutterings. There might be the odd yob that came to fling abuse. John expected the major would deal with that, quite satisfactorily.

Around two, the phone rang. It was unworthy to run away or let Katie answer for him every time. He picked up. He said hello.

'Hello, Rev John Newman, vicar of St Martha's?'

'Who are you?'

'I'm so sorry, forgetting my manners. I should have given my name first. Joe Martin here, Radio Hillford, wondering if you'd like to appear on our show? You'll have heard of our four to five phone-in?'

'*Chat and Cheer with Joe.*'

'That's the one.' Joe sounded pleased. 'Our listeners seem to like it; though we can't claim 69.3 per cent rise in our figures in three years.'

The vicar was impressed. Perhaps they could do business.

'Anyway, this church play which has caused all this fuss? We're keen to hear your side of things? We want to know what the local people think? Are you up for a prepared interview with me? We'll run it first at the start of the show then get people to phone in with their views. How are you with that, John, are you up for it?'

The man's breezy charm was irresistible. He sounded so friendly John did not resist. It would give him a chance to explain his approach, put the record right, make people really understand. It was a great chance to defend himself and the church. At worst, it could not hurt him any more than the paper had.

'Sure, good thing,' he said.

'Great, great. I promise to be fair – tough but fair? I promise to let you have your say. We really want your story and let our listeners react? They're usually a fair bunch, though they do hold strong opinions? Is that OK?'

There was an Aussie lilt in Joe's voice which John, along with most of Hillford, found charming. He seemed really nice. No wonder Joe was so well-liked.

The interview over the phone was all that the vicar could wish. He got the chance to explain, the questions were indeed probing but fair and Joe was civil. 'Thank you,

John,' he said after wrap-up. 'We're very grateful. That went well, don't you think? Hope you can join us at four? Listen in, I mean?'

'Thank you,' said John, 'yes, I think I can do that.'

'Good, good, thank you so much, John, and keep up the good work.' He was gone.

'What a nice man; restores your faith in the media,' said John to Katie.

She smiled sadly and said: 'Let's hope so.'

They both listened in at four o'clock. To their amazement Joe was as good as his word. There was a neutral description of the events of that service. Reference was made to the newspaper coverage. The interview between Joe and John was played in full without editorial spin. It lasted four minutes. John got his message over very well.

Listeners then phoned in. Every fifteen minutes the show was punctuated with the latest music. Joe kept it bubbling along with his breezy and often witty comments.

The public reacted across the whole range. "Tell the police, put the vicar in jail"; "It's disgusting, he's a danger to children"; "What is this crazy man thinking of?"; "Silly vicar"; "Worth a try"; "Church needs all the help it can get"; "This was normal when I was young, can't understand what the fuss is about"; "Wrong to see evil where there isn't any"; "Good try, Vicar, go for it"; "Sounds great, just what the kids need"; "They see far worse on their computer games"; "Tied up ladies in their nighties? I'm going to start going to church"; "Send the vicar for rehabilitation".

Comment was more favourable than not. Hillford on the whole appeared pleased that the dear old dotty church in its funny way was still trying so hard. It was doing no harm to anyone and if anything was a slight force for good in this terrible world. At least the vicar wasn't killing people in the name of some perverted version of religion.

John and Katie held hands tightly at the start of the show. As it went on, they relaxed and smiled to each other. John did a high-five at some particularly favourable comment.

By the end they were happy. They knew everything would be all right.

'That's proper journalism,' said John.

'Lots more people listen to radio than read papers,' said Katie. 'It's going to be just fine. Well done, love.' She punched him playfully on his arm. 'You'll be fine this evening. Well done, you.'

'Yes, I think I will,' said John.

'You're a natural. Second career looming, eh Vicar?'

They now looked forward to the meeting with an easy mind.

By seven fifteen the church hall was packed with fifty people. Maisy who liked to serve teas beforehand to get people in a good mood was flustered. She announced that anyone who missed refreshments before would be most welcome to stay afterwards, and there would be biscuits and cherry cake. But she was worried that not everyone would get the message.

At seven twenty-nine, John sat down as chairman in the centre of a table facing out. The table had a green cloth. He had decided on the protections of formality. It was normally not needed. In previous years, people had been seated casually, anywhere, and the meeting was table-less. John stayed seated, and formal terms of address were avoided. Tonight he was an old-fashioned chairman.

There were seventy people in the room as John stood up and welcomed everyone.

There was a ripple of polite applause, and a few ironic shouts from the back. A group of teenage lads and a row of young mums that no one recognised were sitting there.

'Welcome, welcome, everyone, nice to see so many,' he said. His heart lurched. Among the crowd, he saw Fred Vestal.

Would this be a fine chance for retribution – or would it only make matters worse? Katie mouthed to him to be careful. Meantime, Katie had moved as close to Fred as she could. She intended to glare at him all through the meeting. He would notice all right. What a cheek to turn up, the man was incorrigible.

'Welcome, welcome, everyone, nice to see you all,' repeated John.

'Ha, ha, isn't it, Vicar?' called out a raucous voice. It did not sound friendly. Major Blake swiftly moved himself to the back of the hall. He had foreseen precisely this and had various church members – his dispositions – in strategic places at the ready.

'Before we begin,' said John, 'Maisy would like a word, wouldn't you, Maisy?'

Maisy stood up and said: 'It's nice to see so many but because there's more than usual, we couldn't get everyone their tea or coffee, and cake before we started. So please do stay at the end, everyone, there's plenty of tea, coffee, biscuits, and lots of nice cherry cake. Stay around and chat. Thank you.'

'Thank you, Maisy, and all your helpers. Maisy and Sue and Matt and Ben and Janet, and everyone, you do so much, and don't always get proper recognition. If an army marches on its stomach, a church prays on its coffee and cake.' He looked pleased at this aphorism.

'Ha, ha,' called out two voices. The major gave a nod to two strong lads. They shifted a few seats along their row. It was not yet time to act.

'Now,' said the vicar. 'We'll try not to be too long. You've got the agenda. Usual things, nothing too controversial – just one big decision, but we've already done a lot of work on that. Ah yes, before I forget, one thing before we start. Tomorrow, as we all know, is the election for the county council. This hall is being used as a polling station. So the officials would be very glad if we could be out of here by around nine thirty, so they can come in and set up ready for an early start at 7 a.m. tomorrow.

I'm sure we'll manage that. And – let me remind people – I would not dream of advising anyone for whom to vote. Think of your conscience as Christians, that I will say. But please do go out and vote for someone.'

'— for whom to vote. Very posh!' called out a young woman at the back. Fred made a note in his book. The major glared. He shook his head to his troops. Not yet.

The meeting went on its merry way. 'That's the welcome done,' said the vicar. The apologies, and last year's minutes sped quickly by. Item Four, vicar's review of the year, came next.

'This year, as we know—'

A rough young man stood up. He had his arms covered

with tattoos of hunting dogs. 'Excuse me, Vicar, aren't you supposed to be religious? Don't we get no prayers to start?'

A girlfriend gave him an admiring look. He gave her a proud grin. Major Black signalled to his two best lieutenants. Couldn't have this sort of thing at the meeting. It was time for Operation Eject. He would enjoy grabbing the young ruffian by the lapels if he had any.

Father John cut the major down with a stern frown. They both heard vicious barks from the dogs tied up outside.

'Certainly,' said the vicar, sweetly. 'How silly. I forgot. Let us pray.' He then led the audience in a rendition of the Lord's Prayer. It was taken up vociferously by those who knew it. Father John caused this chorus to stumble by insisting on repeating the section about forgiving those who do us wrong. 'Thank you, young friend,' he said when it was over. 'I believe we haven't yet had the pleasure of meeting. I'm Father John. May I know your name?'

The lad was shocked. 'Call me Fred.' He laughed. The girl squeezed her brave lad's hand.

'Nice to meet you, Fred. You were quite right. We are sometimes in danger of forgetting our priorities. Now, this year, as we know…'

He proceeded with his report. He read it quickly. He had two complementary feelings. The quicker the meeting was over, the less time there would be for trouble. Equally, the longer the meeting went on without trouble, the less trouble there would be. There was no harm in pushing along business, perhaps making it a little dull for once, to get away quickly. Besides, there were the election officials to consider.

The review came out as bland information, including a list of significant events over the past year and congratulations to all who had made the church so friendly and if he dared say so, fun. There was a plethora of unsung heroines and heroes. The congregation had increased cumulatively 69.3 per cent over three years and he took no credit for it. It was due to divine inspiration and the faithful work of so many.

There was the odd muttering during his reading. A loud female voice cut in, 'He sounds just like he did on the radio.' Her boyfriend said: 'It's disgusting what he done. Making excuses. Doesn't he get his frock off or something?'

'It's called defrocked. He should get defrocked, get your frock off, Vicar,' whispered the woman loud enough for all to hear. The major leant forward but kept his troops in reserve. He smiled; quite witty really. No harm in a bit of banter from the foe. Could deal with that.

Polite warm applause rippled out at the end of the speech. Various people turned round and glared at the back of the hall. The unknown elements of the audience kept quiet. The noisy dogs grew silent.

The churchwardens' report given by Polly was received in polite silence. Everything was ticking over nicely, she said, though they could do with a few more people to help Maisy with after-service coffee.

The treasurer guided everyone through the thickets of his charts. He was happy to announce the bottom line, a healthy surplus of one thousand eight hundred and seventy-six pounds eighteen pence, and that was after managing to pay their official Share, the contribution to the diocese, in full for the first time in six years. He could look forward to the coming year with confidence but people could not relax in their efforts. However, all in all, he was pleased and confident for the future.

The meeting was settling down. John threw Katie an encouraging look and she smiled back. Keep up the boredom she seemed to indicate and all will be well.

There now came a particularly dull piece of business, just what the vicar needed. It was the buildings report. The major decided he could leave his post and deliver this as normal, while keeping an eye on the back. His capable aide-de-camp, Dave, was in acting command.

There was some guttering to be attended to, the roof, contrary to their fears, was sound and the Modern Hall continued to attract enough lettings to pay for its general routine maintenance, and no structural problems had been detected.

Now he wanted to talk about the proposed new stained glass window for St Martha's Chapel. This was the most exciting project for years. They had to make the final decision this evening. 'However, before I venture forth on this, I want to say this. I'm sure Father John will forgive me. His report was excellent. It was encouraging. It was also – and rightly, I say – deliberately dull. He chose not to speak of the sensationalist report in today's paper and this afternoon's more measured radio debate. He isn't going to defend himself, so I will.'

He stood tall, like Montgomery addressing the troops. 'Know this, everyone. Father John is the best vicar this parish has ever had. I don't begin to understand the wild workings of the press. Anything to sell papers. Damn hypocrites, probably spin some yarn about freedom of the press, stand up for freedom rot, so they can make people's lives miserable. I tell you, the people who really stick up for freedom are our gallant forces. You know my views. The press is not worthy to lick the boots of those who are really fighting for freedom.

Stick up for the vicar. He's a fine man. I'd welcome him in my regiment any day. Everyone get behind him and move on. We're right behind you, padre, right behind you.' The major glared. 'You've transformed this place in just three years. You've even made us newsworthy.' The major stared. 'Anyone who thinks ill of our excellent padre has me to answer to. We're right behind him.'

'He's behind you,' called out a voice from the back in a pantomime voice. People sniggered.

The dam burst. There was thunderous applause. Some people cheered and stood up. They were relieved that someone had given them permission not to pretend that nothing was amiss. They had wanted all the time to stick up for their vicar. Now they could.

A cool voice called out. 'May I speak? I am afraid I cannot quite agree with you there.' He was dressed well, in a suit as if just back from work, a professional man in his early forties. 'Speaking as a father, I have to say the protection of children is paramount. I shall probably be launching a civil action against this priest. My children certainly will not be attending his church again.' He gathered his papers and walked out. 'My name is Mr Mason; of Mason, Smith and Wedgely.'

People watched him leave in silence. Then they burst out cheering again.

A figure in a lounge suit and a purple shirt and a whopping great crucifix had slipped in to observe. It was the bishop.

John stood up. 'That's enough, Major. Since you interrupted your update on the window to talk about me, I'm taking over.'

The major looked surprised. 'Very well.'

'I hope I may return the favour. I too would like to congratulate the major for being deliberately dull, and for introducing the one exciting topic we do want to talk about, that is the controversial new window for the chapel of St Martha.'

Everyone laughed.

'Who's she when she's at home?' sneered rough voices.

'Ah that is the point. She's very much a home girl. She's an old-fashioned woman in the Bible. I'll tell you who she is, in a minute. First, though, what Bernard and I plus Polly of course, want to tell everyone, is that we have at last got the Faculty, the official permission, to go ahead with the new stained glass window in the St Martha chapel. You've all seen the design. Most of you like it. Some of you may find it controversial. It shows Martha serving her guests with bread and wine. The resemblance to mass is deliberate. She can be seen as the prototype of women priests. Maybe Our Lord got the idea from her.'

The bishop put his hands on his head. This was worse than he feared.

'So if there is any journalist here, who thinks that I — that we — are fuddy-duddy and patriarchal, let him think this. St Martha is the inspiration for all female priests, which we should have had long ago.' His glare drilled into Fred as if fracking through rock.

Fred decided to make a stand. So he stood. 'Vicar,' he said, 'I am sad if I have upset you. But there's no way I am going to apologise. I'm fighting for the freedom of the press. Don't take it personally. Will you shake hands with me here, now in public, to show no hard feelings?'

'Come to service on Sunday. I will forgive you then and there and shake hands. Not before.'

'So you won't. I am sorry to hear you don't practise what you preach.'

'Fling him out,' yelled one of the church lads.

'No.' The vicar sounded like Amos at a volcano. 'That is quite enough.' He resumed. 'Let me just remind our new visitors of the story of Martha. Jesus and his mates went to have supper with her. She fussed about, did all the work in the kitchen, you know what it's like when you have guests, and her sister Mary instead of helping out, just sat around listening to Jesus's amusing stories. So Martha comes bursting in and complains. "Tell her, Jesus, I'm doing all the work, tell her to come and help, so you get a good dinner." He isn't very helpful. He tells Martha she's working too much and Mary has chosen the best bit. Imagine how Martha feels.

It gets worse. Some people say this Mary was the woman who used to sleep around and who poured precious perfume on Jesus's feet later, instead of giving her earnings to the poor. So she doesn't do any work, goes with all the men, wastes money on pouring precious oil over people, and Jesus keeps telling her she's doing the right thing. No wonder Martha gets pissed off. If you forgive the language but you get the idea.'

The women at the back were spellbound. They had never heard anything like this from a vicar. The bishop was shocked.

Fred licked his lips. So the vicar likes this Mary who chases men, and is a drag on everybody. She'd be on welfare if she lived now. Vicar says Jesus liked her. Fred remembered the tradition that Jesus and Mary had a thing going. The vicar seemed to hint at this, else why is Jesus sticking up for her? This was great. This vicar really was weird.

The man was obsessed. Weren't there some rumours that he wouldn't shake hands with people till he got that woman of his into bed? Then he puts her in bondage in his church and gets seen rescuing her. That's in front of children. Weird, just weird. Fred could spin all this for several issues. He was so glad he had come.

One of the women called out: 'I like this Mary.' She turned to her boyfriend. 'You get your own dinner from now on. I can relax with telly. Bible says it's all right.' Dogs outside started to bark again.

'Well,' said the vicar, 'I didn't quite mean that.'

'You're all right, Vicar,' called out the woman. 'Can I join your bondage class? Instead of making his dinner?' She pointed at her boyfriend. The men started muttering. They did not like this doctrine one little bit. The women were in hysterics.

'However, I'm sorry to tell you, folks, there are three Marys, who somehow got confused. We've got this one, the sister of Martha, Mary Magdalene, and the woman who poured oil on the feet of Jesus. We don't know if any of them was a prostitute or chased men. And no, Fred, Jesus never had a wife or an affair.'

That to Fred sounded very much like a U-turn. Did the vicar even know what he believed?

All this time the bishop made notes. He couldn't decide

whether to be appalled or applaud. Dammit, why bring all this religion into the meeting? The man certainly had verve. It would need some thought as to how to proceed at the interview tomorrow.

Chapter 6

John knew it was going to be fine. They finished the last of the business, including the election of the parish council and churchwardens, and everyone was happy to let these people decide on going ahead with the beautiful new window. The great majority were in favour.

It was quiet. The humming of the central heating gave a comforting melody. The people at the back were getting bored. The chained up dogs had gone to sleep. John's strategy of being as dull as possible had paid off.

It was time to round off with Any Other Business. No decisions were allowed under this item and it was just a chance for a few stray comments. Then there would be more tea and cherry cake, some nice conversations and perhaps the chance to meet new people at the back before they sloped off. He'd met far rougher people during his time in London. Overall the evening had gone well. John did not expect any more trouble from Bishop Edward tomorrow than a few rumbles about being careful and avoiding even the appearance of scandal, but thank you anyway for reviving the parish so well.

'Any other business?' asked John. Usually there was nothing other than the organist defending his choice of music.

One by one his parishioners stood up in the vicar's praise.

Maisy said: 'He's a good man who does good things. I've just got good words for him. All of us stick up for him.' She sat down with great force and her chair skidded.

Old Harry said: 'That's right. John's the best priest we've had. Good on you, John.'

The professor thought: 'Where one can't find fault, we must speak but good of our priest. I am glad to do so.'

'Prof, I like your beard. It's rare to see a bush like that,' called a voice from the back. His girlfriend hit him.

'Apologies, I have to leave now and teach my evening class.' The professor left and heard no more of the meeting. No one observed which way he went.

A young lad got up: 'The vicar's great.' He sank down, exhausted.

A young mum next stood up: 'I don't get all this fuss. My kids are quite safe here. They love to act in his plays. They don't do no harm at all.'

The major barked out his views: 'You know what I think. Whole damn fuss. Don't get it. I call on you all to stick by our vicar.'

Polly had been silent for a very long time. She rose to her feet. She was pale and trembling. 'I quite agree, we must stand by Father John, who is so full of good ideas, and so well-motivated. He's fun and inspirational to work with. However —'

She stalled.

The clock could be heard. People perked up. Anxious, leering, expectant faces looked directly at hers, Fred's pencil poised on his notebook. It would be fantastic to have the vicar's female top boss criticise his actions in public.

'However,' continued Polly. She gripped the edge of

the table. 'We have to be aware of the effect on others. We need to know how the world might see us, and the impressions that people might get. I understand, and the church congregation understands, how innocent and spiritual the St George play was. However, I can't help worrying that people outside the cosy world of our church might get the wrong idea. I see where the famous Fred is coming from.'

Fred began to worry. This could be deadly praise.

'So perhaps we can support our vicar by asking him to tone things down, just a little, just for a time. We mustn't give the wrong impression. Nothing is more important than our children.'

She sank down, feeling sick that she might have spoken out of turn. She was willing to resign if she had to. She gulped half a glass of water from the table.

'Too late for that, darlin'', called the voice from the back. A big man in studded leather, brandishing a heavy dog lead, lumbered to his feet.

Another man leapt to his feet. He was bald, of middle height and in a well-made suit. His tie was dark red and he had come straight from work. 'Before our friend here gives his views,' the man looked around, 'may I inject a note of reason? It seems we all – except perhaps the lady who has just spoken – are missing the point.'

He was a mild man who exuded authority. He planted himself in the style of Henry VIII, and continued.

'I am the head teacher of St Martha's C of E Primary School, with over 500 children. You will know of us, as we are attached to this church. The vicar often visits. Last year the Ofsted inspectors gave us an Outstanding grade. They specially praised our child protection strategy, which leaves our pupils feeling free as well as protected. So I may claim to know a thing or two about real children's welfare. My own two children took part in the St George play, as well as other children from my school.'

He turned and pointed at Fred Vestal. 'What that journalist has done is an utter disgrace. He has brought fear where there was none. He sees evil where there is none. He has trivialised a very serious topic. The vicar's play was harmless, and it was showing good versus evil, the children enjoyed taking part, but Fred has sexualised it and made a scandal. In my school we encourage children to go online and see what is suitable for their age about the big world. We are proud to get them to support their local newspaper and read about local events.

I was amazed today. All day kids have been coming up to me and my teachers, and asking "Is that bad? Is the vicar a naughty man, sir? Is it still OK to go to church? Will the vicar go to prison, sir? Sir, what's bondage, is that something really bad?"

I shut down your website at once, sir. Your newspaper is no longer welcome in my school. So much for your seedy efforts to increase sales. Shame on you, Fred. You've cried wolf, you've made it less likely we will take the real horrible stuff as seriously as we should. You're a disgrace and a menace.'

Fred started to get to his feet.

'No, hear me out. Kids have been really upset. They think they're in trouble. Kids who took part are now asking me, have we done something bad, sir? We thought we were helping the vicar to rescue that nice lady from a horrible dragon. We thought it was nice to look after people. We thought we were doing something nice and we liked that, but the paper says we've been really naughty. Are we going to prison with the vicar, sir?

You are a disgrace to your profession, sir, and as well as that, you give ammunition to those who want to reduce press freedom, and I can't say I blame them if you pull these stunts just to boost your sales. I repeat, sir, you are a menace. I am astonished you have the insolence to show your face among decent people.'

He sat down, red and shaking with anger.

The vicar whispered to Katie: 'It's much worse to call a good thing bad than the other way round.'

She said, 'Yes, dear.'

You could have heard a dead fly drop.

Fred struggled to his feet, but thought better of it. He too was inflamed and angry. He was only doing his job, sticking up for freedom of expression and making the news interesting. But there was no point in arguing with these people. They had no idea what press freedom costs.

It was silent as the other side of the moon. The dogs outside were still. There began the sound of rain.

Then Katie called out, 'Fred, go and sit on the naughty seat.' Half the audience laughed and cheered. John smiled and even the bishop gave him a grin and thumbs-up. It was going to be just fine. It was very touching just how much support there was. The major was ready to stand down his troops.

'So, now,' said the vicar, 'thank you everyone, time for cherry cake, I think.'

'Vicar, I got to speak.' The well-studded man was on his feet. His dog chain was swinging. Then his mate stood up, shorter by six inches, but stocky as a wild boar. He wore an identical outfit.

'Aw, I'm fed up with these speeches,' he said. 'We want action. I'm fracking done.'

Major Blake was ready. He signalled to his men. One was heavy, a nightclub bouncer and security expert. A few strong lads were in position. Now. It was time to move in. The major would courteously ask the wild men to leave. If not, the bouncer would apply pressure. These troublemakers would find themselves outnumbered by nice young men in suits, and by a couple of young ladies who knew martial arts and how to humiliate wild men. The major was surprised to find he had been just a little disappointed that things had so far worked out well. No matter, he would enjoy seeing they remained well and calm. A matter of moments and with luck, not many people would notice his swift, clean operation to clean the hall of trouble.

The rough man shouted into his smartphone. He waved along the two rows at the back. Somehow, and the major took weeks later working out how, the hall was full of dangerous types. He had been utterly out-generalled. A dozen or so lads came pouring in from outside. Their dogs were barking and lunging, so far, still on their leashes. The rough general was no fool. Dogs are far more effective as threats. His would leave no bites, with consequences for himself.

Various chants went up: 'Paedo vicar, paedo vicar, paedo, paedo, get rid of paedoes'; 'Hypocrites, hypocrites';

'Can we join your bondage classes, Vicar?'; 'Take me, Vicar; take me to your bondage room'.

The dogs jumped up and turned over chairs. People ran screaming away from them. The men began to smash up the chairs and the crockery. A banner of St Martha was ripped from the wall. Children's pictures were torn in pieces. Maisy started wailing; 'Calm down, have some cherry cake.' She started to cry as several dogs jumped on the counter and ate it.

In the chaos, the vicar stood firm as a chained bear under attack. The bishop was magnificent. He towered like a rock, and remembered his rugby skills. Several men nursed bruises from his tackles for days. Slowly he and the major regrouped against the forces of the Midianites, and in an instant the wild crowd was gone and a trail of destruction was left behind it. The bishop was about to give chase but the vicar and major pulled him back.

'Let them go, sir. I can remember what they look like,' said Major Bernard Blake. 'We'll round 'em up.'

Three council officials arrived. They were shocked to see that the stored election booths were smashed. 'What will happen to tomorrow's election?' wailed one.

'Don't worry, we carry on, there's plenty more we can get in time.' The chief official turned to the vicar. 'I'm afraid, sir, we shall have to charge you for damage to council property.'

People were calming and Maisy and her team made more tea and brought her reserves of cakes from under the counter. 'It takes a lot to stop tea,' she said. 'Carry on drinking,' she smiled. 'Tea or coffee, Bishop?'

People settled. Now it was over they were glad they had been through this together.

'Where's Fred?' someone asked.

'He slipped out, hoping not to be noticed. He must be ashamed of himself,' said the organist.

'No,' said Polly, very worried, 'the mob carried him off on their shoulders.'

Chapter 7

After a night of heavy rain the fingers of dawn flung tender shades of pink and blue across the sky. It was a glorious May morning. The birds were delirious and John was optimistic. The previous evening, though interesting, had turned out well. His anxieties had been reasonable – there was no need to reproach himself for having felt them – but he could not have wished, really, for a better outcome. The worst had been faced and banished.

The bishop himself had seen it and John was now ready to meet his prelate.

John rose with the sun just before five thirty. It had long been light before then. He said Morning Prayer and had a cup of coffee. He prepared for his interview.

At seven o'clock he sat down with Katie for a rare, proper breakfast. He had scrambled eggs on toast and two cups of tea. Katie had her special slimming cereal and strong coffee.

'You'll be all right, love,' she said. 'He can be a silly bishop, but he does see sense in the end.'

'I felt awful when he slipped in late like that. Just what I was dreading. Then when all that chaos started,' John laughed, 'he really enjoyed himself. It was probably the best fun he's had since he was breaking heads in Cambridge.'

'You'll be just fine,' she said. She topped up her cup. 'He needs you, if nothing else, to keep him entertained.'

She glanced at the kitchen clock. It was always ten minutes fast. She had easily gone back to nursing and found a job at the local hospital. They jumped at a trained nurse of her quality who was not afraid to get her hands dirty. 'Must rush,' she said, 'it's not fair to keep the night shift waiting. See you around half eight this evening, if nothing turns up. Don't forget to vote!'

'Oh I forgot. Probably on my way back. I don't know who for.'

'Then you should. Don't be remote, Vicar. I'm voting for William.'

''Cause he's the only one who called?'

'Precisely.' She slammed the door and was gone.

John took his leisurely way down the hill and through the old half-walled city. He loved the early morning before the tourists arrived, workers grabbing a sandwich and coffee, the dust carts clearing cardboard boxes from the streets, delivery vans knocking at shop doors, a few people studying the windows, the world all fresh.

Today was clean, lovely after the rain. The sky was golden blue and far above, a beautiful aeroplane was cruising to some exotic place. John rejoiced in the skill that made these things possible.

He went down Hillford's most beautiful street, Butchers Lane. Councils did not do apostrophes any more. Perhaps they could not decide if it was one butcher or more than one, or maybe they were using a noun as a kind of adjective, like people saying "woman bishop" rather than "female bishop". He wondered how soon the current Bishop of Hillford would be succeeded by a female bishop.

Ah, the bishop. John waved to the security guards as he passed under the Great Gate, without having to pay. They greeted him cheerfully as if pleased to see him.

Bishop Edward was a modern bishop in an old palace. It was one of the few remaining. He was a pragmatic man who did not mind either way. He would have preferred a new house like John's, but larger of course. However, he recognised the implacable logic of his position. It would cost a fortune to update him. The Old Palace was built into the fabric of the precinct. Tourists expected to see a bishop wandering round the place preferably old, in scarlet robes, with a beard and looking faintly other-worldly. Thank goodness the Church Commissioners had seen sense in allowing his old mate the Bishop of Bath and Wells to stay in his lovely old place. The swans, the lake, the bishop; just the right note of beauty, nature and holiness.

Bath was the one place that Bishop Edward had coveted. Instead he got ancient Hillford. He loved the city. He loved wandering round, meeting people, being seen buying his sandwich lunch at Eat Me. He enjoyed chatting to strangers and unlike John, never had problems in shaking a thousand hands a week if need be.

The bishop would have made a very good politician – which in fact he was, though he had never had to face what William and thousands did today, a British election after a gruelling campaign.

John entered the old yard, which was as dusty as when Henry was king. The walls badly needed repointing. Through the entrance he found Janet at her desk. She was in her late forties, cheerful and would have welcomed even Genghis Khan with a cup of tea before converting him into a sweet Anglican. She knew everyone in Hillford, and what they were doing. She found people endlessly amusing.

'Good morning, John,' she said. John wished she were in charge of his case. 'I'm afraid you're in the library today. Still, he seems in a good mood.'

The palace was a building of two halves. The ground floor was historic, beautiful, dark, enclosed by its Tudor past. Much of the administration happened here, though on open days the public were allowed in to marvel at the ancient sunk rooms. Above on the first floor lived the bishop's personal quarters. Normally he welcomed his guests here to the warm, bright lounge. It was here that the bishop spent many hours reading, preparing his talks, and planning. He loved looking out at the tourists. Next door the delicious rose garden of the Canon Residentiary wafted glorious scents in summer.

John smiled. 'Looks like I'm in trouble,' he told Janet. 'Library, eh?'

He went into the large, old reception room, which was two steps down from the lobby. It was half-timbered, with red bricks peeping, and had small windows. Someone had placed Victorian chairs around, in an attempt to make it look authentic. Official functions which could not be avoided happened here. It had the effect of shortening them as people made their earliest excuses. On open days the public poured in to have their romantic view confirmed of how a bishop should live.

John walked through this room and into the corridor.

On the wall was a picture of an old Baptist preacher. The library door was open. He tapped and went right in.

'Come in, come in, John. Thank you for coming, how nice to see you.' Bishop Edward sounded like the host at the start of a cruise.

They shook hands. John noticed someone else in the corner. It was Babs. She nodded, smiled briefly and did not offer her hand. She sat down in a corner and took out a pen.

'Sit down, John, sit down.' The bishop indicated a chair, in the centre of the room. John sat in front of a table with a green covering. The bishop sat the other side of this with his back to the window. The old books on the groaning shelves looked down with interest. Though the day was sunny, the bishop had a standard lamp lit in the corner where Babs was seated. There was a frown on her face. The room was cold.

John was offered no tea or coffee, but there was a glass available on the table and an endless supply of water. Four bottles of mineral water sat close to hand. There were more at the edge of the table.

The three clergy said a little prayer.

'Now, John, now, let's sort this one out. It won't take long, won't take long, I'm sure. Thank you for your hospitality yesterday evening. A most interesting meeting.'

'You acquitted yourself valiantly, Bishop,' said John.

A boyish smile lit up the bishop's face. Then he remembered himself. 'One does one's best,' he said. 'However, we really have to resolve this whole thing, John, won't take long, I'm sure.' He looked across at Babs, who made no recognition. 'I've asked Archdeacon Barbara to come along to, ah, make sure there is no misunderstanding. Now don't worry John, this is not a formal enquiry or disciplinary matter, no nothing like that, we try to avoid that sort of thing, I do especially as you know, but ah well, there are times when—' He looked at a vase of flowers for help.

'It's good to clarify matters and see how to go forward,' suggested John.

'Exactly that, John, exactly that. I'm sure we shall soon sort things out together. I thought we might have a cosy chat. To see how to proceed. Work out the future.'

John waited.

'To go forward on the next stage of our pilgrimage.' Edward looked at the old books. They were not going to help him.

John looked across at Babs, and smiled. She made no recognition. John waited for the bishop.

'What I think is best, John, is if you go on a retreat and sabbatical for say six weeks. The old forty days, eh? Get a rest, recharge the old batteries, do some thinking, meditate, say prayers, that sort of thing, eh, get reorientated. Good healthy food, nice country walks, eh? Think about the next, er, steps, er...'

'Stage of my pilgrimage?' offered John.

'Yes, yes. Good man, I knew you would understand.'

'I think I do, Bishop. You are giving in to the press, you're doing what their editorial tells you to, you are shunting me to one side and hoping I will come back as a boring priest, and stop all my stunts and stop causing you trouble.'

The bishop stared at him, with a look that Nathan the

Prophet would have considered excessive. He controlled himself with a vast effort. He must show leadership here. He looked across to the archdeacon. She was writing.

'I am sorry you take that attitude, Father John. Let us consider your position.'

'My position, Bishop, is that in the three years I have been at St Martha's, church attendance has increased by 69.3 per cent, and rising. Yes, I do employ modern and sometimes amusing or unusual methods. The punters seem to like it. I have more young people, young families, as well as older people, than any other church for ten miles around.'

'Beware the sin of pride, John.'

'You want the church to increase its mission, Bishop. I am only doing my best.'

'While upsetting a whole lot of people.'

'The church was never meant to be a soft touch, Bishop.'

The bishop gripped hard on the pencil in his hand. He snapped the pencil in two. 'Don't be naïve, John. It matters a great deal what impression we make. The church can't afford in these times even the slightest whiff of scandal. You know what they say about us and crazy clerics and children. We have to be cleaner than snow. Your little sketch was so open to misinterpretation. It was a weird mixture of raunchy and on the edge of danger to children.'

'How do you know? You weren't there.'

'The account in the press wasn't made up.'

'You were talking of naïve just now, Bishop? I am sorry, I don't wish to be disrespectful, but one really cannot believe every word in the press, or TV, or radio, or social media.'

The bishop sighed. 'That is hardly the point, John. It is not the actual truth that matters here, but the impression of truth.'

'What is truth, eh?'

'We have to be so careful, John. The church has many enemies. That service of yours and the subsequent reporting has done a great deal of harm. I am only asking you to lay off for a while, consider your methods, and go on retreat for a short time to readjust and redeploy. I am right behind you, John, 115 per cent, really am, and want you and your parish to go from strength to strength. But we really cannot afford to offend the press these days.'

'You know what they are like, Bishop. They can be irresponsible and malicious. Look, they made ridiculous claims over my harmless little play. They are the real danger. When they get silly and sensationalise, they make people less likely to take the real, vile abuse seriously. People just say: there the press go again, putting a vicious spin on harmless things in order to sell papers.'

'We must respect press freedom, John, we really must, especially in these times.'

'And what about my freedom of expression, Bishop?'

The bishop stared at the old books. 'The media make the rules, John.'

'I stand for truth, Edward.'

'Stop imagining yourself as a martyr, John. We don't go in for that sort of thing any longer. Just be sensible. I am recommending nonetheless that you go on a refreshing and comfortable retreat. We look forward to seeing you come back as your old – but renewed – self, John.'

'Bishop, are you instructing me to go?'

'Oh dear, John, don't force me. We don't use that sort of language. But yes, if you force me, in view of the unfortunate scope for recent and future misunderstandings from the press and public, I think it best.'

John smiled. He felt admiration for the man. This silly and muddled bishop had outmanoeuvred him comprehensively. You don't, thought John, get to be a bishop of the Church of England without considerable gifts.

The bishop laughed. 'Happy, John? Let's be friends, John. I'll even take you to Twickenham to see Harlequins...'

They both laughed and shook hands. 'Well done, Edward, you win. No promises, mind, no promises.'

The bishop came round from his desk and gave John a rugby hug. 'Glad you agree, dear fellow, well done,' he said. Barbara put down her pen, grinned and joined the holy huddle.

The phone rang. The bishop looked cross but went to answer it. 'Janet, I thought I said no – ah, oh, I see.' The bishop listened in great silence for a couple of minutes. He paled over and looked sick. He placed the receiver down.

'Oh, oh,' he said. He sounded like an animal in pain. 'Oh no, I've just been told that Fred Vestal has been found dead in the porch of St Martha's.'

Chapter 8

It began badly, got better, then descended into farce and calamity.

Mr Brown, in charge of his first polling station, was not pleased, not one iota, to have found a meeting which delayed his preparations. He left and returned to find a civic riot. One of his polling booths had been smashed beyond repair. After a great deal of effort, calling up reluctant security men, he had finally got hold of a replacement from County Hall at eleven in the evening.

He and the team set up, finished by midnight, well done team he told them, and were back in the morning for the seven o'clock start. Their mood was not improved by the loss of the spare cherry cake which Maisy had kindly promised them for their sustenance during the long voting day of fifteen hours; the dogs had slavered all over it and chewed half.

Things went rapidly uphill between seven fifteen and nine. Maisy brought in a new cherry cake, newly baked, for a late breakfast. There was a steady stream of polite and appreciative voters, and it was a lovely day.

Mr Brown knew that henceforth everything would be perfect. There would be a record turnout and he would be commended for the best and most welcoming team. There was an unofficial competition between all the teams to see who could make their polling station the most friendly, with such things as flowers and even light music in the background. A few had a jar of sweets available. They really tried to make democracy a pleasure.

By nine forty, Joanne was desperate for a smoke. She was down to five a day. She and Jason had agreed not to try for a baby till she was entirely clear. The incentive was working, but slowly.

Joanne excused herself. She slipped past the car park, and along the side of the church. She stood by the north porch door, admiring the flower garden. She thought how lucky she was. She would beat the weed, cuddle up to her man and have lots of babies. They both had good jobs and Jason was doing really well in his home maintenance business.

She wandered into the garden, threw the cigarette stub among some tulips, as it was very compostable. She mustn't spend too long, but the semi-formal garden was lovely. In true local style there were untidy edges. You could not conquer wild nature; it would plant and seed what it wished.

She nodded in approval at a large green heap. This was all very ecological, grass cuttings from the large field behind the hall and church. They must have modernised what was once the graveyard, to turn it into grassland. She wondered if they had picnics and games that side of the church.

The garden too had clearly once been part of the graveyard. It was now a living garden. She imagined it had all been cleared with due respect. It was hard to imagine there were once a lot of bodies underneath.

Time to go back.

There was something strange about the rotting grass heap. There was a green man lying there covered with slime. Joanne screamed. It was a dead body. It should have been underground. It had no business appearing suddenly above ground on this bright May morning.

It was worse than a horror show. She ran to get Mr Brown.

The organist, whose name was Tom, and Major Blake voted at around nine fifty. They drifted along to the church, Tom to practise for next Sunday's service and the major to see what sort of job the Community Payback people had done on the garden. He did not think that last night's rioters would have had the wit to find, much less damage the garden, but he had to make sure. Tom was humming a tune as they walked. He was well aware the congregation thought that if a hymn had two possible tunes, Tom would infallibly choose the duller one, if more than two, the dullest. He planned to surprise them. He would introduce some hot, hippy, happy-clappy chorus tunes next month. That would cheer the vicar up.

A young woman came racing past them. She was crying. She ran into the hall.

The major saw it first. The body lay face down in the filthy compost heap. Someone had rolled it over a couple of times. It was covered with green slime. One side of the face was showing.

It was the journalist who had caused so much grief.

Tom clutched the major's arm. Both men wondered if Father John was capable of so much hatred.

The major took charge. 'Touch nothing,' he

commanded. He and Tom retreated twenty paces. Major Blake called the police on his smartphone.

They went back to the hall. There was no need to inform Mr Brown or Fiona. They were shaken and wondering what to do. Joanne was sobbing quietly and Fiona went to make some cups of tea. Mr Brown was relieved that Major Blake had phoned the police.

'Seal off the area,' said the major. 'Let people come in and vote, but they mustn't go west of the car park. Act perfectly normally. The police are coming.'

'It's a good job that this is normally a low time of the day for turnout,' said Mr Brown. 'If we are lucky no one will turn up for half an hour.' He was surprised at himself for uttering such heresy.

Detective Inspector Mark Ellis scorched to a halt twenty minutes later. It was on the main road – no parking allowed – because somebody had sealed off the whole of the car park with police tape. The complete church site was a forbidden crime scene.

Helen. Trust his sergeant, Helen Roper. She was there a full fifteen minutes before him. With two constables she was preventing any public access. This was a crime scene. To blazes with elections.

Her car was of course inside the car park. Mark blew his horn. The constables raised the tape and let him through. He parked his new white Peugeot by her battered Ford, next to the official police car. She was tapping at his window before he could undo his seat belt.

'Nice to see you, sir,' she said. 'We've been waiting. For your guidance, sir. Traffic's heavy today, isn't it?'

It was the method that entranced and irritated him. If she had not been so damned brilliant, he would have had her transferred long ago. And that smile, enough to melt a glacier.

'Cut it out, Roper,' he said. He mustn't look at her eyes. 'Where's the body?'

She led him close to the scene. Nothing had been touched. 'Forensics are on their way, Mark,' she said. 'In the meantime, we can infer: young, professional, male, apparently knocked unconscious, maybe killed, by a blow, then left to suffocate in that pile of sludge. Not a casual murder, not a prank gone wrong, not a drunken accident. The culprit really hated him – look, the victim has been rolled round and round in the filth. Some sort of point is being made. There is some attempt at humiliation, maybe sadistic not sexual, as none of his clothing has been removed. Indeed, Mark, sir, I know the victim's identity.'

'I'm sure you are going to tell me.'

'Yes, sir. Fred Vestal, talk of the town, the journo who damaged the vicar so much.'

'Are we to draw the obvious conclusion, Detective Sergeant?'

'Let us just say, sir, Father John is at the very top of our interview list.'

Inspector Ellis walked near the body and had a good look.

'We'd better leave now, Helen. We're in danger of polluting the scene.'

'I thought of that, sir.' Of course she had. Her cool eyes appraised him as if surveying the talent at a nightclub. 'I thought it best, though, to let you form first impressions close at hand. First impressions tell us so much, don't you think?'

He sighed. 'Ever heard about grandmothers sucking eggs, Helen?'

They drifted back to the polling station. Mr Brown began to protest. 'Look, Detective Inspector, we have an election here, for the second most important tier of government. Can you not move the tape and let the people in? Otherwise I shall have to inform the returning officer and there is great danger we will have to cancel or postpone the vote. I don't know if we can extend the voting hours by even one minute. The election for this seat will be null and void. All manner of inconvenience will attend this.'

'I am sorry, sir, this is as you know a crime scene.' That was Helen.

Mr Brown turned to the inspector. 'Look, Officer, can't you get your team to escort people in and out, from and to the street? Already people who wish to park will be unable and will be seriously inconvenienced, and there may well be danger on the highway if they try to park there. This unfortunate occurrence will turn people away. Those who try now may not come back to vote later.'

He seemed more upset at the loss of voters than the loss of Fred's life. He sank down in his seat and ruffled his hands through his hair.

Mark took Helen aside for a private chat in the kitchen.

'Why do you always do this, Helen?'

'What, sir, always arrive before you do, and take decisive action?' Her blue eyes bored into him.

'Helen, stop playing the innocent. Why, Detective Sergeant, are you so pedantic, why do you always go over the top? It would have been perfectly adequate to seal off the area between the hall and the church. There is plenty of space. People could come in, park their cars, vote, disappear, and think no more about the police car here than ordinary security. But now you are shouting "Murder" at the public.

Look, the garden is sealed off by a huge hedge. The public will never see forensics working behind the proper taped area. At worst they might think we were investigating some church break-in.'

'No, sir. As you, the public and I know, Mark, the police don't come out for small things any more. *De minimis non curat lex,* as one might say. That means, sir, the law doesn't care about micro crime.' She was proud of the GCSE Latin she had taken before leaving school at sixteen. She devoured the scraps of legal jargon she picked up.

'I know what it means, Helen. You're wrong, we care about it all. But we haven't got the resources. Dammit, Sergeant, let these people vote, they might choose some politicians who give us coppers more cash.'

'Yes, sir,' she said. 'That's very good.'

A constable tapped on the door. 'Sir, there's a man called William. Says he knows you. Says it's urgent. Says he's one of the candidates.' The constable's voice was deep as a Yorkshire cave.

'Just what I need. Bring him in.'

Three minutes later, William arrived. 'Good morning, Brother,' he said. 'Busy morning for us all.'

'Helen, you know William Ellis, my brother? He's one of the candidates in this election.'

'Indeed, sir, I like to be well informed.' She pouted as prettily as a milkmaid in the time of Pepys. She shook hands with William. 'Nice to meet you again, sir; we met at the Hillford Legal Society dinner last year. You gave a remarkable speech.' Her smile was warm.

'Oh, a modest proposal. Call me William.'

'A fine contribution to a great debate, William, on when and where it is right to show restraint in applying law and when to enforce its full majesty, such as when the homeless—'

'Yes, yes,' interposed Mark. He was supposed to be the flexible and reflective one in this team. 'When you two have stopped swapping philosophic notes?'

'Indeed, Brother, you have a murder to solve.'

'With respect, William, we don't know that yet.' Helen gave him no smile this time.

'Quite right, quite right, I do apologise,' said William. 'There is an unexplained death on church premises, which you must investigate.'

She beamed. Both Ellis brothers were capable of correction.

'In which context,' continued William, 'we have a problem. I am reliably informed that said unfortunate body is at a considerable distance from this hall which today is a polling station. You have roped off too much area, Brother, and are preventing people from exercising their lawful right to vote.'

Mark flung a reproachful stare at his colleague. 'We were just discussing that, weren't we, Detective Sergeant Roper?'

'Yes, sir,' she said.

'Hmm,' said William. 'On the one hand you do not wish to give the impression, however wrong-headed, that you opened up the hall just so your brother could get elected to the county council.'

Helen looked hopeful. 'That indeed is one more reason for me to advise we keep the line where it is.'

'On the other hand, Mark, you don't wish to appear to thwart democracy, shut down a polling station, cause unnecessary postponement of an election, at the cost of thousands of pounds, appear officious, pedantic and over the top.'

Helen flushed with anger. Whatever else Mark was, he could not be described like that.

'Either way you are in trouble, little brother.'

'You are both making life very difficult,' snapped Mark. He was normally a fit-looking forty. Today he felt like a weary fifty. Retirement was decades away.

'The press will have a field day, sir. Imagine what they will say if you give the impression that you even slightly damaged a crime scene, of their own dead journalist as well, sir, think of that, makes it ten times worse – just so you could get your brother elected to the council. What would the superintendent say, sir? A month or two's delay is nothing, Mark. I don't really see you have any choice.'

'Hang the press. The superintendent will back me, she'll understand, even if you don't, Helen.'

Helen looked as if she had been stabbed.

'I won't mention the point that if I do get elected two months late, there goes any chance I have of getting a Cabinet post.'

'Hang the council. I am deciding this on purely operational grounds.' Mark stood silent as Buddha.

Helen and William knew better than to speak.

'I am going to overrule you, Sergeant. We're moving that tape back.'

'I really don't recommend it, Mark.'

'It's time I stopped listening to you, Helen.'

The smile and sadness that passed between them was like an epitaph.

'Very well, sir, I am putty in your hands.'

Mr Brown was relieved. No voter, by luck, had turned up at that slack time in the twenty-minute delay. There was no need now to postpone the vote, or ask for an extension of voting hours, or otherwise inconvenience the voters or those who supervised the voters. Mr Brown had already had quite enough of this particular venue.

Forensics arrived and discreetly set up camp. Few people noticed.

Major Blake had already phoned the vicarage to inform Father John. There was no reply and the major remembered the interview. He phoned the Old Palace. Janet took the call and put him through to the bishop, who almost fainted.

In the library, the bishop, Babs and John agreed that John's retreat was out of the question. He had better be available. John agreed to go home, pray, think and await the police.

Chapter 9

Karen trembled as she poured herself a cup. Her hand shook: the coffee spilt and scalded her left arm. She flinched and knocked over the red plastic cafetiere. It fell on the hard kitchen floor and smashed into little pieces. Karen fell sobbing to the ground and curled up like a hurt puppy.

Another part of Fred was lost. It was her last present to him.

They had met three years before in the Lake District. She loved hillwalking and frequently visited Norway. That September she had left Copenhagen for a two-week tour of Cumbria. She was entranced by its beauty and was content to wander happy days in this ravishing land. When she could be bothered she recited Wordsworth. She met Fred sitting on a cairn. He was twenty minutes ahead of her in crossing Striding Edge. She always believed he was waiting for her.

He offered her a swig of lemonade, and a grubby tomato sandwich. She laughed, they talked, and a week later she decided to abandon her studies in Copenhagen. A month later they moved into a flat in Manchester. She transferred her final year of accountancy while he completed his journalism course. Her English was so fluent that most people thought she was a native of some undefined place in the north.

He was an auburn Lancastrian, serious at heart and a very lapsed Catholic. She was a fun-loving daughter of Denmark. Her father was a Lutheran pastor in a cosy part of Copenhagen. She was slightly lapsed: she attended church perhaps twelve times a year, which most of her friends thought was way over the top. Her humour was wicked.

She convinced Fred that, not only was the Little Mermaid statue quite large, contrary to urban myth, but that she Karen Christensen was the original model for it. She showed him pictures and indeed her face did bear a close resemblance, and her body was a similar build.

He took to boasting in the local pub about his wonderful new girlfriend, the original of the Little Mermaid. His friends were impressed at first, then amused, then bored, then irritated. Dave took the trouble to check it on the Internet. He challenged Fred to a round of drinks – if Fred was right, then free drinks to Fred for a fortnight; if Dave was right, then Fred paid two whole rounds for his eight mates.

The truth came out. Poorer in cash and briefly humbled in spirit, Fred went home in a furious mood to Karen.

She laughed as if she would die. "My poor, sweet darling," she said. "You're so innocent, I do love you, I couldn't resist. I had a bet with my dad how long I could fool you. I've just lost, by three days, so we're equal." Her laugh was merry as bluebells.

Fred sulked a bit, saw the funny side, and decided that against his principles he would marry her within the year. This was a woman he could not lose. Plus, he had learnt more from her prank than in the rest of his course. Journalist, check your facts.

They were married at her father's church in outer Copenhagen, in a long ceremony, with a long sermon, and long hymns in a language he could not understand, surrounded by cheerful people who at the wedding feast cracked hilarious jokes in English, drank a lot and kept saying "Tak".

Their honeymoon included a visit to Møllehøj, the highest hill in her happy country, "at 170.86 metres, a mere pimple on the breasts of your Lake District mountains," she said. "I'm the only person in Denmark who prefers it to the much more scenic Mountain of Heaven at a baby 147 metres."

He didn't care – he was with her – what did he care, if they were together. He vowed there and then, he would be the best in his trade, for her. One day he would return with Karen to Scandi lands, to Oslo for the Peace Nobel, or better, Stockholm for the Literature Prize. She laughed and told him not to be silly. He was fine just as he was, men didn't have to prove themselves to women. As a feminist she had no need of that. She would liberate him too.

So would he mind – just relaxing – and accept that, weird as it sounded, she just loved Fred? For himself, just as he was? If that was not too much to ask?

Now she was sobbing on the floor. She curled up as she did the day that her little brother hid her doll. Alas, her doll soon came to light, and the siblings became best friends – but never if she searched the universe would she find her Fred again. She covered her face and wept.

The phone rang. She pulled herself up to the ledge and picked up. It was her father. He offered such help as he could. He quoted the lovely old words about mourners being comforted. Her sobs subsided as her bear-like father's voice soothed her.

'Thanks, Dad.' She said goodbye and sank into the big, warm chair and wept. 'Fred, Fred, you never quite believed me, how much we love our men.' She fell exhausted in the sleep of misery.

The little boy she was carrying kicked her hard and she woke up. 'Fred,' she whispered, 'dear one, I shall call you Fred.'

The police and their twin, forensics, soon decided that this was a case of murder, or at least manslaughter. They found a nasty wound on the back of Fred's head, the bone smashed on the right side. There was a lesser wound on his forehead. There was no sign of any weapon. They were puzzled at the lack of blood. Eventually traces were found in the pile of sludge.

They examined the whole area. In the ancient porch they struck crimson gold. There were smearings of blood along a wall beneath a window, near a ledge where the stonework was old and viciously sharp. There were a few pieces of old stone missing. Fred had suffered a blow in here.

He might have staggered away in his pain and fallen in the slime. Or else his attacker had ceremoniously rolled him over and over again in the filth to make a point.

There was no blood at any point between the porch and garden. The blood in the pile of sludge was below the surface. That helped the police in their enquiries. The rain was fierce in the night but had ceased just before three. The blood had been washed away before then – hence the body was of someone killed earlier. Fred was alive at nine fifteen. There was the window for the killing, and all alibis.

Now released from the bishop, Father John wandered along to his church. He had to see. He went to the hall, where he was courteously turned away because he had not bothered to register to vote. He drifted towards his church and was stopped by the massive bulk of Constable Walker. The vicar explained who he was. 'I am sorry, sir,' boomed Walker, 'but I still cannot let you pass, because as you see this is a protected crime scene. I will inform Inspector Ellis that you called, sir. I am sure he will be in touch with you later.'

The vicar marvelled at the dark, rich bass of this officer, and how wonderful he would sound in a Russian Orthodox choir.

Inspector Ellis heard the exchange and came over. 'Good morning, sir,' he said. 'Something terrible has happened in your church.'

'I know. The bishop told me.'

Ellis looked annoyed. 'Word gets round quick in this small city, eh?'

Helen behind him muttered, 'Quickly.' She meant him to hear.

The vicar burbled: 'Yes, one of the teachers in our primary school told me she once asked her pupils if they could keep a secret, and they said they could but their mums and dads found it hard. The teacher said if I told you a secret, let's pretend I just killed the head teacher, and told you not to tell anyone, how long would it be before all of Hillford knew; half an hour? She smiled at them. Oh no, miss, they said, only five minutes. We'd text our mums from under our desks, or the toilet, then everyone would know, and you would be in jail, miss, in twenty minutes. They thought that was hilarious.'

Inspector Ellis was not amused. Helen Roper behind him stifled a giggle. She made a note of the vicar's need to burble. It was his defence mechanism.

'Officer?' queried the vicar.

'Please go home, sir. I should be grateful if you stayed there till we come to speak with you.'

'Very well, Officer. I hope that will not take long. I do have parishioners to visit you know.'

Father John, as he walked away, pondered on the long centuries. This was the first known killing at St Martha's. The cathedral was famous for its martyred bishop, killed just within his great church. Now St Martha's could be said to have its own martyr – Fred, not a saint, but killed perhaps for press freedom. Each martyr had been killed for his own version of the truth and what was precious in his own age. Martyrs do not have to be endearing.

William Ellis turned up and asked to speak to his brother. They met at the tape.

'How long will this take, Brother?' asked William. 'Word has got out and we think there'll be a flood of spectators turn up who have nothing to do with the election and they will disrupt the whole democratic process.'

'And put off the people who want to vote for you, William? And you'll lose votes and the election. Is that it, William?'

'Such cynicism, little brother! No, of course not. Remember I'm a lawyer.'

'That is exactly my point, William. Just let me get on

with the job, William, and we'll be as quick as we can. Consistent with a full and proper investigation, as you will fully appreciate. And we can still get you elected.'

'Quite so, quite so, I wouldn't want to use my influence with you to hinder the investigation of the facts. I am fully prepared to lose my election in this good cause, Brother, have no fear.'

Both men turned away less than pleased. They were underneath upset at coming this close to a quarrel. Helen looked on and considered whether there had been undue pressure on the police and incorrect personal influence at the scene of crime.

Helen asked Mark if they could have a private conversation in the police car. 'Not now, Helen, not now,' he said. 'Can't you see I've got an investigation to run *in situ*?'

'It is highly relevant, Mark,' she said. 'Sir?' She gave him her second best smile.

'Oh, if you put it like that.' It was the first time he had smiled that morning.

They sat side by side in the car, like awkward teenagers. She took the driver's seat. 'People will say, Mark, that you were seen talking to the vicar at the tape, not in any formal way and he is trying to influence you, and also to your brother, sir, a well-known lawyer, who may later be involved in the process, and worse, a candidate who just wants you to get out of his way so he can have his election in peace and get elected to the council. Just think, sir, what our enemies will make of that. People might say we improperly shortened the investigation under pressure, sir. Think what the chief superintendent or even the chief constable might say.'

Ellis leant towards her. He inadvertently slipped against the car horn, which made a huge noise and startled people. He was annoyed. 'Helen, we know each other well.'

'Indeed we do, Mark,' she smiled.

'So please don't even give me the feeling you are trying to put pressure on me, your senior officer, eh Helen. No matter how well we know each other, eh? And you wouldn't dream of trying to intimidate me, Helen, seeing as we are good friends?'

'I would not dream of any such thing, Mark,' she said. 'I am trying to look after us both.'

'Very good, Helen. Let's get back to work, shall we?'

'I really think we should interview the vicar at once, Mark. He can tell us a lot, especially in the first shock. Who has most reason to hate this dead male?'

'Just listen to yourself, Helen! We don't yet know it was any more than an unfortunate accident.'

She was furious. 'Just being realistic. There was a time when you said I was the best detective in the county; including you, Mark.'

'There's plenty of time to go and see the vicar. He's gone home to rest; strikes me as not a very confident man. Oh, he's not going anywhere, Helen. We can take our time over him. As priority, don't you agree, as my best detective, that we really ought to find out who was at the meeting last night, and go after them first? They might already be on the run. We know where the vicar lives. He's sitting there all meek and mild, stewing as he waits. He'll open to us like a flower when we do arrive. Psychology, Helen, psychology, I thought you knew about that? Eh?'

She said meekly, 'Just as you say, Mark.' He knew that

look. He decided to tackle the major at once. He was still waiting in the hall for his moment of influence on operations.

As she reached for the door handle, somehow Helen became clumsy. She hit the button which set off the blue light and siren. People for two hundred yards around scuttled for cover. Mr Brown looked out in annoyance. Stationary police vehicles do not normally emit such flashing noises at election time.

'Behave yourself, woman!' snapped Ellis. He clicked off the controls.

'Sorry, sir,' she murmured. 'Feeling very tense today.' Her stone-grey eyes gleamed. She tried not to laugh.

Mark gave her a wintry smile. 'If I did not know you so well, Sergeant,' he said, 'I would have said you did that on purpose.'

'It's a fair cop, gov,' she smiled. 'Sorry.' Her mood had changed to one of ineffable loss.

The investigation went along its proper course. Contrary to William's prediction, there were no extra people at the scene. The constables were too efficient for that. They properly allowed into the hall those who wished to vote, no more no less, no fewer. By the time of the usual tidal rush between five and seven o'clock the whole site had been fully searched, mapped and saturated with full enquiry. There was not a thing that the teams felt they had missed. By six o'clock the pathologist in charge and Inspector Ellis were satisfied that the site could be released. By seven there was no sign that anything at all had happened. They departed from the place in peace.

Chapter 10

The vicar planned his escape carefully.

He just had to visit the scene of crime. He went straight home and made his plans. He borrowed three hundred pounds from the vestry safe. Good job it had not been banked yet. He had more sense than to buy his tickets with a card. He pondered very carefully where to go. He badly wanted to hide. Where does a vicar hide? Where would be more natural than on retreat as the good bishop had suggested? John and he had agreed that this was not appropriate, so a retreat could be the last place the secular police might look.

John reproached himself for being naïve. He thought Walsingham, or Mirfield, or Minster would be good to hide in. He rejected those at once. They were exactly where a High-Church vicar would go and be picked up. Somewhere such as Iona, or Holy Island, nice and far away, cut off by the tide half the day? No good. Distance was no problem for the police. Where could he flee from their presence?

Somewhere unexpected, such as a Low-Church place; Lee Abbey perhaps or some other Evangelical outfit? Nope. Not a chance. France and some great abbey? Could he rush to a lovely Swedish refuge in the forests? No, nor anywhere else in the European Union. They would extradite him at the drop of a chasuble. Russia was out of the question. No. John had anyway not bothered to renew his passport, and all ports, air, sea and land, would be blocked.

No, all the attractive places were so obvious that the most junior police officer would easily find him. Hide in the depths of London? Go to a nice seaside place like Blackpool?

He must think of some completely counter-intuitive place, maybe a commune of a pagan goddess, or become the chaplain of some brothel in Soho? He told himself not to be silly – in his panic he was clearly not thinking straight.

Where would the police expect a priest with little money to hide and expect to be sheltered and kept? There were surely places which would give him sanctuary against all secular authority. He could happily do simple jobs for his keep. The superior would easily keep a straight face and a clear conscience and deny all knowledge of his existence.

No, nothing remotely religious would work. That is exactly what they would expect. Think, man, think, he told himself.

In the end John knew just the place. This one was original. He slung some simple things in a bag, checked the three hundred pounds and wondered what to tell Katie.

If only he had agreed to shake hands with Fred at the meeting, in public. None of this would have happened. If only he had not sought Fred out after the meeting. If only Fred had not been so vile.

He decided not to contact Katie. He would leave her a note and ask her profound forgiveness. The vicarage was empty by three in the afternoon.

Mrs Taylor's schoolchildren were wrong in thinking that news sped like arrows round the little city. The editor decided not to put it on the paper's website. He and his colleagues needed time to think. This was personal. Television and radio stayed silent until the evening. The social media were just warming up. Katie at her hospital did not hear till near the end of her shift. Hillford was in denial.

Katie got back at twenty past eight. It had been a busy, productive and happy day. She helped a lot of people and was too involved to hear anything from the outside world. It was a day that made life worthwhile.

'Home, honeycat,' she called as she got in. 'What's for dinner tonight?'

No answer. This was not unusual from her boyfriend. He was doubtless lost in his study in some profound thought of some great saint. Probably he hoped some of it would rub off on him. She smiled. One thing was for sure, he would be doing the cooking tonight, not her. He was good at baked potato and sausage. There was no smell of that in the house, however. Oh well, she was happy with beans and omelette.

She swung cheerfully into the kitchen. There she saw it pinned, with a neat and different-coloured drawing pin on each corner, to the breadboard near the kettle.

Her hand trembled. This meant nothing good. She unpinned the note and read:

Forgive me, my love, I have to go away a little while. I will not tell you where, so that you will not have to face pressure to inform the police. Do not worry. I shall be perfectly safe. I need time to think, to pray, to heal.

I am wrongly accused of being a weird eccentric, a bondage freak, a nutcase vicar, a danger to children. My parish work has been traduced. The bishop has suspended me without appeal. He tells me to hide in the house and take no services, do no duties, "till it all blows over". I am not even allowed to go on proper retreat. I sit here where all may come at me, without defence.

I looked on the social media. It is already starting. A vile campaign, full of horrible things is trending against me, "the vicious vicar of Hillford". It is no consolation, none at all, that the late Fred Vestal is similarly a victim of vile abuse, deceased though he is. It is no consolation that he began the whole process.

I shall miss you, my love; you have no idea what you mean to me. It would have been good to have been with you and known your comfort in these times.

It was only a children's play, for heaven's sake. I weep for the late Fred who so wilfully misrepresented me, my mission, and worse, so trivialised the topic of how we protect children from terrible things.

The man is dead. He was killed at my church. Who has reason to hate him as much as I? I am now a murder suspect. They will say: "The vicar, never mind all this forgiveness stuff, he must really have hated this young journalist, who was only doing his job, and standing up for freedom."

The police are coming. I cannot face them. I can no longer face my people and the community. I shall come back when I can. If.

Pray for me, my love. Resurgam - I shall rise again. (Our little joke!)

Your lover,
John xxx

It had been such a good day. Now this. Katie read the letter three times. She made herself a cup of instant coffee. She read the note again. 'Silly man,' she said. 'You poor, dear, stupid man.'

She made two photocopies and hid them away. She pinned the note back on the breadboard and rang the police. Five minutes later there was a pounding on the door. She walked across and opened the door. It was Inspector Ellis and Sergeant Roper. They introduced themselves.

'That was quick,' said Katie.

'On the contrary, we are far too late.' Helen shot her boss a filthy look.

'Did you really think we wouldn't come for you?' Helen was in no mood to be tactful. They were in the sitting room.

'I beg your pardon?'

'I'm so sorry, Mrs, er? My colleague is tired. It's been a long day.' Inspector Ellis spread his arms in apology. 'My colleague means – in view of recent events, of course you might assume we would wish to interview the vicar and his wife.'

'My name is Miss Katherine Baker, and I am the friend and live-in partner of the Reverend John Newman of this parish, who has been so sorely abused by the press, good man that he is, and you doubtless are going to come and accuse him wrongly of what appears to be a murder because the unfortunate journalist who began all this has carelessly been found dead on church premises. John has found it all too much and has left, perfectly lawfully, to find some solace somewhere away from it all where no one can find him for a few days. I have no doubt he will return when he is ready and will answer your questions. And I too have had a long, harrowing, but ultimately rewarding day, doing some good, I trust, in the world. I have just come in from a twelve-hour shift at the hospital, found the note as you see and summoned you as soon as I could.'

'Then if your man is so innocent, let us know where he is, answer our few simple enquiries and we can eliminate both of you from our enquiries, and leave you in peace,' said Helen, unrepentant. 'And yes, Ms Baker, we coppers also aim to do good in the world.'

'Miss,' said Katie.

'Cut it out, Helen,' said Ellis. 'Oh dear, Miss Baker, we do seem to have made a bad beginning. May we start again?'

'I'll get us some coffee. You need it as much as I do.' She smiled. It was like a teenager offering daffodils to Mum after a Saturday of sulks. She signalled to them to sit on the sofa. Mark sank into its soggy recesses.

Helen sat on a firm, old upright dining chair. She took out her notepad. 'Thank you, Katherine, may I call you that? Or is it Katie?'

'Miss Baker will do, Sergeant Roper.'

The inspector smiled. You could always get a laugh somewhere in the day.

He said not to trouble herself with coffee but Helen said she would love some. 'Poor you,' she said, suddenly sympathetic. 'You did absolutely the right thing to phone us as soon as you could, without even waiting to get some food. We will try not to be long. Why don't you put a quiche, or lasagne or nice macaroni or something in the oven, and it'll be nice and hot for when we're gone?'

Katie smiled. As a nurse she had heard similar talk far too often.

Helen spotted it. 'No, really. We'll leave you in peace and you can eat in peace – or if we do run over, I tell you what, turn it down, or turn the oven off and it will be nice and ready for when you are.'

The women smiled in sisterly understanding. Ellis forgot to laugh and wondered what he was missing here.

Katie disappeared into the kitchen. There were various bangs and clatterings. Five minutes later appeared a cafetiere of coffee and some Belgian biscuits. 'There, all done,' she said.

Ellis and Roper fell on the biscuits like Assyrian wolves. They had not realised how hungry and tired they were. It had been a long day tracking down and interviewing the noisy gang from the parish meeting. Now this; potentially the breakthrough.

It might be some time before Katie could eat her meal, and probably a burnt offering at that.

Katie caught her eye. 'Oh, don't worry,' she said. 'John thoughtfully took out an old hotpot from the freezer, so it would be thawed out and waiting to pop into the oven when I came home. I've put it on a low heat. It won't spoil even if we take an hour.'

Mark wondered what to read into this. Helen was in

no doubt. Katie sat coiled as a child for a story. The three sipped their coffee, like warriors warming up.

Secret messages seemed to be passing between the women. Mark read none of them. He felt better from the coffee. Without a word, Katie went and came back with fresh coffee and biscuits.

Helen took more coffee but no more biscuits. She warned herself to be aware of this preternaturally psychic opponent.

The police officers read the note, still pinned to the breadboard, then read it again, in silence. Neither of them touched the paper. Katie did not think it necessary to tell them of her photocopies and her repositioning of the note.

Helen was the first to speculate where the vicar might have gone, and why. As if musing aloud, she asked Katie, 'Now I wonder where a priest with little money would go and hide and expect to be sheltered and kept? Which place might think it right to give him sanctuary against secular authority?

That is obviously some religious centre, a place of retreat like a monastery? Now the Reverend John Newman is a clever man, so that is exactly where he would expect the police to look – so has he done some completely counter-intuitive thing, gone somewhere quite different? Has he joined a road band? Could he be hiding as an illegal immigrant, or as a rough sleeper on the streets? He will know such people through his work.

Just where are you hiding, John, in the sure knowledge the police will never think to look there? Interesting, very interesting.' She made it sound like a Christmas game.

Katie made a show of being helpful. 'I have no

idea where he is. One thing I can say: don't waste your time guarding all the ports and airports. He hasn't got a passport.'

'Thank you, Miss Baker; however, we shall still keep an eye out on the ports. He might still turn up and try his luck. We'll have to watch the little corners of the coast as well – he might know someone who can smuggle him over.'

'No chance,' said Katie. 'You don't know him as I do. He's very law-abiding.'

'Let us hope so, Miss Baker,' said Helen. 'Now as you know him so well, can you suggest all the places you can think of where he might have gone – including the unlikely ones?'

Katie ran through the names of the religious centres which John had considered, and more. She added: 'Of course, he won't have gone to any of them. He would expect you to look there first. I truly don't know where he might have gone.'

'Has he ever been an actor on the stage, or a musician, for example? Does he know people in that world?'

Katie laughed. 'Not my John. He's just as likely to have been a Siberian camel! He did work for a few years as a teacher then briefly as a social worker, so yes he would have some of those skills and contacts.'

'Thank you. We will find out. Are you sure you are telling us all you can, Miss Baker?'

'What my colleague means, Katie, is there anything you may have overlooked, as every lead is precious?' said Mark.

Delicious smells of dinner were drifting into the room.

Katie did not bother to hide her impatience to have these people gone. She turned round in longing.

Helen was relentless. 'Come now, Katie, he is your partner. You must be desperate to know where he is, that he's OK. You would move heaven and earth to find him. So help us, we'll find him for you all the quicker if you help us. Miss Baker?'

'I don't know, I tell you, I don't know.' Her loneliness and the sweet scents of food were driving her to distraction. 'Please believe me, I can't help you any more.'

'I find that hard to believe, Miss Baker.'

'Stop it, Helen,' said Mark. He too was feeling desperately hungry. It really was time to go home. Nothing more could be achieved this evening. He hoped Victoria had saved something hot for him at home.

Helen took another tack. This was the line she should have taken from the beginning, thought Ellis. 'Right, Miss Baker, please tell us all you know about last evening. You were there and saw everything that happened?'

'Yes, no,' said Katie. She was desperate for dinner and grabbed the last biscuit. She made no move to bring any more. She munched meditatively taking her time.

Helen was annoyed. 'What precisely do you mean by that, Miss Baker?' She made a flourish with her notebook.

'Yes, I was there. No, I did not see everything. Nobody ever does.'

Helen bit her lip. If she was ever to make inspector this was exactly the provocation to patience she was going to need. She flashed Katie her Grade Four smile. 'We shall be most grateful if you would tell us everything you did see that evening.' She waited like a seagull surveying a walker eating fish and chips.

'Absolutely,' smiled Katie. She related all she knew about the meeting, including the excellent business atmosphere, and then the moments of chaos, and final calm. She said that Fred had seemed cheerful but a little disappointed that the vicar insisted that Fred return to church to make his peace. 'He didn't seem to like the idea of going to church for real,' she laughed. 'John would have made him really welcome and been really nice and warm about the whole thing. I expect they'd have gone off for a glass of wine somewhere afterwards and become the best of friends.'

Helen raised her eyebrows. 'So why didn't your partner make friends, like a good Christian, the first chance he got? Why not make a public show of being reconciled? It must mean John deeply disliked this journalist for what he did?'

'These things take time to heal, even for a good man like John.'

Helen scribbled in her book. 'What happened at the end of the meeting? After, you say, the crowd carried off Fred on their shoulders like a hero? That must have annoyed your partner.'

'Most people went. A few of us stayed to chat a bit then just John and I were left. John told me to go home while he sorted out the final details with the election officials. He said he would give them a key to lock up after themselves and he'd explain where everything was. They could keep the key to let themselves in next morning.'

Helen scribbled. Mark happily let Helen continue. She was good at relentless narrative gathering.

Katie continued. 'I'd had that day off work, but was

on duty at eight next morning, Thursday, today, and a twelve-hour shift, so he thought I might like to get to bed early. So I did. He said he might just have a final look around before he came home. He was worried about Fred, knowing the mood of the crowd and might just have a quick look to see Fred was all right. He thought they were members of the local Wolf Gang – I think their leader is actually called Wolf. I told John to be careful then came home.'

Helen and Mark gave each other the most imperceptible of nods. They knew each other's body language. People in the force said these two had an almost supernatural understanding.

'When John came home, did he tell you what he did after you left?'

'No.'

'Let me be clear, Miss Baker, you and John are very close and share each other's secrets?'

Mark gave Helen a warning look. Katie saw this and was amused. 'Oh yes, Sergeant. Don't you and your lover do the same?'

Mark gave Katie a warning look.

'Very well then, Miss Baker, what I find hard to understand is that John apparently did not tell you everything that he did, saw and said between the time of your leaving the hall and his return to the vicarage. Surely, if you were worried as you say, about what John might do after the meeting and warned him to be careful, surely you would have been waiting up and got him to tell you everything he had done or had happened to him? I just don't understand, Miss Baker, seeing as you are as close as you say any woman is to her lover.' She shot a warning glance at Mark.

'John and I did not talk at all, for the very reason I told you. I went home and was asleep in bed when he arrived home. I knew he would be all right. He is very considerate and knows how much I need to sleep for the next day. He was certainly not going to wake me up except for a real emergency. Anyway, he was there all bright and breezy in the morning. He was ready to meet his bishop.'

'So you didn't even chat over the cornflakes before you left?'

Katie shuddered. 'I don't eat cornflakes, Officer.'

'Whatever. Did you discuss things over breakfast before you hurried off?'

'Not a lot. There was not a lot to say. He just said it had all worked out but there was still more to do. That was it, and I had to rush off. I expected we would have a good conversation this evening. But this has happened. So if you don't mind, it has been a stressful day and a horrid evening, I do need some privacy. I've told you all I possibly can.'

'Possibly can? What do you mean by that, Miss Baker? All you possibly can bring yourself to tell us, or all you really know?'

'What do you think, Sergeant?' The smells of dinner were driving Katie mad. She wanted these people gone. She prayed that John would find a way to send her a message before bedtime, and anyway she badly needed more sleep before next day's early and long shift. The dinner might start to be overcooked as well and she was starting to grow faint. 'Have you finished?'

'Miss Baker, I find it impossible to believe that John

did not tell you a great deal more. He, maybe, discussed with you his plans for flight. I believe you are keeping vital information from us, Miss Baker. You really had better tell us everything.'

Katie flared up. 'I have told you everything. You are now starting to bully and there's nothing more you can get out of me. Why don't you leave? I've got patients who need me in the morning.'

'There are other nurses, Miss Baker. Are you going to tell us more, or is it necessary to invite you to the police station to question you in a more formal setting?'

Katie had never smelt a more heavenly meal and here she was trapped at the gates of paradise, locked out. 'Please leave. I've told you all I know. Please understand I am sick with worry about John. I've not the slightest idea where he is, or what he did after the meeting last night. Now, are you satisfied?'

'I think, Miss Baker, we shall have to invite you to come with us to the station. You can help us work out what really happened.'

Katie did something she would regret. It was against all the professional discipline instilled in her. It had been a long day. She was almost insane with worry about John. With a smile she said: 'Sergeant Roper, you are being unreasonable. It is not my job to aid police speculation.'

'That, Miss Baker, is for us to decide.' Helen returned the smile.

'Right,' said Katie, 'I too can be unreasonable. If you persist in harassing me, I shall report the affair you two are having to your superiors.'

'How…?' Mark went crimson.

'So it's true.' Katie's laugh was as merry as church bells over a May meadow.

Helen was furious. 'You have no grounds for thinking any such thing.'

Katie stared at her woman to woman. A slight flush appeared on Helen's cheek. 'Very well,' said Helen, 'you give me no alternative. I am arresting you on suspicion of a) perverting the course of justice and hindering police officers in the course of their duties, strictly two offences but we will roll them into one and b) attempting to blackmail police officers in the course of their duties.'

She read out the immortal words about silence possibly harming her defence.

'Oh don't be silly,' said Katie.

'I'm afraid she is serious, Miss Baker,' said Mark, 'and I'm afraid I have to support my colleague. Come along and get this over as quickly as possible.'

'Can't I eat my dinner first?' said Katie.

'Oh, we'll find a sandwich for you down at the station,' said Helen. 'I do hope you won't require us to handcuff you.'

'Cut it out, Sergeant,' said the inspector. 'That will not be necessary. Clearly Miss Baker is no danger, or in any danger. Of course she may eat her dinner. We can wait. Anyway, Helen, she will be in better shape to answer our questions with some good food inside her, and all being well can be back at home in bed in good time for the sleep she needs.'

'Very well, sir,' said Helen. 'Let it not be said we coppers are cruel. Let us give Miss Baker no grounds for any complaints. We are after all a public service.'

Mark shook his head. 'Stop it, Helen.'

Fighting off the tears, Katie went into the kitchen. Sounds appeared off stage of plate out, oven opening, clatter of cutlery, glass of water, condiments, food banged on plate, tray being loaded. Katie reappeared, little smile on face, and sat down at the table and allowed the police to watch.

Helen stood heavy and close as if observing the last meal of a condemned prisoner. She was damned if she would allow Katie to enjoy her meal. Mark gave her a little glance. Helen ignored it and stood as close as she could, overlooking Katie. She wanted her to feel like a marked terrorist. Mark sat down and picked up the *Guardian* which John had left.

Katie enjoyed her meal. She took her time. She was well aware that each officer was hungry and tired like herself. Normally she would have been full of compassion and given them food. Not today. The police had chosen to make this a contest. If it was to be her last civilised meal for some time, Katie was damn well going to enjoy it and extract the extra fun of tormenting the police. After all, they had their homes to go to, either together, or their respective spouses. She sighed – ah, the infinite frailties of man- and woman-kind. She really enjoyed her last quarter of an hour in her home.

Mark got absorbed in the newspaper and held off hunger that way. Helen concentrated on staring at this remarkably stubborn witness and enjoyed thinking how she, Helen, would break Katie at the station. It would be sweet retribution and then she would get home, gobble lasagne and drink two glasses of Merlot once her son was safely asleep. With luck Katie would tell them enough to solve the case in twenty hours.

Mark enjoyed frustrating Helen, in letting Katie finish her meal after arrest, against normal procedure. This was, after all, Hillford.

Eventually, Katie was finished. 'Time to go, Miss Baker. Bring some warm clothes.'

Chapter 11

Next day William was declared duly elected as Member for Hillford Central on the county council by 597 votes. It was a moderate but not magnificent margin. He was among the last to know.

William was annoyed to receive a call at eight thirty in the morning from his brother. He was eating toast and honey. 'This is most irregular, I know,' said Mark, 'and I shall remove myself from the questioning, but we've pulled in Katie Baker, the partner of the vicar who's run away, to assist us in our enquiries. She's at the station now, and she flatly refuses to say a word without her solicitor present, and she's asked for you, William, only you, as the best she knows who does it pro bono, for free. She hasn't got any money and she apologises and hopes it doesn't spoil your election.'

'Stop!' said William. 'She does realise it means I can't go to the count? We'll never finish your questions in time.'

'Yes, and she's very sorry, but she does need you, and anyway, it won't affect your result. She muttered something about chaos theory not applying in this case.'

'A woman of impeccable logic. She sounds interesting. All right, tell her I'll do it. I am an idiot.'

'Absolutely! That's why you'll get elected. Good man, good man. Thank you, William. It will speed things up a lot.'

The questioning by Detective Sergeant Roper and trainee Detective Constable Debbie Thompson was detailed, meticulous and fair. Helen Roper eventually accepted that Miss Baker had told all she knew. Katie seemed almost relieved by her night in police hospitality. The cell was no hardship; she had known far worse beds in her missions. She slept well, exhausted and relieved of responsibility. Arrangements had been made to cover her shift at the hospital. Katie was convinced that her John was innocent of all crime, even though he had been foolish enough to run away. She stressed to herself, to the police and her solicitor that John had done nothing illegal in moving around in his own country as a free citizen, not being charged or held under any other procedure. Therefore John had nothing to fear. Therefore Katie had nothing to fear. She told all she knew. Helen dropped talk of any charges.

Katie even enjoyed her breakfast. She was given time to eat it in comfort. Sergeant Roper made a point of making sure it was a good one. From the little kitchen she obtained muesli, scalding hot tea in a huge mug and a bacon butty. Katie smiled for the first time in twelve hours.

Her final statement was signed at noon and Katie left. At twenty-three minutes past noon, William arrived at the election count and discovered he was too late to hear his result which had been declared one hour earlier.

At one o'clock, Inspector Ellis read over Miss Baker's statement. It said in essence that Katie had no knowledge of any crime, no idea where her partner was and as a free citizen he had the right to travel as he wished. She thanked the police for their nice bed and breakfast, was keen to get back to her patients, and looked forward to the return of the Reverend John Newman even more than the police did.

Chief Superintendent Barbara Smalledge found the team in the office as they started a hasty and unhealthy preparation dripping with creamy sludge which Sergeant Gutteridge had been so kind as to get them from a local shop, "as you are so busy, innit?" Barbara said to Helen and Mark, 'I wonder if you could spare me a few moments. We can go up to my office if you like.' She looked over them with the interest of a sparrowhawk hearing a songbird.

'Come,' she said.

They feared the worst when they saw the nice lunch prepared for them. There was a large pot of tea, and roast beef sandwiches, with some sushi pieces and seven-bean salad. Helen and Mark stared at it like two children lost in the forest. They took Barbara's warm green seats without being invited. They knew this was what was required. In her usual manner Barbara served them in person. She took for herself only a mug of hot coffee from her machine.

'Sorry,' she said, 'should have asked. Is tea OK or would you prefer some coffee?'

Tea was OK.

They sat ensconced comfortably and enjoyed the food. Barbara said, 'We must look after you properly. After all, at present you are the two most important people in the office.'

They did not think this was a reproach that they were spending too long indoors.

'I mean it,' said Barbara. 'We have every confidence in you and I am more than happy to let you get on with this most unfortunate murder. Murder investigation, I mean. Silly me.' Her schoolgirl laughter did not invite familiarity. 'You are doing well. However, forgive me, there is just one tiny thing I need to mention. I do hope you don't mind?'

Mark and Helen assured the chief superintendent that they did not mind.

'I have noticed a little tension settling between you these days. There's nothing wrong is there? Anything I can help you with?'

'Sorry,' mumbled Helen. She nearly choked on the delicious salad. 'Perhaps I was a little hasty in quarrelling with Mark about his demarcation line.' She shot Mark a furious look.

'She didn't really accuse me of damaging the investigation in order to improve my brother's chance of success in the election.'

Helen glanced at Barbara in mute appeal. 'I wouldn't dream of using that sort of blackmail, ma'am—'

'Of course not, dear,' said Barbara. 'Now Mark—'

Mark felt as if he had been stabbed by an icicle. 'No, indeed no, ma'am. I never meant to imply—'

'Splendid, splendid, all happy again, eh? I know you two are inseparable best friends really. Right, I think I have a nice Victoria sponge in my desk. Do have a piece, both of you and return stronger to the fray.' She started humming one of her favourite hymns.

When they left, the two glared at each other, then fell in fits of laughter. Unseen by them, Barbara watched them retreat in relief. She poured herself a minuscule tot of rum, which she and Albert had brought back from Barbados. Even she could not protect them from the chief constable if they did not solve this one.

Chapter 12

Shortly after three o'clock on Friday afternoon, she came to the garden. It was spring-like and the birds were busy. A stranger would have wondered why this young woman was bringing flowers to this teeming garden.

Karen looked and soon found the pile of grass cuttings, the sludge where Fred's body was found. The area was neatly stacked, reassembled as good as new. No one would have seen any signs of yesterday's obsessive search which forensics had conducted. Dr Jenkins was meticulous in leaving a crime scene clean, just as it was before the crime as far as he could judge.

She knelt and placed the red roses on the pile of sludge. The birds fell silent and local traffic noise was far away. She wept a little and stood up. She walked in the garden and found some sticks. She bound them in the shape of a cross and placed it where the body had lain.

Karen knelt again and cried. She spoke to her lost husband. 'Oh my one, my only one, my true love, my darling, so stubborn, so Fred, who has done this to you, why? Is it something you said, or saw, or did, or something that you wrote?'

She rocked back and forward on her knees, the way she did as a little girl when she cried. Her long hair fell over her face and her tears were inconsolable. 'Fred, where will

I find another Fred? I don't want another one, I want my own. Come back, love, tell me it is just a tease.'

She sang a little lullaby to herself and crooned and rocked on her heels.

'We were happy, weren't we, my darling? You understood and I understood the things that matter. So serious you were, I loved teasing you and you got used to it and loved me, and told me I would always be your Little Mermaid, and remember that time when you got a little drunk and called me your Woman-Size Mermaid, and I hit you and we collapsed and it was funny. You called me your Danish pastry.

You told me things you never told anyone else, so you said. How as a little boy you were bullied because of your ginger hair, a prejudice you never understood, and it made you all the more determined to make your mark in the world and fight against every bit of bullying, and when you spoke out, and were told to shut up, that's where you got your need to fight for speaking freely, however incorrect, and never mind what other people thought. You were a warrior, my darling, my true Viking.

How did we ever get together – me, the daughter of a liberal clergyman and believing the faith, and you, lapsed Catholic, with such a hatred of the church? You saw through the fairy stories, you said, and the monks who raised you were cruel and nasty, but you found a priest who was kind and he was really genuine. He was the only one who understood and encouraged you to follow your truth even if against the church and don't tell his bishop or he'd get in terrible trouble and then he laughed and went back to his whiskey. He was the one churchman you had any time for.

Was that why you were so rough on the poor vicar who's now run away? Was it he who killed you, Fred? Will we get him? Fred, Fred, look down from where you are, look after me and our son.

They will find your murderer, and put him away. I will go back home and raise our son. I might one day find another husband, you won't mind that will you, my darling? It will take a long time to find anyone half as good as you and I will love him and have more children and love them too, but you won't mind, Fred; it will be different, not the same as my first true love, the love of my life as you English say and who says you aren't a romantic lot?

Oh Fred, I adored our life here, in our little cottage. You were getting more gentle by the day, my dear. You pretended to hate it, my love, but I could see you beginning to wonder, give up the nasty side of things, and stay here as a loved local writer. We would have been so happy.'

And she wept and she said a prayer, and kissed the ground and said more things to Fred. A shadow fell over the sunshine. She became aware of a figure standing next to her.

She turned. 'Oh hello, Vicar,' she said. She flinched.

'I'm afraid so,' he said.

She stood up and faced him. 'Everyone thinks you've run away, and they want to know why.'

'Still very much here, I'm afraid,' he said. His smile was like sunshine on an icicle. 'I spent the night in the one place no one would think to look, in the church, in the organ loft. I've got a kettle, food, a radio and bedding, there's a little kitchen and toilet in the church and it's quite cosy. I panicked. It was wrong to hide but I thought people would believe I was the killer. Who else hated Fred so much?'

'You'd be surprised,' she said. 'He annoyed a lot of people. He annoyed even me at times.' She reached out and clung on to him. 'Tell me,' she said, 'tell me it's not true, tell me it's one of your little English jokes and Fred's not really gone, not really dead.'

'I'm sorry,' he said, 'I'm sorry.'

She broke away and smiled. 'Excuse me,' she said, and wiped her face with a huge cloth which she took out. It was decorated with the Danish flag. 'So sorry, such bad manners, flinging myself into the arms of a man I haven't been introduced to. You're the vicar, everyone knows that. I'm Karen, wife of Fred.' She offered her hand in the best English manner.

'John Newman, as you say, vicar of St Martha's. How sad we meet under these tragic circumstances.'

'I'm now his widow.' She fought hard to stay calm.

'You'll see him again. One day,' said Father John.

'That's what my dad says. He's a priest too, in Copenhagen.' She bit her lip. 'I want him now, Vicar. I want him now.' She stared down at the grassy remains. 'They took his body to the mortuary. I can at least remember him here. Maybe you can place his ashes in your churchyard.'

'That would be most fitting. I don't think he would mind, not judging from the conversation we had before he died. He would want to please you.'

She backed away. 'When was that? Did you kill him? Have I just embraced his murderer?'

'Of course not, Karen,' said the vicar. His voice was soothing as baby's milk. 'Of course not. I was upset by his attack on me and my work. He upset my partner. I hated him for half an hour. Then I remembered all I believe. I was so glad we had that final conversation.'

'Tell me.'

'Shall we go and sit in the porch, or have a coffee in the hall? Nobody's there.'

'No,' she said. 'It's best if we stay outside.'

They began walking through the garden. Karen kept her distance. She got ready to flee. Perhaps this man was worse than weird; perhaps her Fred had underestimated him and paid with his life.

John pointed out the pile of rotted grass. 'They've put it back really tidily,' he remarked, 'just as if there had never been a body there.'

She went pale.

'I'm sorry. That was insensitive,' he said.

They walked to the end of the garden. It was like paradise before pain entered the world. 'Let's try again,' he said. 'We built this garden for anyone to come in and find peace. Gardens mean a lot in religion: Eden, innocence; Gethsemane, pain; Easter garden, life.'

'Thank you, Vicar,' she said dryly.

'Sorry. Preaching. It's an occupational hazard. I wish I could heal your pain over Fred.'

'Did you kill him, Vicar? If not, why did you run away? And will you run away again?'

'No. Don't know. Don't know.'

'You were going to tell me what happened.'

They sat down on the bench opposite the red roses. 'After the meeting, I really wanted to find Fred and talk. When I saw the Wolf Gang mob carry him away—'

'Wolf Gang?'

'Alas, yes. They are well known. They turn up all over the place and cause chaos but keep out of trouble with the law. They're very clever. They live on the Autumn Meadow estate. Their leader is called Wolf and his wife calls herself Lupie.'

'Got a sense of humour then. They sound educated.'

'Oh yes. They are not to be underestimated. They keep huge dogs and even bigger motorbikes. They act like local ill-bred hooligans, but do not be fooled. They call themselves graduates against the system, but know how to work it.'

'I've met people like that at home,' said Karen.

'His number two is Fox, and his girlfriend is Vixen. Another gang member is Dog.'

'Don't tell me his partner calls herself Bitch.'

He smiled. 'I'm afraid so. I met her once. She's witty and good company with a great sense of irony. She knows exactly what she wants, and is in fact a highly successful businesswoman with a haulage company. I think she enjoys having the best of both worlds.'

'Fred hated types like that.'

'After everyone left, I saw to the election people, showed them the keys and everything and left them to lock up. I'd get the keys from them in the morning. I told Katie to go home and get some sleep. I wanted to check the church porch and make sure the light was off. It disturbs the people in the flats opposite if we leave it on at night – it's only meant for evening concerts and such in the winter. Maisy has the habit of leaving it on; she thinks it stops burglars. She's wrong. They're more afraid of the dark.

Sure enough, when I got to the porch, the light was blazing away. I switched it off and turned to go. I became aware of a figure under the bench. He groaned and pulled himself to his feet. It was Fred.'

Karen gripped the vicar's arm.

'I put the light back on. He looked dreadful. He was all covered in slime, like a green man. He told me Wolf and his gang carried him off on their shoulders as a hero. At first he was chuffed. Journalists like their work appreciated. He thought they were taking him off to a pub and would tell him how right he was to expose me. He'd been having doubts and wondered if he'd gone over the top. He might even get some more stories from them.

He told me that they marched him round a bit singing songs. Then he realised. This was a highly educated mob that was having a laugh.

It was Vixen who disabused him. "That vicar was good to me," she said. "He agreed to christen Olly even though I can't remember who his dad was."

"It better be me," said Fox.

"Course it is, love," she said. "Could be. Whatever. Vicar didn't preach at me, just said he welcomed little children. He did a lovely service – in the afternoon too and he didn't insist I went to church or anything, and we didn't have to do it in front of a lot of people. He's a good man, got a lot of time for him."

Fred asked her, "Weren't you lot being rude to him at the meeting, calling out 'paedo' and things?"

"Never," she said. Her wide eyes opened in surprise. "That was the lot from Falling Leaf Avenue. We are going to have a word with them."

Fred told me that the Wolf Gang gave him a wide grin. The dogs were barking but the gang kept them away. One great hound bit him on the shoe. "Down, Baskerville," yelled Wolf and Lupie gave Fred a smile. "Just a playful nip," she said. "He won't hurt you."

"What shall we do with our fearless journo?" asked Vixen.

"Let's show him our appreciation. Let's show him what we think of him."

They carried him into the garden and tipped him into the muck-heap.

"Mm," they murmured. "Good place for muck-raking journalist." They took turns to roll him over in the grassy sludge. Wolf and Fox sat on him. He was winded and could not breathe. Then they were gone and he got out and came in here to rest.'

Karen had listened with every fibre to Father John's account. She walked furiously into the porch. 'The swine,' she said, 'the swine. Should be locked up. He was just doing his job. He was one of the finest writers of his generation and by rights should have been on a serious national paper.'

'Yes,' said the vicar, 'at my expense. He was just doing his job.' He and Karen sat together on the bench.

'You sound as if you approve. I bet you put them up to it. Very clever, Vicar,' she said.

He took her hand. She snatched it away.

'I tried to comfort him. I offered to take him home, or to hospital, or the vicarage. He said he'd be all right. He just needed a few minutes to come round. He said once he got back to you everything would be all right.'

'He said that, did he?' Karen started to cry. 'So he really loved me.'

'Oh yes, Karen, yes, indeed.'

They sat quietly. Karen let the tears come, then stopped.

'He said something else. He told me how much he was going to enjoy writing his next piece in the paper – all about hooligan gangs. This lot would regret it. He'd make sure all Hillford sat up, including the police.'

Karen laughed. 'We should have both enjoyed that very much.'

'And I should have enjoyed reading it, very much.'

They sat a little longer. The vicar said, 'Do you want to hear more?'

'Yes, please.'

'Fred's mood turned. "I'd do it again, Vicar."

"What?" I asked. "Get dumped in slime?"

"I'd write the same about you and your dangerous mission. I have to follow truth wherever it leads."

"Truth at all costs, eh?"

"Exactly," said Fred.

"You don't care if you badly hurt people? Or if you spread fear when there's no need for it?"

"Truth at all costs, Vicar. Doesn't your religion say the same?" he said.

"Well, there are other things to consider," I urged.

"There you go. Typical C of E waffle."

"We won't agree, will we? But will you shake hands with me?"

"I won't. Not on the condition you said I've got to go to your church again and write the piece you want," Fred told me.

"Can I just say something? You journalists pride yourselves on holding everyone fearlessly to account; government, church, business, and so on."

"A noble aim, wouldn't you say?" There was a pebble on the ground. He kicked it out of the porch.

"Very good. So when did you lot last publish the salaries and expenses of your proprietors, editors, staff and journalists? When do television companies ever do that, either?"

"That's different. We have to preserve our independence."

I laughed. "Sure," I said.

Fred got quite angry and then calmed. "One day I might shake your hand."

"And not my throat? We might have that in common. Seriously, it seems we have at least three power centres fighting it out. There is government who say they help people; religion, to comfort and give meaning; the media to crusade and entertain."

"And the greatest of these is the press. What about big business and money, Vicar, or the legal system? They can do a lot of damage. Only the press keeps everyone under control." He actually grinned. "The people need us most."

"We need it all. Anything can get corrupt and power crazy. The rich can get oppressive. If religion turns to theocracy, you have control freaks who crush people in the name of God. If the government is too strong you get horrible repression. If the media are too strong you get people torn to shreds. If any of them cosy up, we're in dead trouble. Kept in balance they're all a force for good."

"Too neat, Vicar."

"Maybe." The front of his head was bleeding. I asked him about that. "You should get attention," I said. "How did that happen?" We both forgot about the handshake.

"When those yobs threw me into the pile of filth, I cracked my head against a stone lying there." He was adamant about that. "It didn't seem much. I'll get it sorted."

"We ought to get you to hospital, check it out; or at least get you home. Get your wife to look after you."

His face brightened. "Karen," he said. "She's lovely. She'll know what to do."

Karen smiled through her tears. She grabbed the vicar's hand. 'Thank you. He did love me, you know.'

'Oh yes, Karen, yes, indeed.'

'So then what happened?'

'In spite of my best efforts, he wouldn't go just yet. He said he just had to text his story through there and then, while it was fresh and white-hot. He smiled – "nothing, not even though I'm hurt, must stand in the way of truth."

He assured me he'd be all right. He promised to get help as fast as possible. I left him there, upset, wounded and defiant in the porch.

I shall always regret I never did shake hands with him.'

Chapter 13

At ten o'clock on Saturday morning Maisy, Old Harry and the professor were ready for their great adventure. They were assembled in Maisy's small front room.

'Have you all got your sandwiches?' asked Maisy. She had prepared everyone a bag which contained one round of egg sandwiches, one round of ham and tomato sandwiches, one piece of chocolate cake and an apple. 'I've got the flask of coffee.'

The professor opened the pack and sniffed. 'Sorry, I don't like tomato,' he said.

'Oh, I'll take it out,' said Maisy. 'Is that all right?'

'He can have my egg sandwiches,' said Old Harry, 'I like ham and tomatoes.'

The two adventurers swapped rations.

Maisy beamed at them. 'Good,' she said. 'That's all sorted. Everyone all right with coffee?' The men agreed that they were all right with coffee.

'Right,' said Maisy. 'Plan agreed? We three are going to solve the murder of that poor young man. I don't think the vicar did it for one minute, even though he's run away. He's just upset, that's all. It's horrible what that young man wrote about him. I don't doubt he deserved what he got, but murder's going a bit too far and I don't think our wonderful vicar would do that.' She sniggered. 'Must

144

have been fun watching him being shoved into that pile of sludge.'

'However, we are agreed that murder is going too far,' said the professor. 'That which is inappropriate can never be the right course of action.'

'Agreed. In my day, if a farm lad was rude like that we'd have thrown him into the farm pond and left him there to soak. We would not have murdered him,' said Harry. He stroked his white beard. It surrounded his red face like an aureole.

They sat in silence considering the importance of the moment. They, The Terrible Three, were going to confront the Wolf Gang. They planned to find the truth and get the gang to admit to it. 'It's pretty clear who did the murder,' said Maisy.

Old Harry was confident. 'We'll get them all right,' he said. 'It's the last thing they will expect, three oldies like us confronting them. We'll shock them into saying things to admit their guilt.'

'I'll write down what they say,' said the professor. 'Then if the gang does not admit what it has done, I can take to the police what it does say as evidence.'

'I expect the police have already interviewed the gang,' said Maisy. 'They will have thought of that. I also expect that the gang will be used to the police and know how to protect themselves from them. But they can't protect themselves against The Terrible Three.'

'People like that usually listen to their grandmas and granddads,' said Old Harry. 'It's their culture. Say nowt to the police but listen to Granny and Granddad.'

'Those who will not speak to one set of people have

not thereby precluded themselves from speaking to others,' said the professor.

'Quite right,' said Maisy. 'Now have we all got our plans clear? Go straight to Wolf House, speak to Wolf and ask him to get the others to come along for a chat. If he won't tell them we'll go ourselves house to house till we have spoken to everyone. There's a fair chance the women will feel ashamed and say things even if the men won't. They are bound to be so surprised to see us that they will let us in. If they don't, we park ourselves outside till they do. That's when we might need our rations.

The gang will think we are a soft touch, might as well get it all over with, so they will tell us a pack of lies, then we'll believe them and tell the police and the gang will be in the clear. They think they are being so clever. But we'll be able to see the truth. They will give away enough information.'

'That is a good plan,' said the professor. 'That which aims to deceive may even so lead us to the truth.' He stroked his face.

'That's right,' said Maisy, 'though I expect they will tell the truth first time. They think it won't do them any harm talking to a bunch of barmy old people who won't be believed anyway. The gang will make the truth sound unbelievable, if it reaches the police via us.' She checked the room to make sure all was tidied for the day. Domino had enough food and the cat flap was unlocked. 'Right everyone. Loins girded? Let's go.'

The three marched out of her door determined and confident of victory by the afternoon.

They arrived sooner than expected. Maisy had

expected some difficulty in finding the location as it was not normally a part of town she frequented. 'Do not worry,' said the professor. 'What we cannot find ourselves, we can ask someone the direction thereto.' They parked Harry's ancient Fiesta at the end of the street. They sat for a moment in Harry's car, weighing up options. They decided on a frontal attack.

They strode to the front door of Wolf House. It was a detached dwelling with four bedrooms in a sea of three-bed semis. The area was smart, having been mostly sold off as private housing since the days when the council owned the houses. Some were showing signs of new neglect. These, the three assumed, were rented to students by absentee landlords.

Humming a happy tune, Maisy rang the doorbell. They were surprised to hear a strong, confident tone of Big Ben chimes. The professor gripped his walking stick. You never knew if a strong fat dog would come biting out as the default position of this house.

It was Wolf himself who answered. He was wearing a leather waistcoat, and his arms were bare. Maisy was taken by the rippling muscles. The tattoos appeared as moving men of action. 'Hello,' said Wolf, 'how may I help you?' His voice was lyrical and soft. It was impossible for the three to read whether it was soft sarcasm or public-school charm.

Maisy for once was thrown. 'Oh, er, Mr Wolf?'

'That's me,' he said. He grinned. His teeth smiled.

The professor gripped his stick. No noise of any dogs yet.

'Oh, er, we would like a word with you. If that's all right. May we?' Maisy realised this was all a mighty mistake. 'If it's not too much trouble. Er, sorry to bother you. Perhaps another day.'

Wolf laughed. It was like apples falling softly to ground. He could have been an actor, movements graceful, under control and voice modulated on demand. Lupie was always nagging him to get involved in direct political action.

'Come in, come in – if you don't mind the animals,' he said. 'Lupie and I aren't doing anything – just at present. Bit early for it, if you know what I mean.' He laughed at the discomfiture of the three. 'Never let it be said that Wolf House is inhospitable.' He called out, 'Lupie, we got guests.'

Lupie came in. She smiled. 'So long as it's not the police.'

'Don't know these people,' he said, 'but don't look like it.'

'That's what worries me, Wolfie,' she said. 'If they are police spies, they're not going to look like police spies, are they?'

The professor was impressed.

Maisy was anxious to reassure Wolf and Lupie on this point. 'Oh no,' she said. 'We're from the church. We're very upset about what happened, you know about—'

'Not half as unhappy as that journalist bloke, eh, Lupie?' He gave the biggest grin that Maisy had ever seen. She could see three metal teeth. 'Shame what we done to him.' He laughed. 'Shouldn't have gone attacking that nice vicar.'

'Drop it,' said Lupie. 'We don't know these people. They could be police spies. We had enough bother with the real police.'

'You are right as ever, darlin' canine. Still. Don't let's talk of old, unhappy things. We got guests.' He turned to the three. 'Tea? Coffee? What can I get you? We've got some nice carrot cake, ain't we, Lupie? Take a pew, people.'

Maisy's eyes misted over. Lupie, modern as she was, sloped off to the kitchen to look after her guests. They were harmless, anyone could see, and it might be good to talk things over.

The three squashed together on the low sofa with its blue cloth. They said little while Lupie got the refreshments together. Two German Shepherd dogs entered the room. In utter silence they took position either side of the door, and regarded the strange people. They were like security men in dark bulging suits in attendance on their affable master who is working the cheerful crowds, adoring his charisma. The guards are unsmiling and yet pretend to be mere members of the happy meeting. Most people are not aware of them. There are other layers of security which even the observant do not see. Maisy and her friends were well aware of these dogs in the house of the Wolf. The professor told himself to prepare. He gripped his stick and found it of little comfort. Still, that which cannot be avoided must best be borne with grace. They did seem decent individuals. He really mustn't judge people of a different background by his own standards.

Maisy cast her eye over the room. She admired the pictures of hunting hounds chasing a fox. She wondered where Wolf's sympathy lay. He noticed. 'Oh,' he said, 'I like both fox and hounds. I'm on both their sides.'

The professor was still puzzling the logic of this when Lupie came in with a big old biscuit tin. She laughed. 'I still can't stop doing what Mum used to do. Well, sort of. How do you like my lucky bucket? Full of stuff.'

The lucky bucket held a new supermarket cake and chocolate biscuits from the pound shop. Lupie then brought a tray of six knives, five teaspoons, three cups and saucers, two mugs, a sugar bowl with its own spoon, milk in a green jug, a teapot and a cafetiere of coffee. It smelt fantastic, thought Old Harry. It was a long time since someone had served him in this way. They waited. 'Shall I be Mum?' enquired Lupie.

They were severally served exactly as they wished. The manners of Wolf and Lupie were impeccable. They gave the appearance of thoroughly enjoying the unexpected honour of guests from church. Clearly they wished to help all they could, concluded Maisy. Just shows you cannot judge a human by his or her cover.

'Now, how may we help?' asked Lupie. In the lair of the Wolf she was clearly in charge. She wore a leather skirt and top. There were two rings on her face, unsymmetrical, one on her nose and one in her ear. Round her neck was a necklace of shark's teeth. Her bare lower arm was tattooed with a picture of twin wolf cubs being fed. The professor was startled. He had just noticed the famous Romulus and Remus print on the wall above the acre of television.

'We want to know who did the murder,' said Maisy. 'We know the vicar wouldn't do such a thing, even if that horrible journalist was so nasty to him. Trouble is, the vicar has run away, so the police are sure to think he did it. Forgive us, but you were the last people seen carrying off that journalist. You seemed so pleased carrying him off, like a footballer who scored the winning goal at the World Cup. So we don't think you had anything to do with it.'

'Otherwise, of course, we wouldn't have come to see

you today,' said the professor. 'It would not be logical to put ourselves in the power of anyone we thought did the murder.'

'Naturally,' said Wolf.

'Anyway, you've been so nice to us and you were so nice to the journalist, we wanted to know what you know. Please tell us it wasn't the vicar and he just ran away because he's upset,' said Maisy.

'He's such a good man, he would feel guilty for causing all this trouble with his modern methods, and getting that journalist to write about him and then getting killed for it,' said Old Harry. 'He's like that, our vicar; blames himself for what isn't his fault. Some of our weaker lads on the farm were just the same.'

'What he could not face, that he ran away from,' suggested the professor. 'We cannot bring ourselves to believe the vicar committed such a crime. So we rather hope you can tell us what happened when you released the journalist from your embrace of honour. Did you see or hear or notice anything which can shed light on the mystery?'

Wolf took a long, thoughtful sip of his strong coffee. It was triple espresso strength. 'Nice one, Lupie,' he said. 'Shall we tell these lovely people what we know?'

Her long brown hair fell over her eyes. She shook it back. 'All right, Wolfie mate, or police will be back and stitch us up. They are sure to come back and this time they won't be so gentle.'

'Maybe they have come back,' said Wolf. He nodded at the three. 'Cunning bastards, police. Think we'll let our guard down with these nice guys. So, people, assuming you are from the police, here is the truth, the full truth and nothing but the truth. We did not do it, we do not know for sure who did it, but we think we know.'

'Thank you,' said Maisy. 'Tell us everything you can.'

'We like the vicar,' said Lupie. 'I don't want to be rude but we think he did it.'

Maisy reacted. 'Don't you dare say that.'

'Look, darlin', you come to our house, invite yourselves in. Where we come from that is considered rude, but thank your stars, Wolfie and me and Dog and Bitch and Vixen and Fox got over all that and where we are coming from now is this, we have open door, so long as you take us as you find. That includes our right to tell the truth. The truth, the whole truth and nothing but the truth. Eh, Wolfie?'

Wolf gave a perfect imitation of a wolf howling at the moon. 'Spot on, sweetheart,' he said. 'Spot on. So darlin', now tell 'em what we did and saw, just like the lady asks.' He looked at his guests. 'More tea, coffee, anyone? Sorry we ain't got no crumpet.' The dogs at the door moved from couchant to crouchant. They growled.

The door sprang open. Vixen and Fox came in. They also had large dogs with them, chocolate Labradors.

'Party time,' said Wolf. The dogs went to the sofa. They stared at the three guests. Their muzzles were at knee level. Maisy and the professor said a silent prayer. Old Harry said soothing words to them. 'Off,' said Wolf.

The dogs went into the kitchen. Lupie shut the door on them. 'They like their food,' she said.

'See you have guests then,' said Fox. 'Can anyone join?'

'We was just telling these nice people from the church how we think their vicar did the wicked deed,' said Lupie.

'They first said they want to hear what happened, now it seems they don't want to hear.'

'But they are going to hear, aren't you?' said Wolf turning to the three. 'Then you can go to the police, tell them again what they want to hear, what we already told them. All points one way; motive, clear opportunity, witnesses, that's us, we'll tell you in a minute, and the vicar admits his guilt by running away. Maybe that's why the police gave us an easy time and for once I think they believe us. They are busy chasing the vicar from one end of the country to the other. They'll get their man.'

'So do you want to hear? The mission finished, you can go away unhappy,' said Lupie.

'Be careful what you wish for,' said Vixen. 'It's a shame. Like you, I like the vicar too, very much after the way he looked after my baby, and I'll always think nicely of him for that. I might even visit him in jail. But you can't ignore what we saw. He always was a bit strange.'

'OK,' said Wolf. 'Tell them, Lupie.'

'Are you sure you want to know?' Lupie stared at Maisy.

'Yes,' whispered Maisy. She stared out of the patio doors. More people were arriving. There was a man and a woman with dogs in the garden. Lupie followed her gaze.

'That's nice,' said Lupie. 'It's Dog and Bitch. Look, they've brought the family.' Two Great Danes were running round. Dog appeared to be doing a dance with one of them. 'Hard to control that one, he's big as a baby horse,' said Vixen, 'but he won't hurt you, he's just being affectionate.'

The professor wiped sweat from his forehead. There was no comforting logic.

'Open the doors, let's have some air,' commanded

Lupie. 'Don't worry, sir, we'll keep the Danes outside. They get excited over new people. They'd love to meet you but you'll probably find them a bit much.'

There were now nine people and six dogs. The German Shepherd dogs took up position by the patio doors, the chocolate Labradors were allowed back from the kitchen, and the Great Danes gambolled round the garden. A small spaniel with glossy ginger coat turned up and sat at Maisy's feet. Correction, seven, pondered the professor. Why are the big dogs not eating the small one?

'I'll get us more coffee. This is turning into a wicked party.' She called out. 'Come on in, you two. Tell Baskerville and Wilberforce to stay in the garden.'

'That's cosy,' said Wolf. 'Now, where was we?'

'Just give us the facts, please,' said the professor. 'Tell us what you did and saw that unhappy evening.' He wiped under his collar with a spotted red handkerchief. He could not understand what there was to keep those vast animals out.

'Very good, sir,' said Lupie. 'We carried Fred off on our shoulders. He thought he was our best buddy. We marched him around a bit singing, "For He's a Jolly Good Fellow". Then Vixen told Fred how good the vicar had been to her baby and asked him why he was so nasty to the vicar. Long and short is, penny finally dropped, Fred realised he was no friend of ours. We marched him round a bit more and found the garden. We took him in and dumped him in the filth.'

'Just where he belonged. Lupie didn't say we was looking for somewhere good to put him in, like a river, so he was lucky it wasn't worse,' said Wolf. 'He got all upset, but we told him we wouldn't hurt him no more.' He licked his lips appreciatively. 'We couldn't have found a nicer place for him.' He took a sip of tea. 'Poetic justice,' he mused.

'Was he hurt?' asked Old Harry. 'I've seen men hurt when falling over things in the field or barns. If you're trained how to fall, it's no problem.'

'This one wasn't trained, was he, Lupie?' enquired Wolf.

'Course not,' said Lupie. 'But he didn't seem hurt to us, didn't see him bang his head or anything, just made a mess of his nice clothes and fancy hairstyle. More a case of hurt pride. He got up and we waved a cheery goodbye. He yelled at us. Something about nasty scum and he'd be writing about us in the next paper. We laughed and said we looked forward to it. Last we saw he wandered off towards the church.'

Vixen said, 'Tell him what you told us, Bitch.'

Bitch said, 'I don't like to see anyone really hurt, not, really. I'm kind like that. So I stayed behind just for a moment after the others had gone. I saw Fred went into the church porch, maybe to gather his thoughts, or wipe his clothes before facing the world, or writing his piece, who knows? I saw a vicar with a cross round his neck come along. I was just near enough to hear they had a long chat. Then it got angry. I saw the vicar go away, and I didn't stay to see if Fred came out. I reckon the vicar would have not gone away if Fred hadn't been OK. I expect the vicar told Fred he got what he deserved and don't be a sinner no more.'

'Later you got worried, didn't you?' said Dog.

'Yes, I told the police when they came to ask all about it. They was very interested. They didn't say much, but I

155

reckon that young policewoman thought that the vicar did it, and left Fred in there, or maybe moved the body or made Fred so ill, that Fred just crept away to die in the pile of sludge. Her mate didn't say much but looked worried. He was an older man who kept looking at her. He wrote a lot down.'

'So, I'm afraid, darlin', Maisy you said your name was, we think it was the vicar, all dressed up in church costume he was, got his revenge in the end, and now he's on the run and the police are after him.'

Maisy fumbled in her bag for a tissue. 'He's the best vicar we ever had. I loved him, I really did and it's awful if you can't even trust a good, kind man like that.'

Old Harry put his fist on her shoulder. 'Bear up,' he said. 'Worse happens on the farm.'

'Have another cup of tea, darlin',' said Lupie. 'Look, we in the Wolf Gang look horrible and rough but we're nice. We know how to look after people.'

The Great Danes had their noses pressed against the patio window. The German Shepherds were getting restless. Then it happened. A cat strayed across the lawn. The Great Danes went wild. One barked into the room. All the dogs went loose. For several moments seven dogs ran round the garden. Their owners shouted at them. The animals came in and raced round the room. The cafetiere was smashed and mugs bounced on the carpet. Stains spread on the walls. A crack appeared on the glass panel of a bookcase which contained motor manuals.

Maisy, Old Harry and the professor struggled to their feet, thanked the gang for their help and fled through the front door.

'That was a nice party, wasn't it?' said Lupie. They sniggered and with a snap of their fingers brought everything to order. 'I liked the fun ending best.'

As they got in the car, Maisy started crying. 'Now I know who did it.'

Old Harry said, 'They've as good as confessed, haven't they?'

'No,' cried Maisy. 'It wasn't any of them. If only it was, if only it was.'

As Harry drove back, the professor pondered the logic.

Chapter 14

It was later agreed that Karen had experienced a lucky escape from the mad vicar.

When he expressed his regret to Karen that he had not shaken hands with her husband, she took this at face value. She understood that Father John might have been upset over the press coverage of his pranks in church, but she also felt he understood the imperative needs of journalism. He had on his own admission engaged in philosophical discussion with Fred about the role of religion, state and press in a free society. After such discussion, you do not normally kill the man you argued with.

She was comforted by her conversation with the vicar. He understood her and her late husband. Everything would be all right. The true killer would be found. The vicar would learn from his encounter with her dear Fred. She would always remember this time and would bring up her son with a love of England where he was conceived. She did intend to begin a new life back at home, but not yet. She had to see the killer found and justice done and whatever harmony was possible restored.

Karen was surprised how the vicar disappeared into thin air as mysteriously as he had suddenly appeared at her side. One moment he expressed his regret, next moment without palpable motion, he was gone.

Back home she began to think. All Friday evening and Saturday morning she brooded. What if her conversation had been a mighty bluff by the priest? Why had he gone back to check the scene of his crime? At noon she could bear it no longer. She phoned the vicarage to see if she could meet Father John again and ask a few more questions.

There was one ring and Katie answered the phone. It was clear to Karen that the phone had been snatched off its stand. 'Yes, John? Is that you, love, where –? Oh, Mrs Vestal. You're the last person I expected.'

'May I speak to Father John, please?'

'You could if I knew where he was. Sorry if I don't sound very calm, but it's nearly two days without any word.'

'Oh, I spoke with him yesterday.'

Karen told Katie the whole story.

'We'd better tell the police, don't you think? Come over now, tell me everything again, and we'll get the police here.'

Karen jumped in her car and arrived at the same time as Helen and Mark. Katie made no attempt to offer the police any refreshments and the two women told them all they knew about Father John. Inspector Ellis expressed admiration at the brazen cunning of the vicar at hiding away in church and his own exasperation at not thinking of this. Helen Roper stayed silent. She had not thought of it either.

Karen related to the police in full detail her conversation with the vicar in the garden. It was word for word what she had told Katie on the phone.

'So he's scarpered again,' Helen observed. 'I think we have our man. Or, we will have once we find him.'

'Don't say that,' whispered Katie. 'You've got no evidence. He can do what he likes. You never told him he can't leave. He's not under any caution or anything.'

'You have to stand by him, Miss Baker, of course, but I am afraid the evidence is not good. Innocent people don't run.'

'You don't know my John,' snapped Katie. 'He's creative and takes things to heart. Why do you think he was so hurt by that journalist? Sorry, Karen.'

'If he is so hurt by the journalist, and the journalist is found dead on church grounds, and the vicar then runs away once, then visits the scene of the crime, maybe to reassure himself he's left no clues, chats up the widow to persuade her he is innocent and then runs away again – well, I'm no psychologist, Miss Baker, but you must admit it looks pretty difficult? Prima facie at least?' said Helen.

'Cut it out, Sergeant,' said Ellis. 'My apologies, Miss Baker, but perhaps you can see how it might look?'

'Yes,' said Katie. 'Do your worst, Inspector, just find him and bring him back safe and sound. We'll persuade you he is innocent.'

Helen bit her lip. 'I'm sorry, Katie,' she said. 'We'll do what is right, I promise.'

'You'd better go now,' said Katie to the detectives. 'Karen, I'd be ever so grateful if you could stay. We can have some lunch. We're both victims of a sort.'

The two women embraced.

Mark and Helen left in silence. They both looked forward to the rest of an uninterrupted weekend. By Monday the man would be found and the case would be stitched up. For the moment there was nothing to do but wait. Helen could take her son Aaron to the seaside and Mark looked forward to Sunday lunch with Victoria and whoever of the family was around. William would join them, in a mood of high celebration. Mark expected William to bring a particularly tasty offering from his excellent cellar. It was almost certain to be a Chilean Carménère.

Maisy and her friends got back to her house breathless and excited. They took out their sandwiches and ate them, as it seemed such a shame to waste them and anyway it was time for lunch. Maisy found a half bottle of Chardonnay for herself and the professor. She took out a bottle of pale ale for Old Harry. They sat in the garden and pondered what to do.

Old Harry went first. 'Nice dogs,' he said. 'Need working though; on our farm we'd have found a job for them, or five.' He rearranged his beard.

'What we have seen, we have two options for. I am sorry to end my sentence with a preposition,' said the professor. 'Let me rephrase that. What we have seen and heard on the one hand we must report. What we have seen and heard on the other hand may harm our splendid priest. Thereby we have a dilemma – that which we must report, must not be reported if it will result in more harm than good.'

'Haven't you heard of the duty to help the police in their enquiries?' asked Maisy. She was very worried. How could she hurt the vicar whom she adored? What was the right thing to do? If the vicar had killed a man, was he so worthy of love – or more in need of it – or was love unconditional and where did her loving duty lie? If the vicar was innocent, which she most fervently believed, would it betray him to tell the police what she knew? This was too much philosophy for Maisy and she turned to the professor.

He explained. 'You must do what you think best, Maisy.'

They ate the rest of their food in silence. Maisy went to make a nice big pot of tea. The three came to their own decision, individually.

'Can't let our man down. Let the police do their own investigations. If they are any good they will find him. Keep out of the way of the law,' said Old Harry. He remembered a few past secrets on the farm. 'Let sleeping dogs lie, unless you need them for work.'

'Professor?' asked Maisy.

'I cannot let down a man today from whom I took guidance last Sunday.'

She was turning her mug of tea round and round in her hands. She looked out and saw the most beautiful goldfinch perched in her laurel tree. It sang to her. Maisy smiled at the bird. She made up her mind. 'I'm sorry,' she said. 'I shall have to tell the police. I have to. He's been a wonderful priest, and I shall always respect him. But you can't go round killing people even if you are my lovely vicar.'

'That which we cannot do ourselves, we may respect in others,' said the professor.

'What you have to do, do quickly,' said Old Harry.

Maisy winced and left the garden. 'Let yourselves out,' she said. The others did not see her tears.

Maisy walked up to the police station. She swallowed hard and tried to open the door. She was surprised to find that it opened of its own sweet will, like Ali Baba's cave without the need for a magic password. It was easy to enter, but would it be easy to leave? She strode to the counter. There was nobody there. After all her efforts to steel herself, the police might at least have had the decency to welcome her.

There was scuffling behind a wall. A young man came out. 'Oh, sorry,' he said, 'short-staffed, how may we help you?' Maisy was glad there was no one waiting at the counter before her. She would not have had the courage to stay and wait.

'I need to talk to someone about the murder. Someone senior,' she said, looking at the young man who looked all of eight years old.

'The journalist one?' he asked.

'Do you have any more?' she said.

'Oh no, sorry,' he said. 'How may I help?'

'Perhaps you did not hear me. I wish to speak to someone senior. I have some information to impart.'

The eight-year-old was not as young as he looked. He had been warned at college about dotty punters. 'Oh,' he said. 'That's good. I mean, that is interesting. Do you want to tell me first and I can pass it on to the relevant person?'

'Young man, it is not every day that someone enters these doors and admits to first-hand information regarding a murder. Either you get someone senior and serious NOW, or I walk and you will not easily find me again.' Maisy was impressed at her own resolution.

'Oh quite, or yes, er, I will—' He pressed a buzzer. He spoke to someone above in hushed tones. 'Yes, I think we

163

have to take this one seriously,' he was heard to say. He replaced the receiver, and said to Maisy, 'Thank you, madam. My seniors are very grateful. Someone will be down to see you. Please take a seat. There's a coffee machine over there if you would like. It's free. Any problems let me know.'

Ninety seconds later, Sergeant Gutteridge appeared. He heard an outline of what Maisy had to say. He invited her past the counter, through some doors with high security codes and into secret corridors. He took her to Chief Superintendent Smalledge at once, in her upstairs lair. It was a terrible risk bothering such a senior personage with what might be a silly snippet. Heaven knows there were too many of those. Yet, to ignore what might be a breakthrough would be inexcusable and the chief superintendent would have plenty to say if she had not been informed. There was something about this Maisy person that compelled respect. Oh well, take the risk. It was only his career.

It was mid-afternoon on a Saturday and the station was normally quiet, before the evening rush. The chief superintendent said, 'Thank you, Sergeant, no, please stay, we can both hear what this lady has to say.' Barbara's steely grey hair gleamed sleek in the sun from the window.

Oh no, thought Gutteridge, it's her way of telling me off. I'll be in her presence as we discover this witness is just a nutcase. He wondered if he could still get on that accountancy course.

'You behaved correctly, Bill,' she said.

Hell, she could even read his thoughts. 'Thank you, ma'am,' he said.

Maisy had perfect recall and within five minutes,

both sergeant and superintendent were impressed by the evidence of this witness. It confirmed the truth of the Wolf Gang's account. A priest wearing a cross was seen walking away from Fred that night. She too had seen something similar.

They thanked her and she gave a written statement and her address. They persuaded her that she had done exactly the right thing and promised to follow up.

When Maisy had left, the two police officers knew what to do. The chief superintendent was confirmed in her view that she had been correct at noon in sending away the fractious, tired duo, her most successful team, for what remained of the weekend, to take their rest, prepared for the rigours of Monday. Barbara had no doubt that by then they would have found the vicar.

By Saturday teatime Polly was going frantic and the major was muttering about lack of proper staff-work by the generals. It is one of the manifold duties of the churchwardens to make sure there is someone to take the services. Father John was lucky – so far his parish had not been absorbed into a team ministry system, with many churches combined into a soft or hard federation, parishes combined and a rota of too few clergy to take on the lot. In the Hillford diocese there was indeed one conglomeration called St Ethelburga with Saints Pancras and Nereus and James the Lesser and Jude. It was doing well.

It was a matter of time before a similar fate befell St Martha's. The vicar's successes had been so welcome in staving off that day. Now what had been an asset, his funny ways – would surely hasten the day. Polly and the major were in despair. They phoned all the known clergy for twenty miles around and could not find one at such short notice to fill the slot. The church was sure to be packed next day with the curious, the faithful and the amused. Trust their strange vicar to disappear again just when he was needed.

The phone rang in Polly's cottage. Caesar barked to inform his mistress that the phone was ringing. She answered. When she put the phone down, she was in smiles of relief. She rang the major.

'It's all right,' she told him. 'I've just been told by the archdeacon that she is coming to preach tomorrow, and guess what? The bishop himself is coming to celebrate. So they are caring for us after all.' She spoke in tones of wonder.

'Looks like the generals are finally doing their job. Left it damn late to tell us. I wonder what the bishop will say. Maybe Father John will emerge from wherever he's hiding, and join the party.'

'Don't delude yourself on that point, Major,' said Polly. 'We've seen the last of him; unless we choose to visit him in prison.'

Chapter 15

The church was packed. Father John it seemed was able to gather in even more by his absence than by his theatricals when he was there. Maisy, Old Harry, the professor in possession of a troubled conscience were in need of prayer. The churchwardens were pleased the show was still on the road. The Wolf Gang sent along two representatives, Bitch and Dog, to see if there was any news about the murder and possible progress towards arrests. Parents made sure to accompany their golden children, to snatch them away in the event of any threatening little stunts. Three extra teenagers turned up hoping for some fun.

Chief Superintendent Barbara Smalledge also decided to give it a whirl. She was a regular attendee at her local Baptist church, as she especially enjoyed a good sermon. It gave her time to switch in and out at will and she did a lot of meditating and thinking during a good twenty-five minute exposition. The minister was young, good looking and he never lacked offers of help. He was engaged to a very nice girl called Lucy from Essex, and the matrons of the church were making the most of their final opportunities to look after him. She was, unlike the local vicar's partner, not living with him, and had no intention of doing so until the wedding had taken place next month.

He was away on leave in Essex this weekend,

staying chastely at her parents' house, while making final preparations. Barbara thought she might as well try a new service. It would be fun to try the smells and bells which St Martha's was reputedly so good at. Even if the sermon was not up to much, it would be something new to try. And who knew what clues she might glean? Someone in the congregation might let slip the sort of place where the vicar would go to hide. It would be amusing to confront Mark and Helen tomorrow with the case solved. Oh no, she had not lost her own investigative skills.

She packed up a bag of lemon sherbets and sat down near the churchwardens' seats with a good view to the pulpit. The sidesperson gave her a warm welcome as she came in and asked if she was new to the town.

It was a lovely warm day, when May excels itself and makes puritans want to set up maypoles. It was a day for sea, frolics and fun. In the local park, by eleven o'clock a number of young people were wrapped around each other, while others looked at the flowers, and children chased cricket balls and skipped. Mums and dads were getting out the picnics. Church was the last thing on their mind.

St Martha's was not worried. Today it was difficult to find a good seat.

At twenty seconds past eleven, the procession began. Chief Superintendent Barbara especially enjoyed the swirling incense. It wasn't quite Santiago de Compostela, as seen on TV, but the teenage lad in charge achieved a racing horizontal swing. It gave a delicious cedar of Lebanon smell, and Barbara made a note to get some for the bathroom.

Next in line came the crucifer, netball captain of her school. She held the tall silver cross by one hand. She kept a discreet distance. Too close and she would be struck by the burning censer. Too far back she would hold up the others. It would be like detaching the train from the engine.

The dignitaries swung left, along a bit then left again and up to the front. Towards the rear came Archdeacon Barbara, determined of step, looking neither to right nor left, but missing nothing. The churchwardens came next. At the rear swung the bishop in glorious canonicals, more lovely than any rugby strip he ever played in. His mitre was half a metre high. He beamed at everyone in sight, right, left and centre, and reckoned he was doing a good job. His crosier clicked at the tiles like a gangster stalking a dead man. The bishop's chaplain, last of all, protected his back.

They bowed to the altar, swept round and took their positions. There was no announcement. Barbara found this very odd. She did not think it usual, but who was she to say, for a local parish church to be blessed with a visit from both archdeacon and bishop. If such great clergy arrived, would there not be some welcome at least, or explanation? The chief superintendent found this both odd and satisfactory. There would be a lot of clues to pick up during the service. She was very glad she had come. Already she was enjoying it enormously. She did not think she would like such richness every week, but like a stuffing of chocolate once in a while it was very acceptable.

She took in the beautiful windows, the rood, the statues, the enchanting roof rafters. No, this would not do at her own church, but never mind, it took all sorts. She wondered if they would let her take Communion.

The service proceeded. The archdeacon took the lead and finally the moment came when the bishop ascended the steps for the sermon. Barbara laid out five lemon sherbets on the ledge in front of her. No sermon was any good if it required less.

'Please sit,' said the bishop, and the people sat. He spoke on forgiveness, new beginnings and an end to the regrets of the past while learning their lessons. The two Barbaras listened to every word. The chief superintendent tried to like the sermon but the poor bishop was not a patch on her own minister. Never mind, her minister was not so brightly arrayed.

She had popped only the third sweet into her mouth when things got interesting.

'Now, some of you may be wondering why you are honoured – if I may call it that, or perhaps pestered – by both your archdeacon and your bishop. It is not every day that a local church gets even one of us. Indeed you might say that one was a misfortune and two is a bit careless.' He looked round for appreciative little nods. Nothing happened.

He proceeded. 'As we know, there have been some unfortunate events recently surrounding this church. First your beloved pastor was, let us say, the subject of unkind misunderstanding in the local newspaper. Then came the appalling event of the death of the young journalist, here on holy ground, on church premises.' He allowed himself a theatrical shudder. 'And now your pastor has gone missing. I have nothing to say about the investigation of this case. I say nothing as to the cause of his precipitate running away.'

He had better not, muttered the chief superintendent to herself. She had taken a dislike to this man. His sermon was poor, he used worn out techniques, and he was more worried about the effect he was having than on his message. Barbara told herself to be more charitable. Perhaps this was how it was done in the Church of England. She liked his outfit, which seemed to be predominantly Lincoln green underneath the outer garb. She liked the huge cross swinging round his chest as he swayed under the force of his oratory. It was quite something.

'My friends,' said the bishop. He leant confidentially on the edge of the pulpit, like a kindly prosecutor charming a jury into convicting the accused.

'My friends,' he said, and swept his gaze round the congregation. 'As you can imagine, your good pastor was deeply troubled by being so misunderstood in the local press. A lesser man would have been tempted to hatred. When the poor young journalist was found dead on church premises, Father John, good as he is, felt that people would blame him for, indeed accuse him of, the crime. I understand why he decided to retreat, foolish as that action may have seemed to some. He told me that he slept one night in the church – where indeed would be the last place one would expect a priest to hide?'

He paused but saw no smiles. 'He tells me he then had the opportunity for a reconciling conversation with the young widow of the poor young man. I naturally advised him to go to the police and tell them all he knew.

For you see, on Friday evening, as is proper, he came to visit me. As his bishop it is my duty to look after the pastoral needs of my clergy, however troubled, however errant. He assured me that he would indeed visit the police but might he have refuge with me for a short time? He needed to meditate, find peace and discover the right thing to do.

Tell me if I did the right thing. I reluctantly agreed that he could stay in my private little flat near the old chapel at the top of my palace. It seemed imperative that he be given temporary sanctuary, find his healing and be reconciled to whatever awaited him after his visit to the police. We indeed have a duty to the civic authorities. Only Father John and I knew where he was. I ask forgiveness from his wonderful partner Katie, for forbidding him to speak with anyone at all during this time of purdah. She must have been out of her mind with distress, but it was the only way, I still firmly believe.

It was agreed late on Saturday after much prayer that Archdeacon Barbara and I would take this service. I am happy that your excellent churchwardens agreed.'

'Damn right,' muttered the major. 'Least the fellow could do. And why's he wearing the wrong colours?'

Polly seated next to him, hissed, 'Shush.' She prayed no one else had heard.

'Do not worry, people of St Martha's. Your priest is well and alive and is feeling very much better. He will do his duty. Perhaps he will be restored to you in the fullness of time.

Now, so that he may say his farewells, I have a little surprise for you.' The bishop turned his head to the right and shouted, 'Come forth, Father John!'

Nothing happened. The congregation waited. A door clicked open. From near the choir stalls, a figure appeared. It was the vicar. He stood sheepishly at the front of the chancel, waved and sat down in the choir stalls. He said nothing, and took no part in the service. The congregation greeted him with prolonged applause, and a few gasps.

'You may speak briefly with your good pastor at the end of the service and shake hands. We must all say goodbye properly.' The bishop concluded with some holy words and made his way back to his chair.

Barbara made no sign. She smiled. She had got her man. There was no chance for him to escape. She was at peace during the rest of the service, and was very pleased to be allowed to take Communion, which she did at the hands of both bishop and archdeacon. The service ended, the last hymn was sung and as custom dictated, the clergy went to the porchway door to say hello and goodbye.

The three clergy stood in line. Some of the people would go straight home but most would stay for coffee in the hall. The bishop had sent his chaplain ahead to talk to people there. It was a moment of great triumph – here was Archdeacon Babs, quite right at first position, then the errant local priest, then himself. Bishop Edward pondered on how far the odd but strangely likeable vicar had come, now he was in line with his bishop shaking hands and not kicking the bishop's leg in for daring to ask. Redemption indeed.

Only Babs overheard his whisper to John. 'Glad now you can stand next to your bishop and shake hands with people? It's not so bad, don't you think?' The kick still rankled. Pity the vicar didn't play in the diocesan rugby league.

The people lingered and many said "Good luck" to John, and some said "Nice to have you back" and "It will all get sorted" and similar remarks. John smiled and said very little. It took longer than usual for the people to file past. There were many more people, with a lot to say. It was a treat for people to speak to a real living bishop in their own church. He shook hands with vigour.

The chief superintendent hung back and finally approached as the very last person. She introduced herself to the archdeacon.

'Oh how nice, another Barbara,' said the archdeacon. 'I thought our name was nearly extinct.'

The bishop lent over and boomed, 'Like buses. None for ages and then two come along.'

The Barbaras ignored him. 'Tell me,' said the archdeacon, 'do people ever call you Babs or even Babe, as they do to me? And do you mind? It's good for my humility, stops me taking all these robes and status too seriously.'

The policewoman shook her head imperceptibly. 'Oh, I rather think not.' She smiled. 'Though Albert has other names for me.' The women laughed.

Father John had not expected this. It had been explained very clearly in the sermon that John would be going to speak voluntarily to the police at some point after a farewell handshake with his parishioners. He could certainly stay for coffee and cake in the hall. Suddenly here were the police, and very senior too. Someone must have texted them. Yet he had not noticed anyone arrive. So they must be staking him out. It was cruel of this senior person to engage in banter with the archdeacon before the cobra strike.

Chief Superintendent Barbara turned to speak to him. 'Thank you for your offer to speak with us,' she said. 'Any time tomorrow will be fine.'

He said nothing. This must be a new method. Let him stew and worry for another day, then he would say anything tomorrow. This was unjust, and he was about to protest.

She put her hand on his arm. She whispered. 'Don't worry, John, don't worry.'

She moved on to the bishop.

'We are honoured indeed,' boomed the bishop. 'We are honoured indeed. The police are here in person, a chief superintendent too. Called Barbara.' He lowered his voice. 'You will treat him gently, won't you? He's been through a lot. I must look after my clergy.' He nodded knowledgeably at his protégé.

'Edward, Bishop of Hillford, I hereby arrest you on suspicion of the murder of Fred Vestal. You do not have to—'

The bishop did not hear the rest of the words as he dropped his crosier to the floor.

Archdeacon Barbara nodded at Chief Superintendent Barbara. 'I'll go and tell people the bishop has been called away on business.' She stared at Father John and one or two of the parishioners who were still lingering. 'Understood? Discretion, please everyone, discretion.'

The bishop nodded gratefully. He had recovered quickly. He felt it best not to show anger. 'Thank you. I'm sure we can sort out this misunderstanding.'

'I am sure we will come to the full truth, sir,' said the chief superintendent. The others left and the bishop and the police officer were alone. She phoned for a police car. 'Good, good, Gutteridge and Walker will be here in five.

Very good.' She turned to the bishop. 'Would you like us to retrieve your jacket and things from the vestry, sir?' she asked.

'That would be very kind,' he said, 'but if you don't mind I shall stay in my canonicals as you take me away. One must preserve a certain dignity for this sort of thing, do you not think?' He looked superlative in the robes; no fashion house ever set off purple and green in more lovely style. The green chasuble was embroidered with pictures of fields, smiling families of all nations working the land and fisherfolk toiling in the seas. There were rice paddies and birds flying overhead. It was nature most innocent, beneficent. His mitre with its golden cross towered over the whole show.

Barbara was sorry for him. If he thought that he could appeal to her that way, or in any way, to divert her from her duty, he did not yet know his woman. She was sad. Even a bishop could sin. There was no need to be discourteous however. 'Would you like to wait privately in the porch, sir?' she said. 'Less chance of a stray person wandering back in and seeing us here, and asking—'

'I think we will be all right here, if you are happy.'

It made her all the more determined to detain the bishop in the porch. 'Let's go there, sir,' she said. When Barbara spoke in that way, it was hard for even a bishop to refuse. 'Very well,' he said, as if it were his own plan.

He shuddered involuntarily as they entered the porch. He looked round and Barbara noted a sense of something close to terror as they stood there. He swallowed. 'Sorry,' he said, 'I always find these porches dark and gloomy areas, not places really, but transition points going somewhere else, not a place of their own. Do you know, in olden times people had to be married here, as the church couldn't quite bring itself to bless the union of man and woman as being connected with naughty bodily deeds, and not even marriage was fit for the altar.'

'I've heard something like that, yes, sir,' she replied.

'Good we live in more enlightened times, eh, Officer?'

She said nothing. She was studying his reactions. He started to sweat. He took off his mitre, wiped his head, and put his mitre back on. He looked majestic even in this place of gloom. He looked around intently. He seemed very interested in the rough stone wall opposite to where they were standing. Barbara thought he was looking for something.

The marked police car drew up, full sirens blazing. It skidded to a halt. 'Sorry, sir, that will be Constable Walker. He does nothing by halves.'

'Are you sure you are not making a point, Officer?' said the bishop. He was regaining the formidable strength and insight which had promoted him so far in an organisation not backward in understanding human nature.

She led him outside. There was an audience waiting. Somehow the people in the hall had heard. The car left them in no doubt. Crowds three thick stood by the hall. People started gathering along the pavement near the church complex. Teenagers waved and texted. People took photographs. Some tried to position themselves for selfies. Barbara wanted to take him quickly to the car.

The bishop had other ideas. Defiant, ashamed, majestic, lonely in his glory, he insisted on standing firm. He waved a blessing to his flock. He was dressed in a style worthy of a coronation and he revelled in it. In his humiliation he was a teacher still. He seemed about to give a speech. Let the police do their worst. The church was solid as a rock.

Maisy came running up. 'I found this, Your Grace,' she said. 'You left your stick in church.'

'Crosier,' he said and smiled. There would always be a generation of old ladies to keep the church alive. 'Thank you very much. I wondered where that had gone.'

The crosier was made of olive wood. It was unvarnished and rough-hewn and just smooth enough to handle without splinters. Barbara saw a dark stain two thirds along its length. She nodded to Gutteridge to take charge of it. The bishop noticed and he went pale. 'Let's go,' he said.

Watched by a crowd of nearly a hundred, the bishop was carefully placed in the back. Walker tried to press down the mitre to make sure the bishop did not hurt his head while getting in the car. The bishop waved him away angrily. 'I played rugby for England, man, and can look after my own thick head, thank you, Constable,' he said. 'Keep your hands off my mitre.' It was the one outburst he permitted himself.

Constable Walker made sure everyone was in safely and seat belts fastened. He walked round to his seat and drove them away, with no siren. The crowd watched in silence, and one or two waved. St Martha's was living up to its reputation for entertainment yet again.

Chapter 16

It was another lovely Sunday of an amazing May. Helen's mum Kim drove over and picked up her and six-year-old Aaron from Helen's flat. Kim always made up the sandwiches the evening before so as not to waste time. Helen brought along the flask of tea and some fizzy drinks. Aaron was awake early and found that unlike Christmas it was light. They were going to the seaside. It was great, said Kim, that Helen was really free today and not on call. Just in case, they had better get away quick, 'cause you never knew what her bossy inspector might grab her for even on her day off. The murder could wait.

They were gone by nine thirty.

They drove in Kim's blue Honda the twenty miles to Seaway that had a cosy, safe bay and lots of ice creams, plenty of sand, a harbour and some nice old houses and a famous writer's house which smugglers had used. There were loads of lovely cafes, and a promenade with grass that looked down on the beach and out to sea. On a good day there were boats to ride and children's fun activities.

Aaron was perfectly happy to be with his mum and Nan. He rarely saw his dad who was away on business in London.

After an easy journey of forty-five minutes they were settled on the beach for the day, in a really nice position. Helen got out a book, but soon decided it was more fun to chat with Mum and watch Aaron defy the sea to destroy his castle. Bliss, nobody could get at her, not today. She was better organised than Mark Ellis, so even if something came in, it would be he that got caught and not her. Anyway, Barbara, who did have her good moments, had told them, hadn't she, not to worry, nothing would come in before Monday. Helen slapped on more sun blocker.

Kim took out some of the hamper. There were tomato and cheddar sandwiches, three other varieties of cheese, a mountain range of salads, coleslaw, cold ham, Scotch eggs, little sausages, tuna rolls, cakes and crisps. There were some little oranges.

Aaron placed pirate flags on his castle. It was a work of art and the sea was about two hours from reaching it. He was working on a series of impregnable fortifications, tunnels and moats.

He worked on intently. He forgot the bag of chips that Mum had promised. The sea was creeping closer. He dug deeper to protect his work in sand.

It was two o'clock when the call came. Helen was asleep. Kim ignored Helen's smartphone. It would not stop ringing. Kim got worried. She longed for her daughter to have some peace and family time, but she did not want Helen in trouble or any danger of losing her good job. Torn, she woke Helen. 'Sorry, love,' she said. 'It sounds like work.'

'Maybe they're just updating me,' said Helen. 'Maybe they've solved the case and giving me tomorrow off. How kind.' She was angry with herself for bringing her phone.

Why couldn't she just be inefficient like everyone else and forget, or not care anyway?

It was Barbara, of course. There was no obligation but Barbara would be ever so grateful if Helen could come in at once as something which could not have been predicted had arisen and she didn't know how things could progress properly without Helen's expertise. It would be lovely if Helen could see her way… and so on and thus forth.

Helen saw her way. An invitation from Barbara was like a courteous invitation from the government to pay your taxes.

Helen bit her lip. 'Yes, ma'am,' she said.

'I am sorry, Helen dear, I would be angry too,' said Barbara. 'It truly can't be helped. I'll explain at the station. Let me see, it'll take you half an hour to get in from the beach—'

How did she know? Helen sighed. You could not beat this woman. 'Forty minutes, ma'am, forty minutes.'

'I know, love,' said Barbara, 'it's all right for me, my two boys grown up and gone; she's forgotten what it feels like. Tell Aaron he can come in and try out the helmets next time we haven't got a murder. Sorry, love, but I would be most grateful. See you in thirty-five.'

Helen agreed to drive back to Hillford. She was fully insured on Mum's car. Kim would take Aaron home by train and taxi, paid for by Helen, to stay the night at Kim's house, because there was no telling how long Helen was needed. Helen would pick Aaron up from school on Monday, if she was free.

'We got half a day, Mum,' she said. Helen wondered if it was time for another career – or whether her fierce ambition to get at least as high as Barbara was still worth the sacrifices that Barbara herself had surely made. Helen resolved to stay with it. She was certainly going to outstrip her nominal boss Mark Ellis. She intended to come back as chief constable while he was still stuck as sleepy Inspector of Hillford.

At the police station the bishop was given a lunch of corned beef, warmed up baked beans and potatoes from a tin. For pudding there were tinned apricots. Sergeant Gutteridge served it in person. The bishop thanked him, and said it was better than he usually got for Sunday lunch. He had been spared yet another church Sunday offering of canapés and the cold lettuce and cheese nibbles and creamy prawn sandwiches generally offered. He offered prayers of hearty thanksgiving before the sergeant had time to leave the cell and the sergeant never knew if the bishop was taking the mickey – or whether all church people were equally weird.

The bishop was sitting in his full canonicals. He had laid aside his mitre, as not being on parade. You arrest me in canonicals, you get me in canonicals, he told Barbara in the car. Sergeant Gutteridge had taken charge of the crosier as being a dangerous weapon, and one moreover which would help the police in their enquiries.

Barbara looked into the cell. If he thought that being in church robes would intimidate her officers, the bishop had another think coming. As a Baptist she was not the slightest bit impressed. She did not think that Helen or Mark were bothered either way. They will be mad at being called in from their peaceful Sunday, and that would add an extra edge to their professional interrogation. Great, but

I'm a wicked person, she told herself. Perhaps I need a bishop to confess my sins to.

In the cell, Bishop Edward awaited. He determined to say nowt.

Victoria had surpassed herself. She was very fond of brother-in-law William, who was coming for a hearty lunch to celebrate his great victory in the polls. He was now a county councillor and could not help showing he was pleased. She loved Sunday midday meal when there was every chance that the family would gather, the one time of the week. Food was the official great attraction, and none of the children would admit that they really quite liked this time together. Mark was usually free.

Today, in honour of the great victory, and to a lesser extent to relieve Mark's mind over the dreadful murder, Victoria had arranged a traditional dinner, never mind the warm weather for the time of year. There would be Yorkshire pudding and beef, nut roast for daughter Sarah, with the usual roast potatoes and veggies. To follow there would be Eton mess, which drove William into ecstatic mumblings – "Victoria my dear, you are too good for him, marry me instead."

William still grieved over his adored wife Clare, lost to cancer at the age of forty, ten years ago. There were no children of the marriage. Brother Mark was his nearest family and he often joined them on Sunday. Sometimes they provided a new woman at table. William was infallibly courteous, and it never went further.

This time William brought in real champagne and two bottles of his beloved Chilean Carménère.

'Sit up, everyone,' sang out Victoria. Sarah was first at table, then William and along came Mark struggling with the champagne. 'I'll get Sam,' said Sarah. She had sympathy – she was in the same exam obsession last year.

'Careful, little brother,' said William. 'Here, let me, can't have you shooting the cork through the window.' He made no move to help, and clapped when the bottle opened properly with the correct plop.

Sarah, Sam, Mark and William were seated. Mark poured the champagne. It was a day to celebrate and to forget there was murder in the world.

'Hey,' said Victoria, 'you're supposed to get food on the plate before serving the drinks. And no, I don't want any help in the kitchen, thanks.'

'Sorry, Mum,' said Sam. He was studying for maths GCSE this week and had dispensation.

Mark started to carve. It was twelve minutes past two. The land line rang.

'Don't answer it,' said Victoria. She had an intuitive dread of unexpected phone calls on a Sunday.

'I have to, love,' said Mark. 'In the midst of lunch I am in murder.'

William accepted two hearty slices of beef.

Mark came back with a pale face. 'I'm so sorry,' he said. 'Barbara's arrested someone and I have to go and interview.'

He grabbed a couple of beef slices and stuffed them into his mouth. He swallowed two roast potatoes. He went and got his things. 'Don't wait up,' he said. 'I may be a long time.'

He gulped a glass of champagne. 'I'm walking,' he said. He slammed the door and went into the bright afternoon.

Victoria did not wave. 'I might take up your offer of marriage,' she told William.

'All the more beef for us,' remarked William. His face reddened. Didn't the police have reserve staff for this sort of thing? Murderers really had no consideration. They nearly stop him getting elected, then a fellow can't even have a decent celebration. Still, there was always Carménère and Victoria. Well done those Chileans for saving that noble grape.

Victoria piled her husband's unused portion onto William's plate. The two children stared at her as only teenagers can.

Helen stormed down the dual carriageway at twenty miles above legal. She doubted that anyone would stop her and she could always claim a detective's privilege in speeding to a case. She was fuming and ready to sort out the suspect. Barbara must be certain she had her man. It was a matter of getting the evidence to stand up in court. Helen would get that all right; even if Mark was in the room. He had his uses. They had a terrific style of alternating the roles of soft cop and hard cop, altering without warning which one took which role, so the interrogee had no idea where the questions were leading and had best just answer truthfully.

She realised with a shock that she was not very sorry to be leaving Mum and Aaron on the beach. It had been nice but enough. She was looking forward to the old chase with her hunting partner, Mark, for all his foibles. Maybe when it was over he would have coffee with her.

She smiled. Neither prisoners, nor Mark, and sometimes not even Barbara, were a match for her. Once she got her inspector's exam she would fly. She put her foot on the accelerator, overtook a high-sided vehicle from Spain, and hummed. She was looking forward to the encounter. She was determined to beat Mark into the office. Back on the beach her little boy started crying as the ocean destroyed his castle.

Mark dawdled to the end of the road, before turning right to go down the hill. All Hillford lay before him and it was lovely. He seemed stuck in the middle track – content enough not to wish promotion with the risk of leaving this lovely city, but not unimportant enough to be guaranteed family time. He was sick of it. He must speak with Victoria. He stopped. He could go home, and finish his dinner. The suspect was not going anywhere. Be like Drake with the self-confidence to finish his game of bowls before bothering with battle.

He lacked that sort of self-belief. It worried him how easily he jumped to Barbara's bidding. Worse was that Victoria had not protested, but just looked sad. He should definitely go back, tell Barbara he was delayed, and get a taxi down. Dinner first. He took out two Yorkshire puddings that he had secreted in his pocket. He chewed them and his problem slowly.

He shook his head and proceeded on his way to town. He was sure that Helen would beat him into the office. She at least understood him, even though she could be difficult. And that smile! He sometimes got her Grade One smile, the one which set the county alight. Helen wa a good mate, in spite of her funny ways. She was incomparably funny when she chose.

Barbara was waiting. She called them into the famous office. There was no tea, no coffee, nothing to eat. She briefed Helen and Mark and told them to get on with it. She told them all that Maisy had told her. She told them what the bishop had said in church. They stared at her.

Mark, for once, as senior subordinate, took the initiative. 'Do you mean to tell us, Barbara, that you have dragged us from the peaceful Sunday you promised, hurt my family meal and my brother's once-in-a-lifetime celebration on being elected for the first time to the council, taken Helen from her little boy, you have arrested a senior bishop, in his robes, in church, dragged him here in broad daylight, all on a hunch, and on such flimsy evidence? I… we…' looking at Helen, '…don't believe it. All these years you tell us not to go on hunches but to follow the evidence, get it and follow wherever it goes. What has got into you, Barbara?'

For any other chief superintendent this would have been enough for discipline. Barbara was made of senior steel. She was so self-confident she had no time for grudges and picky discipline.

'Believe me, I'm right,' she murmured. She looked over his shoulder into the middle distance. 'His pectoral cross had a green ribbon wrapped round it, as if remembering someone, the way people do when someone is lost. Bishops normally don't tamper with their cross of office.'

Helen led the second charge. 'Ma'am, you think the bishop of our peaceful city murdered a young journalist because the bishop did not like what the young man wrote, in accordance with what the bishop privately thinks about his dotty vicar, but was so defensive of his clergy like 'em or loath 'em, that he kills aforesaid journalist?'

'Yes.'

'As your evidence, ma'am,' said Helen and she counted to five, 'ma'am, and you drag me from the seaside with my little boy for this, your evidence, your evidence – is that, as the gang already told me and Mark, one of them saw a priest with a big cross on his chest talking to aforenamed journalist in the porch and no one saw the journalist after that till after he was dead? And that only the egotistical bishop wears such a bloomin' great cross on his chest and so is the one? Even though the vicar is the priest who ran away?'

'Absolutely. Moreover, the bishop comes parading into church in all the wrong colours. It's still Easter season and he's supposed to be wearing celebration white and gold. In my humble experience bishops are fussy about that sort of thing. This bishop turns up dressed all in green, completely wrong, as an unconscious sign of the green sludge pile where he left a young man to die.'

'Very good, ma'am,' said Helen. 'Very, very good.' Her eyelid drooped. 'Amazing.'

Barbara ignored her. 'There we have it, quite enough to establish motive, opportunity and evidence.'

'Ma'am,' said Mark, 'if we built a case on such evidence, you would make us walk the plank.'

'The bishop is guilty.'

'And you require us to get the evidence to back up your hunch and secure a conviction?'

'Exactly that. Believe me, I am correct. Now go about it.' And Barbara sent them packing. The eyes were implacable behind the grey steel glasses. 'There will be real evidence, believe me.' She looked them over. 'You two are fine partners, there is no doubt you will find it, together. Now, go get, shoo.' She started writing at her desk.

As she turned, Helen sent a Parthian shot at the chief superintendent, so many ranks above her. 'Are you quite, quite sure, ma'am, that the priest that the witness saw speaking to the victim, just before he died, is really the bishop – and not the vicar who ran away and then came back to the scene of the crime?'

Barbara raised her eyebrows. 'Very well then, you compel me. I wanted you, without being influenced by me, to discover this for yourselves, as corroborative evidence. Very well.' She stared out. 'When exactly are we next due for a clean? These windows are a disgrace. I like to see over the city walls.'

'I'll ask Gutteridge, ma'am,' said Mark.

Helen had a defiant glint in her eye. Barbara liked that. 'Very well,' she said. 'It won't damage the evidence if I tell you where to look. I made the bishop stand with me in the porch while we waited for the car. He became agitated, and was looking for signs of something on the stone wall opposite. He seemed relieved he couldn't find anything amiss. Later, when the parishioner came rushing out with the crosier, I saw distinct dark signs on it, which may well be blood. The victim had a wound on his forehead and another on the back of his head.

It is my belief the bishop hit him on the forehead, which made the victim fall back against the stone wall and cause a smash on the back of his head. So there is something physical to work on. It's not just my hunch. I will admit the hunch came first – but as you see, the evidence was not long in coming. Perhaps as the bishop processed in I subconsciously noticed the dark stains on his stick, I mean crosier. Find out how the victim ended up in the sludge pile, if the bishop didn't drag him there.'

'That's much better, ma'am,' said Helen. 'That's very much better.'

Barbara stared at her and Mark was afraid. He really must teach his lover some better politics. It would be a shame to lose her.

Barbara laughed. 'Oh young lady, you'll go far, either back on the streets, or shoot past me to chief constable. You'd like that, wouldn't you?'

'Yes, ma'am.'

'Commendable ambition. Don't let your friend here stop you. However, you have to solve this case.' She looked out again. 'And tomorrow I must see to those windows. You would have thought I might have some privileges with this job.'

'Yes, ma'am.' Helen was trying hard not to laugh.

'Run along now and solve it. If we get the forensics back by Tuesday morning – as I am sure we will – then there will be quite enough evidence. Don't you think? Both of you? Happy now with my hunch?'

'Yes, ma'am,' they chorused and fled while the going was good.

Outside in the corridor, Helen and Mark did not need to say it. Barbara was just as barmy as the vicar. They went down two flights of stairs before either said a word.

'All the world's weird, except thee and me and even tha's a bit funny,' said Helen. It was part of their private code. 'She's clutching at straws. If the bishop did it, he wouldn't bring his stick dripping with blood back into church, would he?'

Mark smiled. 'Not quite dripping. Stained, I think she said. But no, it stands to reason. It's just a dark natural mark in the wood. She's clutching at straws.'

'As I said. Plus, anyone trapped with Barbara in a cold church porch waiting for the car would be terrified and stare at stones.'

As an act of rebellion they decided to spend half an hour in the canteen, and get a cup of tea. They remembered the canteen was shut because of the financial cuts. They went off to The Garden Caff. They could pretend to be planning their strategy. Mark grabbed a caramel biscuit.

'She's flipped,' said Helen. 'How many years does it take?'

'You are not wrong,' said Mark. 'Not many.'

They marched back to the interview. They were hopping mad, which is exactly what Barbara had planned.

They found the bishop asleep curled up in his cell and canonicals. He was clutching his great pectoral cross. It had a green ribbon wrapped round it. There was a great temptation to kick the bishop awake after causing all this trouble, but they contented themselves with letting Gutteridge shake the cleric vigorously. The bishop stirred, remembered where he was and gave them all a blessing. He swept his arm over them.

They led the bishop off for interview. They chose the shabbiest room in the suite. They took him back again. His lawyer had still not turned up.

Mark and Helen asked to see Barbara again but she

shooed them away. 'Must catch up with my paperwork,' she said. 'When he turns up, you'll make such rapid progress, we'll be done in time for *Songs of Praise*.'

Mark and Helen walked away for another cup of tea in the park. Happy people were playing in the sunshine. Helen thought of her little boy alone on the beach with her own mother. They meandered back to the station. They found the bishop set up waiting for them in the interview room. He was arrayed in his glorious robes.

Helen whispered to Mark as they looked in. 'He's trying to intimidate us. How can anyone so pretty and impressive do a murder?'

'It's not going to work, is it, partner?' said Mark.

'You bet not,' said Helen. 'Even you know better than to provoke me.' They both laughed, the most carefree they had been all day. They were certain they would break the bishop before the sun went down.

But he was gorgeous. His alb was next to his chasuble and his chasuble was next to his cassock and his cassock was next to his rochet and his rochet was next to his pleated cuffs and his pleated cuffs were next to his bishop's ring and it was all next to his phenomenal cope and topped off with his golden mitre. While they were watching he took off his mitre and laid it on the table. The pectoral cross which had so impressed Barbara was golden and silver, and wrapped still in a ribbon of green. Green was the predominant colour and it went well with the purple vest peeping out of the assemblage. There were flames of red and gold on the garb. No one would dare convict such a man.

Helen and Mark exchanged a nod and went onto the

field of play. The bishop had held them up long enough with his tricks. They were half-convinced that he had not asked for a lawyer till reminded to do so.

The bishop rose courteously as they entered. 'Good afternoon,' he said, as if welcoming them to the palace. 'I hope this unfortunate timing is not too inconvenient to you.'

'Not at all, sir,' said Helen. She had no idea how to address a bishop but as he was to be treated as any other prisoner, "sir" seemed good enough.

The bishop remained standing. 'I am sorry to keep you waiting,' he said. 'Only I had to find a lawyer and my usual ecclesiastical advisers are not available on Sunday, so I phoned Janet my secretary. She said why don't you try a person I can recommend highly? She managed to locate him eventually, and why, I believe, here he is at last.' He sat down, the door opened and the bishop's lawyer came in.

'Hello again, little brother,' said William Ellis.

Furious, Inspector Ellis walked out and demanded to see Barbara. She agreed and five minutes later, the bishop, William Ellis, Helen Roper, Mark Ellis and she were assembled in her famous office. It seemed colder than before. Barbara insisted that their whole conversation be recorded.

'It would appear there is a conflict of interest,' she said. 'My top interviewer is related intimately to the suspect's legal adviser. How may we resolve this? On the one hand I want my best team available to seek out answers to police enquiries. On the other hand, will he be inhibited as his brother is bound to contest any undue, not error, but appearance of error? What is the bishop's opinion? Will he feel that his adviser is inhibited from pointing out any error or appearance of error on his brother's part? May I ask you all how we may proceed? Bishop?'

'No objection. I have every confidence in your professional arrangements. As I am totally innocent of any murder, I have nothing to fear.'

'You may trust my little brother and me to act both vigorously and impeccably at all times and in all places,' said the lawyer.

'Amen,' said the bishop.

Helen felt she had been transported to Wonderland. 'In that case I have nothing to add.' She wondered if Mum would give Aaron his favourite meal of beans and chips, which he thought was so wonderful it must be very expensive.

'So is it agreed that we may proceed?' asked Barbara.

'Indeed,' said the bishop.

'Then proceed,' said Barbara and turned to her paperwork. She clicked off the machine.

As they walked down the stairs, William whispered to Mark, in a booming voice. 'The call came through on my phone, little brother, just five minutes after you left. The third sip of Carménère was hovering on my lip. The rest is waiting for me when this is over. I was jolly well going to finish my dinner first however, unlike you. Damn fine repast, even wineless. Brother, you should have stayed. Victoria says she will leave you some to warm in the microwave when you get in at midnight or whenever. Don't sup all the Carménère will you, dear chap?'

They sat at the table and the machine was switched

on. The bishop sat opposite Helen, and the brothers sat opposite each other. The bishop rose. 'Before we begin,' he said, 'does anyone mind if I say a little prayer and ask God's blessing on our endeavours?' His voice was as deep as in his cathedral.

Helen crossed herself. Mark had never known her attend any place of worship or show the slightest interest in religion. He bowed his head and looked at the floor. Her shoes were almost as pretty as the bishop's.

The bishop prayed for blessing on all prisoners and captives, that the innocent might speedily be delivered and the guilty duly and mercifully punished, brought to repentance, the acknowledgement of their errors and to redemption.

'Can't speak fairer than that,' said Mark.

'What about the victims?' asked Helen.

'And we pray for all victims,' said the bishop.

'And their loved ones?' asked Helen.

'And their loved ones,' said the bishop. Who was this young lady?

'Now, sir, may we proceed? Is your chair comfortable?' asked Helen. She put on her maternal act. She smoothed her hair, and the bishop noticed. It was her second best smile.

Fine, thought Mark, she wants me to start as hard cop and she will be mother, then in a swift reversal, we might knock him off guard and finish this business before nightfall. That should leave the bishop plenty of time for all-night prayer in his cell.

'Thank you,' said the bishop. 'Let us proceed.'

Helen was ready to pounce. The bishop held up his hand.

'Sorry,' he said, 'silly me. I am undone by the excitement of recent events. I have not yet had opportunity to consult my attorney. Please may we have a half-hour break?'

Helen's look could have scorched a glacier. Mark said wearily: 'Meeting adjourned at 4.14 p.m. Turn off the machine.'

The two groups went their several ways. Mark and Helen marched straight into Barbara's office.

'There's no need to knock,' she said. She listened as they let off steam. 'Another sign of his guilt,' she said. 'But don't let me influence you. OK, let's get you ready.'

She went to her best cupboard, the one made of real wood. She took out some pastries, and made coffee. 'Looks like Albert won't be getting these for his tea after all. I'll wait till you start again.'

They felt much better after proper food. Barbara glanced at the clock. 'Five o'clock,' she said. 'They've had plenty of time. Get them together again, refuse all further delays. Right, I'm going home to cook Albert's and my dinner. He likes his Sunday evening roast. You won't disturb me, will you? When the bishop confesses, lock him up for the night. You two then go home and get a good sleep.' She gave them an old-fashioned look.

Chapter 17

'We can dispense with the prayers, may we, Bishop?' Helen's voice was smooth as newborn snow.

'Indeed,' said Bishop Edward. 'They remain valid for our whole session; which, I trust, will not be long. I don't suppose I can get back for Compline?'

'We shall see, sir, we shall see.'

They had switched to the second best interview room, as befitted a bishop. It had low chocolate-coloured cup chairs on both sides of a low table. The walls were a warm ginger. It had two real windows three metres above ground, with discreet wire mesh which was itself a designer feature. People felt at ease here as much as they could in any custody room. The low chairs were uncomfortable enough, with an awkward back, just within legal limits, to remind people why they were here – to give information useful to the police.

The worst room was austere, with ice-blue walls and a shabby table bolted to the floor. Old school dining chairs stood round the room. One window was like a six-inch frieze along the whole north wall. It was never cleaned and a clan of solitary spiders made a good living along its length. There was no need for reinforcement as only a small child could have wriggled through, to fall five metres into the courtyard beyond. Above the table swung a single light bulb on a long flex. It was just what suspects expected. Sergeant Brown, a great supporter of gangster movies, had insisted on this in the refurbishment which took place just before he retired. Even Barbara had not been able to prevent this sentimental legacy, which the whole station applauded.

She had, however, insisted on the modern suite. She reckoned it was kinder. She was sure that the guests would be more relaxed. She was certain they would unburden themselves of secrets more readily. She was right on all counts.

Here the bishop was made comfortable. Helen was sure they would be done by eight.

They got absolutely nowhere. He was affable, he was courteous, he told amusing anecdotes and told them how much he admired the police and their work and how much he wanted to help them, and how he regretted he had nothing to say which could help them here, and how he was not at liberty to express more than he had in his sermon regarding the actions, words and thoughts of the Reverend John Newman who liked to style himself Father John, High-Church nomenclature, which he Bishop Edward could respect though he Bishop Edward was Low-Church Evangelical himself and as the Reverend Newman had confided in him as his bishop under sacramental seal and also entrusted himself as guest of the bishop, he Bishop Edward was not at liberty to say more, but perhaps the police would like to interview Father John in person and then—

'STOP!' said Helen, exasperated. 'Tell us your own words, actions and thoughts between the time of the meeting and the murder.'

'I cannot,' said the bishop. He spoke sorrowfully as a father who has to refuse his child an unhealthy treat. He checked that all was well with his robes. He smoothed the lush damask chasuble, which was raging green in Glastonbury pattern. He twirled the purple stole which was embroidered with twining Tudor roses.

'Bishop, you are obliged—' Helen wondered if bishops had fashion shows.

It is the catwalk at Lambeth Palace. The world's journalists are gathered. What is the trendy bishop wearing this season? Here is Bishop Jim in a lovely Ely pattern of embroidered silk available in purple, green and gold – thank you, Jim; here is Winchester in an updated style of stole, of astonishing beauty in a clever mix of linen and cotton for the less expensive market, beautiful in purple and red, thank you, Bishop; and now for the pièce de résistance, the Archbishop of the West herself, and we are lucky to have her with us today in the very latest female bishop garments, beautifully adapted to liturgical processions, silver with celebration gold, available for cope or chasuble. Just look at that glorious cope she has on today, fashioned by the Order of St Belinda's. Thank you, Elaine. Now, for those family services, a homely but lovely brocade in silver and green appropriate for the mitre you see here, thank you, Laurence. This afternoon we have the procession of the mitres, you will not believe such lovely designs, all tastefully modern to reflect ecological concerns.

Helen shook her head. What was she like? She was getting as bad as her partner Mark with his off-piste imaginings. It had been a long day and she was tired. What was that about this season's clothes for bishops? Barbara thought the bishop was wearing the wrong colours for the time of year and this was a mighty clue.

Mark admired her cleverness in drawing out this silence. The bishop waited, poised as a panther.

'Bishop?' she asked.

'I cannot, can I, young lady?' said the bishop. 'It is a matter of logic, do you see? You ask me my deeds between the time of the meeting and the murder. One: we do not know there has been a murder. A young man has, tragically, been found dead. Your forensics team has not yet reported to you. Am I correct? He might have fallen simply and banged his head. He may have been pushed, or set upon by a dog and stumbled. Thus the *terminus ad quem* – the putative murder – has not been established. There may be no such thing.'

'The boundary up to which,' explained Mark.

'I know that much,' snapped Helen. 'Very well, Bishop, let us, just for the moment, call it the death.'

'Two: since I have no knowledge of an alleged murder, I can have no idea of when alleged murder took place. Thus I am unable to discover the time limits within which you wish me to explain myself.'

William Ellis sat impassively while the bishop flourished his logic.

'Just say what you did and said and thought and felt and saw from the start of the meeting till you went to bed that night.' Helen felt like adding: "like a good boy." She had got the honey back in her voice.

'Oh, another point of logic,' said the bishop. 'We shouldn't talk of an "alleged" murder or alleged anything. If you say "alleged" next to murder, it sounds just like an ordinary adjective, e.g. brutal, horrible, sly, type of murder. You are assuming there has been a murder for you to describe – as if "alleged" was a regular adjective, and this is an alleged sort of murder, like a brutal sort of murder, etc. But that begs the very question of whether the death was actually murder. The word "alleged" is very misleading. One should say – "it is alleged that there has been a murder." Do you see?'

Helen nearly head-butted the bishop. If he wanted an indisputable murder, she was very near providing him with one. Only he would be too dead to appreciate it. She would bury him in his golden robes.

William Ellis put his hand over his mouth. Bravo.

Time to switch roles. Mark Ellis said, 'I believe, sir, my colleague would be grateful for the fullest information you can give us of all you know between the time of the meeting and the time we believe the young man met his end, our best estimate being just before midnight; so, sir, between 9 p.m. and midnight if you please. Can you help us, sir?'

'I believe I have given full and frank answers on this point, Inspector. I attended the meeting. I left. I have no more to say.'

He glanced at his lawyer. Only Mark knew his brother well enough to spot the undetectable raising of William's eyebrow.

'But, sir, you've told us nothing about what happened after you left the meeting.'

'Ah, alas, I can help you no further. I have no more to say.' He glanced once more at his lawyer. 'I am entitled to say no comment, am I not?'

William confirmed that this was the case.

'Remember the words of the caution, sir. If you fail to

mention something which you later rely on, it may harm your defence—' said Helen.

'Ah, but I have nothing to defend, have I?' The bishop was serene as Croesus. Even Helen felt the open warmth of his genial smile. He spread his arms in self-deprecating friendship, as if thanking her for this valuable experience which would add so much to his pastoral understanding.

'I believe the correct words are: "You do not have to say anything. But it may harm your defence if you do not mention when questioned something which you later rely on in court. Anything you do say may be given in evidence." We bishops tend to be good at liturgy, forgive me.'

'But you have nothing to defend.'

'Exactly,' beamed the bishop. 'I have not committed murder, alleged or actual.'

Every further question elicited the response: 'No comment.'

The recording machine was switched off. Helen and Mark thanked the bishop for his time and remanded him in custody. They all wished William good evening. Everyone left the room.

Helen and Mark were convinced that Barbara was right. The bishop was guilty as sin. But how to prove it?

'Come back to my place for coffee,' said Helen. 'We can talk there.'

They got into her shiny old red Ford. It was battered but perfectly maintained. This was in memory of the happiest three years of her life as a young police officer in London. There she met Wes, who had served with distinction in

Afghanistan and Iraq. He was prosperous and indeed described as a man of wealth at his trial. For the three years Helen ignored any clues of the current occupation of Wes – he was often out with his mates on consultancy work. She was too besotted to enquire further. The police work absorbed her and in her leisure hours with Wes, she did not want to bring home her critical approach which was bringing her such success at work.

Wes was now serving Her Majesty in another capacity. He was convicted of being a player in a drug-importing gang. In honour of his distinguished service to country, the judge gave Wes the lowest sentence he could get away with, eleven years. Wes was a model prisoner and now with full remission was due out in the next eighteen months. Helen did not know if he would come back for her, and if he did whether she would take him back.

The car was his final present to her. It was glorious, brand new, and a flaming red symbol of their mutual passion. After the shock and trial, Helen came home to Hillford and joined the local detective branch. Driven by a mission to do well for herself and her son, and her hatred of the misery caused by drugs, she vowed never again to let her guard down, especially with charming men. Aaron was just old enough to have a few hazy memories of his dad, who was a wonderful parent, even Helen admitted it, and from time to time the little boy asked Helen where Dad was. She gave vague replies that he was ever so busy in London but had not forgotten Aaron; which was perfectly true.

In spite of Helen's vow to have no more to do with men, or at least to stay faithful to Wes until the moment of choice, disciplined as she was, she found that work was not enough even for her. She was human. She could not remember how and why she and Mark had embarked on their foolish affair – but she had to admit, she was enjoying it. She knew it would end, as all things do, but hey, make sunshine while she could and make sure it helped her career. The moment it became a threat, she would end it. She would know when the moment came.

They drove to Roper Row, named in honour of her ancestors. She would leave her home town now only for promotion. Helen was perfectly serious about becoming chief constable of the county.

They dispensed with the coffee.

Later they were propped up in her big double bed. They were as naked as the day they were born. Steaming mugs of tea were in their hands, and a packet of ginger biscuits. Mark tried not to get crumbs on the rich quilted counterpane. Helen had standards.

'Will you still love me when I am chief constable and your boss?' she asked.

'Do you love me now when I am inspector and your boss?' he countered.

They always said this afterwards. There was increasing sadness in this banter. They knew the days were coming to an end. It was a miracle that Barbara did not know about them. It could not take her much longer to find out. Better bale out soon.

They got to discussing the case.

'He's guilty all right,' said Mark. He looked at her glorious body and smiled. 'The bishop's guilty, but how to prove it?'

'You, sir,' she said, 'are in danger of losing your judgement under the influence of my charms. I'm beginning to have doubts. Now I've had time to think.'

'Helen, Helen, I thought you weren't one to be swayed by plausible men. You've been seduced by his pretty clothes. Of course he's guilty. Helen?'

'No, lover boy,' she said, 'no more than by your lack of them. The bishop is as innocent as Adam. Come on, let's do some more thinking and consulting.'

They laid aside the hot tea and snuggled again under the bedclothes.

Chapter 18

That afternoon John and Katie walked hand in hand through the bluebell woods to the north of the city. They chose the middle way, a circular walk of around two and a half miles, or as Katie preferred, four kilometres. This is where they always came to resolve problems and to compose any quarrel. This time they had a lot to compose.

Katie for once had been at leisure in the house. She spent the morning doing light tidying work. She listened to her favourite serial on the radio. She made a pot of coffee and indulged in half a chocolate bar. She had no intention of going to church. After a half-hearted lunch of pilchards and lettuce, she wondered whether to change the sheets on their bed. She decided there was no point.

She had been on the sofa reading a celebrity magazine. The door opened and there was John.

'Oh, there you are.' He had not expected this. There were no tears, no recriminations, no "where have you been, I've been worried sick, how could you just vanish?" – just a weary acceptance that she could expect no better from her eccentric boyfriend.

'Aren't you pleased to see me? Do you want to know where I've been? Weren't you worried?' His abject apologies, so carefully composed, were put back in his pocket. She knew him too well. It was wonderful and it was disappointing.

'My love, I have been out of my mind. You just disappear, leaving a crazy note. How do I know where you went? Are you dead or alive? Are you in some hellhole jail waiting to be extradited to stand trial for murder? Have you just gone off on retreat? Are the police even bothered you're missing? Do they care? Have you become chaplain to a London drug gang in return for safe lodgings? Oh no, my love, since I had no idea and every option was so bad, the only way to cope is not to care. I knew you would turn up, just like this.'

'So you won't give me the satisfaction of—'

'No, John, no. I don't want prodigal son stuff, or grovelling take me back stuff. We know each other too well.' She sat. She could stand it no more. She rushed at him and nearly knocked him over. 'I knew you'd return, I knew you'd return.' She nestled in his arms and then slapped him across the face. 'And that's the only reproach you're getting. You can tell me your story when we've had some food. You are an idiot, Father John, you are, what are you?'

'A man with a story. We have a lot to talk about.'

She made him beans on toast and a mug of tea. There was not much else in the house. He ate it as a gift from the gods. 'You've spilt sauce on your shirt,' she said. 'You'll expect me to wash that for you.'

He told her briefly about his night in the church and how the bishop gave him refuge. He went over the events of that morning's service. She listened and said little. That worried him.

'Maisy did report hearing a strange noise in the church that night, and she said she saw a light flicker in the window, then it was gone. She thought she must be mistaken, in all the excitement.'

'I thought I was being ever so careful,' said John.

'You know what Maisy's like; always hanging around. How long has she had that crush on you?'

They went on their walk. That way they would be sure of privacy. People would be sure to notice that the vicar had returned from God knows where and pop in to reassure him that they knew he was not the murderer, and was he all right, and Maisy would be sure to squeak along with some cake or other excuse. It was best to hide among the bluebells.

They wandered at leisure as if it were any other afternoon. In fact such afternoons were far from usual. Either his or her work blocked off most such times. They were almost grateful for the strange recent events, which gave them this time alone. They said not much, just glad to be together for this short space. They were well aware of trouble ahead and possible separation.

She clung to his arm. 'It's not fair,' she said. 'After so long apart, we get together by a miracle, courtesy of Babs, and then we get so little time. If they send you away, young John, I am not losing you. If they put you in jail for twenty years, I'll wait for you, I'll wait. I'll never find a man as funny as you even if I search the world.'

'Funny strange or funny ha ha?'

'Both.' She pinched his cheek. 'Both, my darling.'

They walked on. The path was dry, but there were hollows in the uneven path which still had mud and water from the rains of April. The sun did not penetrate some of these sections. They avoided the rough places where roots coiled close to the path. It was wild and perfectly managed at the same time. There was no one else in sight. The birds rang with the hollow sounds of echoing woodland. They swooped from branch to high branch. There was rustling in the bracken. John thought he heard a woodpecker working at his trade. She nudged him and said, 'S'sh, there's a nightingale singing for us, hear?' He nodded. It was not far away. She was dreaming. 'Believe me, love, it was the nightingale.'

They walked further. He squeezed her hand and pointed. A rare heath fritillary butterfly floated past. 'And that is just for us,' he said.

They turned a corner and gasped at the fields of bluebells on the forest floor. They were at peak. The fragrance was fresh as a new-made world. They cried out and smiled at each other. 'Our own, our very own paradise,' she said.

They walked on. Each pointed to the other a long selection of common birds, and recognised two spotted flycatchers, and several varieties of finch. There was another woodpecker, and some brightly plumaged bird which neither could identify. It seemed like a visitor from another planet. Neither wanted to speak, neither wanted to spoil their moment together, though they knew the time would have to come. They would have to grill the past events and plan for their uncertain fate.

'Paradise indeed,' he mused, 'and only us two in it. But it's a paradise with a snake. It's time to wake up.'

'Don't, love,' she said, 'don't spoil things. We heard a nightingale, not a lark. You don't get larks in woods.'

'Nice try, Katie, but we have to face what we must.' They sat upon a mossy log and slipped. They laughed and made the seat more secure. They saw two squirrels scampering near some hazel for the fun of it. They sat hand in hand for five minutes. Above them swayed sweet chestnut trees. Still no one else walked by.

They could not bear to end it. Just a little longer. They stood up and walked further. A long tree tunnel threw green shadows across their path. Shafts of sun flung themselves to earth between the branches. The patterns wove among the leaves and none had ever been the same design since the beginning of the world. The two people strolled on hand in hand. Ahead was a cleared glade, and bracken dotted between clumps of grass. A swallow zoomed along their tunnel and out the other side.

The couple reached a bench reserved for all-comers. They sat down and watched the whispering undergrowth. Without warning, the ground stirred and a lark shot to the sky.

'This time it is the lark,' said Katie. 'Now we must talk.' She turned her head and waited for John. 'No escape now, my darling,' she said. 'You have to tell me every last thing, and we can plan together. I need to know, did you hurt Fred in any way? Did you kill him? Why did you really run?'

He smoothed her hand. She took it away.

'So?' she said.

'I'll start with my Oxford days,' he replied. 'I went there from a not very distinguished comprehensive school in the Midlands, read history. I had a wonderful time. They say Oxford used to be quite monastic, nearly all men, but by the time I got there things had changed.

Organ music, Evensong, and women. I never wanted

to leave. I loved it – but you're the only woman I ever adored.'

'Not quite everyone's idea of heaven.' She was trying to suppress her laughter. 'Thank you, sire, for the adoration.'

'Even then I was getting quite religious and when the tutor called me in at the end of my second year to enquire what my plans might be, I shocked him and especially myself by saying I shall be a priest. It was the first time I had even thought of it, let alone said it in words. He was a kind, sweet atheist of the old school who hated all the violence and madness which religion has caused from time to time. He foresaw earlier than most the rise of terrorism in the name of some perverted form of religion. Still, he quite liked the dear old Church of England – at least it's a very courteous religion, nice prose style, he used to say, and if you've got to have religion, which sadly the human race seems to be unable to wean itself from, then it had better be a civilised one where the practitioners don't take it or themselves too seriously.

I did take it seriously, but I knew what he meant. I duly got trained at St Stephen's – I liked the incense and ceremony and all that, but was not too bothered with the theology stuff, much to the despair of my principal. "John," he used to say, "if you're going to be an Anglo-Catholic, be a bloody Anglo-Catholic." I told him that was exactly what I had no intention of being. He got it. It all went sailing along and I had no problems getting through the system and to cut it short, we first met, didn't we, in my last parish? It was all too easy.'

'Never looked back,' she said, 'till I disappeared.'

'I understood about a well-mannered religion. But I

couldn't help seeing that the church was mostly getting made up of older people. I was sure I could reverse all that. Here was I, with my modern methods, who would soon revive my parishes with new people of all types and sizes, all ages, and I'd show 'em. I was going to save the dear old C of E.

I always put on a good show, was determined to have lots of fun and make church a merry place. Do you think I am unaware of being regarded as half mad, bonkers, eccentric, a vicar who has no idea what is going on in the world? That's why Fred's article hurt so much. He really hadn't got it. He thought it was the real me. In fact, I was a showman for the sake of the Gospel. And it was working. He just wanted blood on the carpet.'

'He got that all right,' murmured Katie.

'Now my work is destroyed, St Martha's will fold, or worse, be amalgamated under a grouping of five or so churches who'll be lucky to see a proper priest once every month.

The funny thing is my bishop understood perfectly. He pretends to be a bit distant, but he's a shrewd fellow. I got to know him a lot better these last two days and I can see how he will fight to the death to defend his priests. He did understand, Katie, he did.'

'So one or other or both of you conspired to bump off Fred who was destroying your work.'

'Do you think so, Katie?'

'Tell me you didn't. I asked just now if you killed or hurt Fred. You haven't answered.' She stood up and glared down at him. 'Long-winded answers mean you don't answer the real question. Did you kill Fred or cause his death?'

He groaned. He looked at the marine-azure sky above

his head. He got up and walked around the bench. He turned and spoke to her. 'I can't answer that, my love.'

'So you did.' She plucked at her peasant blouse. She twisted the beads round her neck as if she could atone for this by strangling herself. 'Say you didn't, say you didn't, I'll believe you, I'll flee with you to the ends of the earth. Say you didn't kill or hurt Fred.'

'I hurt Fred but did not kill him. I do not know how far my hurting Fred contributed to his death.'

She tried to absorb this. 'You sound like a lawyer, playing with words, avoiding the truth. Stop it, John, we both deserve better.'

'The bishop and I had huge conversations. We confided in each other. I'm not sure how much—'

'Stop all this religious hiding, John. I'm your woman, aren't I? You can tell me every bloody damn thing. And I may be using those words in their literal sense and I bloody well hope not. So spill, John, spill.'

A family of four came into view. There was a father, mother, in their early forties, and a boy and a girl. He was chasing a red ball and the little girl in claret and blue was riding a tricycle. Mum and Dad looked as if stress was draining from them. It was sunny and they were happy. They passed, waved and moved on. They disappeared into the tunnel of green. The sky sang with blue, and fluffy clouds drifted above.

'You were saying?' She patted down the threads of her blouse that she had damaged. 'Damn,' she said. 'I was fond of that one. You never noticed its ivory shade.'

'After the meeting, I went to check the porch. You know how Maisy is, she insists on keeping the porch light on all night. It's a sort of game between her and me. She doesn't realise how much it costs. There was no sign of her but sure enough the light was blazing and I went to switch it off. I found Fred huddled in a corner and he was in a bad way. He was covered in green slime. He told me how the Wolf Gang dumped him in the sludge pile, rolled him over a bit and left. They didn't see he banged his head against a sharp stone in the pile. He had a very nasty head wound above his right eye. It was pouring blood.

Still, he seemed OK, covered his head with a red spotted handkerchief and insisted on a long discussion. He seemed to get worse and he asked for my help. I told him I was happy to help him all I could. He asked to shake hands on it. I did the worst thing in my ministry. I refused to shake hands. Not till you come to church on Sunday, I said, and write about it properly. I was still very angry. He pleaded, and it was probably his way of asking for some sort of understanding. I refused, but said I would do the practical thing and drive him to hospital. Not until you shake hands with me, padre, he said. He was upset and wanted to make friends.

He seemed otherwise OK. No, I said, if you won't accept my help there is no more I can do. So I left him, in that dreadful state. I might as well have signed his death warrant. Next I heard, he was dead. I suppose he had wandered off, fallen into the sludge pile where he fainted from his wound and died of asphyxiation.

So for my pride in not shaking hands, Fred died. No, Katie, I did not kill him, but I might as well have done. You see why I ran away? The law may find me guilty of manslaughter. At the very least my ministry is over.'

'I see,' she said. Though he knew her well, it was impossible to read her reaction.

'There's worse, Katie, there's worse.' He described his meeting with Karen on the Friday afternoon. 'She was pleading for some sort of comfort. I think I was a good pastor to her. She was consoled and I felt a little atonement. I'm afraid the version I gave her of my meeting with Fred was not quite the truth. I told her that Fred refused my handshake; when it was I who refused him.

Maybe I didn't want to tell Karen I'd rejected her husband. It was very wrong. I let that poor woman think Fred had caused his own death by his stubbornness.'

'You did exactly the right thing.'

'We all need forgiveness. Me, more than most.'

'Didn't you hear me? Stop your guilt trips.' She took both his hands and caressed them. 'Oh my poor dear, don't you see? You did exactly the right thing in lying to Karen.'

'What? Are you feeling all right?'

'I'm ahead of you. Karen came to see me. She told me about your meeting. She was so proud of Fred. She told me how he stood up for his principles even though he was dying. No way would he shake hands with you, even for comfort, she said, if it was only on condition of going to your church again and having it dictated to him what sort of thing he should write. Oh, John, you were a great comfort to her. She is so proud of her Fred.'

'Oh.'

She stared across the clumps of bracken. 'Now what?'

'The bishop knows everything. He understands why I ran away.'

'You'll be running away again, I take it.'

'Yes. The arrest of the bishop has come at the right time. It gives me time to get away. I'm not due to see the police till tomorrow.'

'It hasn't occurred to you the police might have good reason to arrest the bishop?' Katie said. 'Forgive me for stating the obvious.'

'The good man is covering for me. It's to give me time to get away. When he knows I've gone, he'll give them the evidence clearing his name.'

'He could be guilty.' She was relentless.

'Now you're being silly.'

'You want to be the guilty one, don't you, John?'

'Now you're being very silly.'

'Don't call me silly. Because of you I spent a night in the police cell. I was trying to defend you.'

'Sorry.'

'Don't be. Now I know who did it, we have to get you out of trouble.'

'Thanks, Katie. Stand by your man and all that. Let's run away together.'

'Yes, I will. It will give time for the bishop to be convicted.'

'But—'

'It's quite clear. The bishop did it. Oh darling, he's been playing you all along. I bet he told you nothing about his own movements. Listened very carefully to your story, made you confess, feel guilty, but told you nothing about himself. Played the concerned pastor. Played you for a fool. He got the shock of his life when the police saw through him.'

'You can't know that—'

'Yes I can. He's guilty all right. Don't worry. Even bishops can't destroy the church.' She seized him by the hand. 'Come on. We're packing. I know just where we're going, my love. When we get back he'll be awaiting trial and your only job will be to provide extra evidence. Trust me, my love, trust me.'

She kissed him. 'And while we're away, I want us to make a baby. I'll need more than a handshake for that.'

He started to protest. 'How can I leave you with a baby if I'm going to jail for years?'

She put her hand to his lip. 'No argument, my love. You're as innocent as mountain air.'

They got home and made plans to go away. Katie reckoned it was best to leave it till nightfall, so that the police would not get to hear of their departure too soon. Barbara would be expecting them to sit at home, watch some wholesome nature programme, go to bed early and for John to report to the police station at a decent hour such as eleven on Monday morning. The grilling of the bishop would be well under way again and John's evidence would prove the butter on the toast. He would get a kind reception and thank you, sir, for being so helpful, have a nice day. Well, they could wait.

Father John and Katie drove away towards the West. Traffic was light and they travelled a hundred miles by midnight. They dropped into a motel which asked no questions. They planned to stay no longer than two days in one place. They left no forwarding address. John considered that Barbara had given him an open invitation to turn up at his convenience, any time he chose. Anyway, didn't Katie believe the police did not really need his corroboration, and wasn't it a bit unseemly anyway for a priest to give evidence against his bishop? Anyway, the hospital had been so good in allowing Katie such sudden leave, so they must think she needed the break, and they knew about health needs.

Katie told him more than once to stop justifying himself with his anyways and would he please kindly just enjoy their perfectly legitimate, if hastily arranged, holiday?

Chapter 19

The phone rang at 8.08 a.m. the next morning. It was the chief constable. He normally knew better than to argue with Chief Superintendent Smalledge. She had a way of peering into your very soul like a headmistress who gave refresher courses to the Gorgon. It made no difference that Barbara was known to have an inner core of gold.

This was different. He was in a furious mood. He controlled it.

'Barbara. It's Monday morning and the first thing I hear – what's this about you arresting the bloody bishop? Himself? For murder? In church? When he's busy shaking hands with people? All happy? And he doesn't get to stay with his flock for coffee?'

'Is that an ascending or descending order of outrages?' enquired Barbara meekly.

'Tell me you didn't take him out in handcuffs.'

'I didn't have any with me. I was after all in church.'

This set off the chief constable. 'Don't come the mock innocent with me, Barbara. At least you showed some decency. Just imagine – "Bishop arrested for murder. In church. Carried off in chains." As it is, some of our nobler newspapers will want to know why he wasn't carried off in cuffs – "unfair society, one law for the powerful and religious".' He seemed to be setting off on one of his reveries. He recovered. 'Full briefing, by noon, please. On my desk. Evidence, reasoning, likely outcomes. God! I'm not a religious man, Barbara, but pray you know what you are doing.'

'Is that all, sir?' she said meek as a daisy.

This enraged the chief even further. 'No, it bloody isn't, woman! Oops, inappropriate language. No, Chief Superintendent, no, that is not all. It's only my daughter, due to be married by said bishop accused of being a murderer. Due to be married in the cathedral next bloody Saturday!'

'I can see you're upset, sir.'

'Upset does not even begin to get a sniff of describing it. Damn it, woman, I've got half the county coming. What on earth will I tell Susan?'

'Oh, the archdeacon does a lovely service, sir. She's called Barbara, like me. Though I can see how Susan might be upset – but she will be resilient, I'm sure, sir.'

The chief constable snorted. 'No comment. What is your evidence? Had better be stonking good.'

'All in the report, sir,' said the chief superintendent sweetly. 'Indeed we are making progress with the interview as well. There may be more this morning also. Noon, on your desk. Will do, sir.'

The chief constable put the phone down vigorously on the chief superintendent. He smote his desk with a heavy fist.

At eight minutes to ten, the phone rang on the editor's desk. He decided to answer as a distraction from his worries. He did not know what on earth to put in Wednesday's paper regarding the murder of his maverick young reporter from London. The rest of the paper was ready to go but the Monday 4 p.m. deadline was approaching. It would be cowardly to put nothing. It would be disrespectful. The local people would not understand it.

Perhaps he should just put the known facts and wait till next week when surely the matter would be cleared up. It was unsatisfactory but safe. Yes, he would put it on page five, with a little spread, an appreciation of the boy's great work in his all too short time among us, with a nice picture of his blonde wife, and splendid obituary. People would like that and some could have a good cry. Yes, sorted. He picked up his cup of tea. He would call in the senior team; he reached for the phone.

The editor went through all this thinking in the six rings he allowed the phone. He was smiling as he answered. He was grateful for the distraction. He decided to be especially gracious to whoever it was had got through to his own line.

'Alan, Editor, *Weekly Bugle*,' he said and he put his smile into it.

'I know who the hell you are, Alan; circulation 12K; readers, let's be generous, 21K, when it should be 100K. We know who you are. You took a hell of a time answering. Are we too early for your sleepy little town?'

Alan spilt his tea on his nice new tie. 'Who is this?' he asked. He wiped his tie. It was a gift from the Hillford Horticultural Society and featured spring vegetables.

'Martin, your editor-in-chief, London, editor of the world's finest paper, *The Daily Render*, readership one million and rising. I hear you've killed one of our finest young reporters.'

'We haven't killed him. Who told you that?'

'You nearly killed him with boredom on your sleepy little paper. You're being pedantic, Alan, and we don't want that, do we? All right, someone got there first. The poor lad's gone and got himself murdered, have I got that right?'

'You can't murder yourself, Editor.' This for Alan was a sign of extreme annoyance. He liked his job as the editor of a local sleepy rag. He liked its provincial take on things.

'You're a bore, Alan. The lad is murdered. That's bloody marvellous and we only get to hear through other channels. Why didn't you tell us, local flavour and all?'

'We didn't think the sleepy local news was of any interest to you, Martin.'

'Don't be insolent. We further get to hear it's the local bishop wot done it. That is big, Alan, that's big. That's bloody miraculous. Not many bishops get arrested for murder. Me and my team want to do a big and I mean massive front-page story tomorrow. Lucky the other papers haven't got hold of it and we go big tomorrow, Tuesday. We print extra. Look, Alan, I've got my daily editor's meeting in four minutes' time – or whenever I say – to discuss this. We've got lots of angles already: corruption in church, what is the world coming to if even bishops murder people.'

'You don't know that, Editor. He's only been arrested on suspicion of murder. In this country we have presumption of innocence till proven guilty—'

'Will you stop being so bloody pedantic, man? It's good enough for us, guilty or not. Grow up, sunshine, to the modern world. You are sadly misinformed about presumption of innocence. Haven't you noticed, dear boy, in the last fifteen years this has been whittled away? Just try being accused of a sex crime, for example—' he mused. If Alan could have seen him he would have seen a stubby over-fed figure staring in meditation at the rooftops in east London. 'And a good thing too. Makes our job much easier.'

'I don't believe you. Magna Carta and all that. Are you telling me—?'

'What I am bloody telling you, man, is this. This is fantastic. It's bloody marvellous. Bishop arrested for murder. Dragged in chains out of church in his fancy robes and big hat in front of shocked and weeping worshippers. Excited chattering among the faithful. We thought he was such a lovely man, now turns out to be a monster. Alan, this has got everything. More ongoing scandals of the church; can't trust even them any more; what is the world coming to, etc. Bloody wonderful. Even the timing's right: start of the week.'

'You shock me.'

'It's even got our own in-house story. Wonderful, fearless, crusading, dazzling young reporter with the world to live for, sent down to local paper to further his experience, murdered in sleepy cathedral town.'

'City—'

'And the locals do him in, turns out to be bishop of said sleepy town. It's bloody marvellous, Alan, can't you see? Am I dreaming or am I just hallucinating? Bloody marvellous. I tell you that young man has done us wonderful service in getting himself killed.'

'Editor, have you taken—'

'Colleagues hardly able to work through their tears, etc., carry on for his sake. That lad really has delivered. We were thinking of taking him back. I see you liked him. Circulation rising, good man, good man.' There was an unusual pause. Alan wondered whether to offer a prompt.

'Bloody marvel, that boy,' said the editor-in-chief. 'Goes to church, how dull is that, sees routine kids' play and turns it into the biggest scandal your little town has seen in twenty years, bloody miracle, he's nearly as good as me at that age. Then he goes and gets martyred for it. Bloody marvellous. Bishop tops him in revenge. Bloody-fan-bloody-tastic. Even you support him. Nice editorial by the way.'

Alan smoothed his tie in search of comfort. He didn't reveal that Fred had written the leading article as well.

'And jam on top of cream on top of jam he leaves behind glamorous grieving young widow. And she's bloody Danish and blonde and she's bloody pregnant. I tell you this will run for two weeks. Lots of ongoing syndicate rights, TV if we can get an exclusive interview with grieving widow, might even get archbishop to give us a quote, maybe worth a question in Parliament. We might get the Americans to notice. It was worth sending Fred down to your place. He's proved his worth in gold.'

'Are we not being a wee bit cynical, Martin?'

'He's a martyr to the cause, Alan, a bloody martyr to press freedom. That's ideals, Alan, highest ideals. Where do you get this cynicism attitude from? Join the modern world, sunshine; we got to defend press freedom. It comes at a price. Thought you had all those ideals. Alan? Ideals we are all imbued with?' He roared with laughter down the phone.

Alan felt sick. 'Thank you for phoning and telling me

what you intend to do. There is no way I can persuade you not to, or to tone it down? We got very fond of Fred during his short time with us.'

'Listen up, man. Pictures; I want lots of pictures. People in the church audience must have taken pictures on their phones of the bishop being arrested and being led off in his fancy robes and hat. Mitre, before you correct me again. Track down everyone who was in the audience – they do have smartphones?' The first note of doubt entered his voice.

'Congregation.'

'Whatever. Track 'em all down. Speak to the vicar, his wife or mistress or lover, whoever he or she fancies, speak to the church bosses—'

'Churchwardens, Martin.'

'Whatever. Speak to the bloody church cat, anyone. Get me those pictures, Alan. I must have them by four. I want lots and lots of quotes. And the biggie: you have got to, must, it is of necessity, your career depends on it, do I make it clear, whatever it takes you have to get me a filmed interview with the grieving widow. What does she think of England now? What does she think of the Bishop of Blood? You get the idea. I don't want to have to lose time sending people down of my own. Do I make myself absolutely bloody clear? Do you think you are capable of all that? It's your big chance to save your sleepy paper. And your job. Otherwise Beachy Head ahead.'

'Perfectly. Yes.'

'Good. Talk again at four. We sent you Fred to rescue your paper. If you play it right you can help him do just that. Last chance, Alan, last chance.'

The phone snapped down. Martin stared over the London rooftops. He sucked at his e-cigarette. He slurped his fifth coffee of the morning. He patted his fine stomach, and rewarded himself with a fat chocolate muffin. Yes, this was going to be a champion issue. He summoned in the waiting team.

Alan in Hillford started to compose his resignation. This Wednesday's edition was going to be his best, and he would restate his beliefs in the finest traditions. He would give Fred Vestal, that poor young man, the most marvellous and heartfelt tribute. He would make sure that Fred's widow received a generous settlement.

Then Alan would turn his hobby into his new profession and grow food for people.

The editor-in-chief was not a fool. At his bidding, *The Daily Render's* best two reporters, a man and a woman, plus a film crew were already speeding down the Hillford motorway without rest at one hundred miles an hour. He did hope that gormless local editor did not make a fuss and insist on anything silly. If he came up with a local angle, that was fine. If he refused, he was perfectly dispensable. The London guys knew how to find and write.

Chapter 20

The bishop's behaviour was becoming more and more erratic.

Hearing that he was to be detained overnight, he sent out for a change of clothing and his wife Georgina was allowed to send in his night garments and a change for the day. Questioning had ended at 7 p.m. and the police got nowhere. William managed to persuade everyone to retire for the night. Gutteridge asked the bishop if he could come back in the morning and earned a rebuke from Ellis for disrespect to a distinguished guest. For supper Constable Walker microwaved up a pleasant dish of lasagne and French beans, followed by a sticky supermarket bun. There was an instant coffee. The bishop thanked him with exquisite courtesy.

Duty staff looked in at the bishop's cell from time to time during the night. He showed increasing signs of eccentric behaviour. He spent several hours in prayer on his knees and reading the Bible which he had naturally been permitted. He stared into space and recited what appeared to be rugby football scores from his student days. He prostrated himself on the floor, wandered round the room, hit his chest, groaned, made motions as if he were pushing things away, and finally crept into bed at half past three in the morning. He slept like a baby until half past eight. Gutteridge was back on duty and by way of reparation allowed Bishop Edward to sleep in. He took him a breakfast of muesli and a nice bacon butty. There was a large mug of strong police tea.

By ten o'clock they were ready to go. Helen and Mark were side by side as they renewed the charge. The bishop stared at them as if he had never seen them before. Next to him, William sat impassively.

The bishop spoke. 'I wish to change my lawyer.' William perked up. He might yet get away to the induction day for county councillors. A lot depended on this by way of networking, possible choice of committees, promotion, solidarity with the other Members and vital training. He was already furious at having his election day messed up, his celebration dinner disturbed and the thought of the triple whammy, of missing Induction Day was all but intolerable. He said nothing.

Mark read the signs. 'Careful,' said his inner voice. 'Play this one by the book.'

'Why is that, sir?' asked Helen. She was seething underneath. She already knew the answer. The bishop was determined to play them for fools and milk the system for maximum delay and nuisance. He knew such a request could not be denied, but it would eat away the morning and knock them off their stride.

'During the night I had a lot of time to think,' said the bishop. Mark and Helen exchanged glances. At least the man was talking. They had been briefed on his disturbed behaviour. The team had found a bishop in prayer half the night a disturbing phenomenon.

'I decided it would be most unfair to insist on my

original choice of legal guide, even though he is the best in the business,' said the bishop. He smiled at William. 'It was selfish, forgive me. I know you want to get away to your council. Here am I keeping you from your big day. I now realise, also, it is most unfair, seeing that the lawyer is the investigating officer's brother. There would be pressure on the officer to pull his punches in asking me difficult questions. It would be difficult for my lawyer to be fierce in my defence, as it would impede his brother's job. I now consider, in spite of our agreement yesterday, and I say this without any aspersions on anyone's integrity, it is simply asking too much for this potential conflict of interest to continue. Yes, indeed, some would say I had selfishly sought an unfair advantage, since any court could not fail to take into account that the evidence was gathered in this way and it might be discounted or held to be contaminated. We cannot have that, can we?' He smiled the smile of angels.

Helen was wary. Since when did any prisoner throw away the slightest advantage? This was a really cunning counter-bluff. The recording machine was on, and such honourable behaviour from an honourable man *in extremis* would be bound to weigh in his favour. No wonder they had made him a bishop.

William tried hard to restrain his feeling of exuberance. Yes! He would make it to Induction. He gripped his hands firmly together. Mark tried not to look at his brother.

'Moreover,' continued the bishop. Helen thought his voice was really sonorous. No wonder at all they had made him a bishop. She could fall for a man with a lovely voice like that. She shook her head to bat the thought away. Mark gave her the merest warning nod. 'Moreover, as I am innocent and there is nothing for me to say, I intend to remain silent, so there is no need for an attorney to be at my side.'

William urgently whispered into his ear.

'Oh, very well,' said the bishop. 'Mr Ellis advises me most earnestly that it would be most unwise to rely on my own counsel and that I will certainly be well advised to retain a lawyer. He tells me he can have his partner Mr Smith at my side within half an hour.'

So it was arranged. The bishop went back to his cell, Mark and Helen went to the kitchen for a consulting cup of tea and William went rejoicing on his way.

Within forty minutes Mr Smith arrived indeed, all parties were reassembled in the best interview suite and proceedings definitively started. The bishop had a smirk on his face.

They had moved the bishop into the Supreme Suite. This was the very best interviewing room to be used when all else failed. Normally the investigating officer decided between the chocolate room and the ice-blue room with the swinging light bulb. The Supreme Suite was special and never the first port of call. Selected guests went direct from one of the two other rooms.

There was a low coffee table between comfortable armchairs. The walls were a warm lilac, and the room had proper windows with sweet matching curtains. It was kept spotlessly clean, which was easy as the room was not often used. An indefinable lovely perfume pervaded the air. The lighting was soft and friendly. There was a coffee and tea machine in the corner. It was not used but made people feel better. It reminded police guests of a cosy room in a local country inn. You would have expected music of a soft and soothing kind to play in the background – and it sometimes did, so softly as to be almost undetected.

It was the sort of room where the staff could enjoy their short leisure moments together. Barbara strictly forbade this. She said she would shoot the bollocks and breasts, as relevant, off any officers she found using this room as a purely social centre. She said it with a smile and they were amused. No one had so far disobeyed. Barbara reminded everyone of the strictest teacher in their school, respected and loved as much as feared, who always got superb results. The sort of teacher who kept order, made you feel safe and able to take on the world, who always had a twinkle in their eye, with a fund of knowledge and permitted fun. Such people are gold dust and you never cross their line.

Barbara dreaded that some reforming commissioner would hear of her set of suites. Human rights people would denounce her Supreme Suite as seductive in making people feel too much at home and carelessly spill their secrets as to an intimate friend. Others would denounce the set of rooms as unequal and undemocratic and too tailored to the person. Others she feared would denounce the Supreme Suite as a waste of public money and demand a modern allocation of resources.

She would face down the whole tribe of them. In fact, there was little difference between conviction rates. Maybe it was because each room was chosen according to the psychology of the suspect. This was the one concession that Barbara would have granted to her critics and it worried her. The middle room seemed if anything to have the best outcomes. People were indeed alert to danger as they enjoyed the Supreme Suite. They knew it was too comfortable to be safe. Tougher suspects thought the very worst suite was only to be expected, and somehow proper to the situation with its naked swinging light bulb, which was only right and it didn't scare them. Indeed, it showed respect.

Whatever, Barbara's differentiation of room for suspects resulted in higher conviction rates than neighbouring police stations produced and she did not know whether she would be praised or blamed for this.

Here proceedings recommenced at exactly ten fifty seven. The bishop shambled in and before they were seated insisted on going round and shaking the hands of everyone present. Helen thought of a victim's courteous forgiveness of the executioner before the head came off. At least the bishop had dispensed with the opening prayers. Perhaps he had prayed himself out overnight.

The man clearly wasn't right and Helen was determined to find out if this was the measure of his guilt. Perhaps he was shielding some other secret she should know. She was sure she would find out before the day was old.

Today the bishop was dressed in black head to toe with the one permitted bright spot of his purple vest. That it seemed he could not give up. He looked like a penitent on retreat, or a martyr under protest. Helen admired his cunning plan – was he guilty and sad or a forgiving, reproachful saint? He had wrong-footed them again. He was good, she had to admit that. However, she was better.

She lobbed him the first ball. 'Bishop, are you comfortable enough? Any complaints about the way we are holding you?'

'Oh none at all, thank you. People have been most kind and given the circumstances could not have made me more comfortable.' He sounded as if he would give them a good recommendation on a holiday comparison site. 'Yes, thank you, no complaints.' He looked eager for the next question.

'Happy to hear that, sir,' said Mark. He nodded to Helen to carry on.

'Bishop, why did you kill Fred Vestal?'

Mark admired her. Go for it, girl. He knew about Helen's direct approach.

The bishop was unfazed. She might as well have been an insignificant bug. 'I did not murder him.'

'Did you kill him?'

'Interesting, Sergeant. Are you making a philosophical distinction between murder and some killings? I concede there may be a difference. Very reassuring to hear the police understand the nuances of death. Sergeant,' the bishop leant forward, 'true he was a little shit who defamed my priest and did his best to destroy the church, and deserved to be dumped in dung. "Dung thou art and to dung thou shalt return." I made that up by the way. Even so I did not murder him.'

Helen was jubilant. It was only a matter of time.

Mr Smith was shaking his head. His legs started to do a dance and Mr Smith held them down.

'Sir,' said Helen, 'has it occurred to you that this "little shit" you speak of – hardly church language – was someone's son, someone's beloved brother, someone's adored husband?'

'I'm sorry. I should not have said that. I get too zealous in defending my clergy. It was wrong. I apologise.'

'Pity that Fred is not in a position to hear it.'

Mr Smith was about to remonstrate, but contented himself with another leg-shake. He recrossed his legs several times. He folded his elbows.

Not long now, thought Helen.

'I really am sorry,' said the bishop.

'Sorry for what you said, or what you did? Sir?'

'I have plenty to repent of in my attitude and words just now, without having murder added to the charge sheet. And that, young lady, is all you will get from me.'

Helen in the next forty minutes asked him a series of devastating questions. The bishop did not so much as say "no comment". He looked steadfastly at the floor and at his shoes. He lolled back in his comfortable armchair. He gazed at Mr Smith and stared down at Helen. He clasped his hands and closed his eyes in prayer. He noticed on his purple vest a splash of tomato ketchup which had escaped from his bacon butty at breakfast. He took out a red handkerchief and dabbed the stain away with a spot of saliva from his mouth.

It was magnificent. It required only a couple of fast balls, the odd googly and a few yorkers from Helen and the bishop was gone. Yet somehow he was pulling Team Bishop away from the abyss, slowly, steadily, question by question, ball by ball, determined, dogged as does it.

Helen was tiring. Mark took over. Maybe it was time for the gentle approach, slow spin after fast seam. A few kind lobs and the bishop would gratefully relax and be caught.

The bishop looked at Mark in compassion as to a sick spaniel.

'Sir,' said Mark, 'I understand why you may not wish to say anything. My colleague can be a little brusque at times.'

The bishop turned with a smile to Mr Smith. He looked back at Inspector Ellis as one might to a promising young curate who yet has much to learn. He found a knot in his sock and smoothed it down. He looked back up at Mark in surprise to find him still there.

'We'll take a pause for some lunch soon, sir. I wonder if in the meantime I might ask some background questions.'

The bishop glanced at Mr Smith, who remained impassive as a cabbage.

'Sir, in your youth – forgive me, your early youth – you were a great rugby player. You played for England. That must have been wonderful.'

The bishop sprang into life. He gazed towards Mr Smith whose face was ambiguous as a crumbling cliff. The bishop stood up and walked round the room. He found the curtains very interesting. He gave a little kick in the air with his foot. He sat down and stared at Helen. He turned to Mark. He pondered if here was real danger. Oh, what the heck. He spoke for the first time in fifty minutes.

'Second team actually. I played only three times.' His mind was on the roar of the crowds. Oh, the colours! They cheered the muddy March day.

'Tell me, sir.' Helen almost clapped as Mark spoke. She put on her best maiden's rapt look.

'It was fabulous. Twickenham, against Australia. I was on the edge of selection for the first team.'

'It sounds perfectly wonderful, sir.'

'And,' said the bishop, 'I scored a try.'

Mark and Helen both called out, 'Oh, well done, sir.'

The bishop reminisced: 'It was the best moment of my life. It was far above wonderful. The match was ferocious, no mercy, each man playing for a place in his respective national team. We were losing 12-8, with four minutes left. I broke on the right and scored in the corner. Sadly it was not converted – but, well, it was 13-12 to us. The last few moments as you can imagine were Armageddon. We hung on and were the victors.'

'Glorious indeed, sir,' said Mark. There was unfeignable pleasure in his voice. He was truly impressed, never mind the investigation. Steady, his voice told him, don't let the fish go. A bit more tickling is required, but still, the bishop is a fabulous catch. 'You surely got a place in the first team for that, sir: the winning try, at Twickenham, against the Aussies. Magic, sir. I bet they jumped on you for the full England team.'

'Alas, no.' His sadness came from some ineffable deep. 'Alas, no.'

'Sir?' The room was silent as an underground lake. The bishop was in profound recollection of a lost world. He stirred and spoke. 'Alas. The Aussies forced a scrum two metres from our line. We had forty seconds to save the match. The scrum collapsed on me, a dozen men, average weight then fifteen stone. My leg was snapped in an unnatural position. Still, by my sacrifice we made sure of the victory. The injury ended my career.'

'Oh, sir, I am so sorry.' Helen could not help herself.

'In the midst of life we are in death – one might apply that. At my moment of maximum glory came my maximum loss. You can, perhaps, see why I became religious.' He smiled the warmest smile they had seen from him, unguarded, vulnerable. He shrugged and spread his hands to them.

'Enough as you say, sir, to make anyone religious and join the church.' Helen was back on message. Mark shot her a warning stare.

'I have not known such pain before or since. It needed several steel bolts to pin my shattered right leg. Some of them are still in place. I never played again. It was three months before I could walk. I was already keen on church in a hearty sort of way – but yes, Sergeant, this sort of thing makes a man ask where he is going and what matters. I became committed enough to train as a vicar and, well, here we are.'

'How is the injury now, sir?' asked Mark.

'Not bad. Some days I do not know it's there. Occasionally it plays up and normally I walk with a limp.' The bishop paused. 'People think I'm vain, always carrying my crosier. They think I'm so proud of being a bishop I can't help showing off wherever I go.' He snapped. 'It's not vanity at all – it's a sign of weakness. That crosier is my walking stick. I need it all the time to walk and hide as far as I can my limp. Vanity, rubbish! Huh, it's my perpetual reminder of frailty. Who needs a hair shirt?' He was getting worked up.

Helen was furiously writing notes. The bishop took no notice of her.

'This is very moving, sir, and you have our sympathy. We're grateful that you shared it with us.' Mark meant it. Helen rolled her eyes at Mark.

The bishop leant across and offered his hand to Mark. They shook hands. Mr Smith looked on disapprovingly. He coughed, twice.

'Shall we take time out for lunch, sir?' asked Mark.

'Good man. Let's do that.'

Barbara, Helen and Mark were in conference. They were munching delicious spicy wraps, burritos, pitta with turkey and hummus. Barbara had brought them in. 'It's no more than you deserve,' she said. There was some excellent non-alcoholic beer.

'Right, let's review—'

The phone went. 'Yes, sir,' Barbara said. 'I know I promised a full report on your desk at noon. No sir, we have not released the bishop with an apology, without a stain on his character. Quite so, quite so. I am very sorry, sir, but we've been too tied up with the investigation. Yes sir, indeed, by two. If we have anything to report.'

The others fancied they could hear the far-off phone explode as the chief constable smashed it down on the other end. Helen grinned. Mark wished he had the cool self-assurance of his colleagues.

'Now, where were we? Eat up, eat up.'

'We're getting nowhere, ma'am,' said Helen. 'He won't say a word.'

'Except occasionally to offer to say prayers.'

'That's one thing at least in his favour.' Mark thought Barbara was teasing. She must be worried. Her career could be on the line. Not even she was unassailable.

'Don't worry about me,' said Barbara. She offered Mark another beef burrito and beer. 'Don't worry. We'll crack him this afternoon.'

They sat and enjoyed the food. Helen became restless. She said: 'How exactly are we going to crack him, ma'am?'

'It's obvious, isn't it?'

'Are you serious, ma'am?'

'Good girl,' said Barbara. 'You've got it.' She beamed as if she had caught the winning fish for her country in an international angling competition. Mark was left musing on what this was all about and what could happen if he referred to Helen as a girl in front of his boss. In bed that was another matter.

'We tell the bishop exactly the evidence and thoughts we have against him, point by point, and invite him to respond. If he replies, good. If he does not, we shall still learn a lot by the manner of his refusal. We are in the clear since we have played it by the book with open questions until now. Gloves off from now on.' Helen explained it as one does to a two-year-old.

Mark said: 'I see. We have no choice.'

Barbara said: 'We'll make detectives of you yet.'

Helen recapped. 'We ask him why he was wearing green robes at the wrong time and if that has any subconscious bearing on the murder in the green sludge. He will bat that one away easily and will get a false sense of security. It will, however, unsettle him. We ask why there are bloodstains on his bishop's crosier. We tell him a most reliable witness observed a priest wearing a large cross like the one he always wears speaking to Fred Vestal as the last person known to have spoken with him. This, furthermore, happened in the church porch at the correct time.'

'And we mention your hunch, ma'am,' said Mark.

Barbara looked at him as if admiring a particularly foolhardy but glorious act of bravery like the charge of the

Light Brigade. 'Oh, I don't think we need refer to that, do we, Mark?'

'We won't do that, ma'am.' Helen grinned.

'I am perfectly sure you will not,' smiled Barbara. 'Now go get 'im. Let's see, I arrested him at let's say noon–fifteen on Sunday, so we have twenty-four hours and another twelve on my own say so, takes us till this midnight. If he doesn't co-operate enough for us to charge him then I will get Magistrate Jimmy to give us till noon on Thursday. Oh, that will be enough. If we haven't enough on him by then, well he's clean. Don't you think?'

They got back to work at 2 p.m. precisely. Helen and Mark were full of optimism. No one, not even a bishop of the Church of England could be so obdurate or so vague as to impede them in the pursuit of such obvious information, directly demanded. Mark reminded the bishop that as a senior member of a body by law established he had no choice but to uphold said law established.

The bishop smiled and nodded in appreciation of an elegant point well made. He said, 'Bless you' and then spoke in general fashion of other and possibly conflicting goods and duties. Helen felt like beating her brains against the bishop's.

They got absolutely nowhere, and the bishop remained silent until four o'clock. He was exquisitely charming and utterly unhelpful. At one minute past four, Mark apologised and said, 'We need to take a tea break, and are now a minute late. Please excuse us, Bishop, for keeping you waiting for your tea.'

Helen looked at Mark in new admiration. 'Is it Earl

Grey, sir?' he said. 'Or is it English Afternoon tea? I think we may also be able to locate a muffin or two.'

'Thank you,' said the bishop. 'Earl Grey.' He was enjoying the game which he was so manifestly winning. 'Thank you, that would be most agreeable. Have you any chocolate cookies? It is kind of you to think of it.'

He was taken away for his tea and Helen and Mark went away to their sitting area. They had strong coffee and a large sticky bun. Helen had some cheesecake left over from lunch. 'It's dinner as well,' she explained.

'Time for the evening session,' said Mark and got up heavily from his chair. He did not expect any progress. He was beginning to worry, as the hours were ticking by until they had to charge or release the bishop or apply to a magistrate for an extension. He had no idea what the magistrate would make of the bishop's silence.

The final session was transformed. A complete change came over the bishop. He took the lead. 'Since we last met,' he said, 'some information has been relayed to me by Mr Smith who has just heard on his phone. It appears that Father John has disappeared. He has gone away without telling anyone where. It appears he has gone missing. He may be on the run. He may simply have gone on holiday.'

'We get the picture, sir,' said Helen.

'It changes everything,' said the bishop. 'You may have thought me uncommunicative and perhaps unhelpful over the past few hours.'

You can say that again, thought Helen but she said, 'Perhaps so, sir.'

'You may ask me anything now and I will endeavour to answer to the best of my knowledge. Who has the first question?'

The bishop was in expansive mood. He smiled warmly at Helen, Mark and Sergeant Gutteridge. He shook hands with Mr Smith and patted him on the back. Mr Smith winced. 'Good man,' said the bishop, 'good man.' Bishop Edward stood up, expanded his chest, arms and shoulders, did some jogging on the spot. He moved his upper body side to side, as if warming up to go on the pitch. 'Excellent, excellent,' he said to Mr Smith.

'Right, where were we?' he asked Mark. 'Remind me of the questions. I'm ready to give answers as fully as I can.' He looked like a boy with a new iPad on Christmas morning.

'This is good news, sir,' said Helen. 'Was it something we gave you for your tea?'

The bishop laughed. 'No, it's not that, but thanks, your food is impeccable, delicious, just what I like and Mrs Bishop doesn't let me have – and what with all these functions I have to attend as a bishop and be polite at – you know they've put a lot of thought and love in the food – so you feel – you know, I was talking to Archbishop David, when he was archbishop, and he told me—'

Helen coughed.

Bishop Edward ignored her. It was like the thaw of a Russian winter. He spoke on. 'Anyway, I congratulated him on putting on so few extra pounds – he's a lovely man – then we discussed his latest book, it was about the spiritual in poetry. Your food has been excellent by the way, ordinary food like everyone else eats, really pleasant and just the right amount. I must commend the police custody diet. It's a pity I shall be coming off it, just as it's starting to do me good, when you release me.'

'Are you sure, sir, that we shall be releasing you?' asked Helen. She spoke like a courteous hangman anxious to offer the customer a civilised and personal service. Thank you for choosing us.

'Had you not better answer our questions then, sir?' said Mark. 'That would be logical, sir, would it not, in order for us to ascertain if it is indeed appropriate for us to let you go?'

Helen tried not to laugh. At last they were getting somewhere. When Mark spoke to her like that, only in private and between consenting adults, she invariably thumped him.

'Very well,' said Mark. 'You remember our previous questions. I will ask them again one by one. Unusually, I will explain to you the reasoning behind them, and the way the evidence appears to us.'

'That seems reasonable and logical.'

'Number one, sir. Why were you wearing green vestments? These are completely the wrong colours for the season.'

'Quite right. Especially at the joyous Easter season, which we are now in, when we wear celebration white and gold. Good question. Well noticed.'

'Well, sir? You see, we wonder if you were wearing green, against all the rules, as a sign of subconscious reminder of, and repentance for, your role in killing Fred Vestal in a pile of green sludge.'

'I see. I see.' The bishop leaned back. Helen thought the body language was forced.

The bishop leaned forward. He placed his fingers in a

steeple. 'It's a rather tiresome affectation of mine. I annoy some of my colleagues. I always wear green vestments, all the year round, whatever the season. It's my one rebellion against established custom.'

'Murder is also against established custom, I'm told, sir,' remarked Helen.

'No, no, that won't do, Sergeant,' snapped the bishop. For the first time, cracks were showing in the carapace. 'You misunderstand, young lady. I always wear green to warn people about climate change, to warn people what we are doing, to remind us we are stewards of the earth, not its rapists.' Gone was the polished prelate – he was now as passionate as any student activist. 'There is nothing more important on earth—'

'Not love or justice, sir?' enquired Helen, soft as baby oil.

'Are you preaching at me, Sergeant?' There was lightning in his eyes.

Great, thought Helen. At last. We're getting somewhere.

Mark carried on. 'So sir, your green vestments have no bearing on the case. We've misread this completely. You always wear green robes in church in support of Mother Earth. Plus the green ribbon?'

'Precisely,' snapped Edward. 'Next?'

'Question two,' said Helen. 'A most reliable eyewitness saw a priest who wore a large pectoral cross speaking to the journalist outside the porch. It seemed an animated conversation. You, sir, are famous for wearing the chest cross everywhere and it was noticed at the meeting. We believe, sir, you were the last person to be with the deceased the evening he died.'

'That's better, Sergeant,' said the bishop. 'This one does need explaining. You place me in difficulties.'

'Because this evidence will help convict you, sir?' pressed Helen.

The bishop got up, glanced at Mr Smith, walked around the room. Gutteridge stirred. Mark waved at him to stay still. Helen stood. 'Sit down, sir,' she said and the bishop sat.

'Very well, you compel me.' The bishop was troubled. 'Very well. Perhaps there is a higher duty than keeping confidential what Father John told me. Very well. What few know is that after the meeting, when most people had gone, Maisy Dwyerson who everyone knows is half in love with the vicar, felt sorry for his recent troubles and gave him a little present to cheer him up. It was — would you believe — a pectoral cross, which he has never worn before. He felt obliged to put it on there and then. It made Maisy very happy.

John told me, after the meeting he felt very bad. He felt he had been unkind to the journalist. He went wandering off to the garden to pray a little and to think. He told me that he found Fred outside the porch and they conversed. So you see, there was indeed a priest wearing a cross who spoke to Fred and was witnessed. Only it was the vicar. You see why I have been reluctant to answer your questions?'

'So why answer us now?'

'To give John time to run away. Now I hear he has gone, so I am free to answer.'

Mark scraped back his chair. 'You are informing us, sir, that you have been shielding your priest, who you imply may be a murderer, and have been stalling us to give him time to flee from justice?'

'Do you realise, sir, how very serious such an admission is?' asked Helen.

'Yes, yes,' said the bishop, impatient, as if this was beside the point. 'Yes, yes. He'll come running back. I know Father John. He'll spend five days, hide in a retreat somewhere, compose his mind, come back obediently to you police here and tell you everything. He needs time to get himself ready for his ordeal. Do not think me a good bishop for taking pastoral care of my clergy? When I said in church yesterday that he will go to the police, I didn't stipulate at once.'

'Explain, sir,' said Helen.

'That sermon of mine was like one of John's stunts. I approve his methods. They fill the church. I was appalled what that journalist did to such a good man. I was appalled beyond words when that journalist died. John poured his heart out to me when I sheltered him. I told him he would have to surrender sooner or later to you.'

'So it's later. Do you realise, sir, how much this delay has cost us?' Helen was biting her lip, almost to the point of blood. She tugged at her hair. She undid and did up the buttons on her cardigan.

'I'm sorry, it can't be helped. I have to protect the mental state of my priest. Don't worry; you'll get your man. I can protect him no longer. He'll be back.'

The bishop mused. Helen and Mark let him talk. 'It all went wrong. I could hardly have foreseen that your police officer Super Barbara would be in church. When she introduced herself as we shook hands at the end, I thought it a mercy. John would go along at once and be arrested. Better to get on with such things.

I was astonished to be arrested myself. I soon realised it was for the good. The longer I could hold things up, the better. John really did need time, and this most unexpected development provided just that, with the benefit that the police would not be so vigorous just yet in pursuing John.

Where was the harm? He would get away, have time to think, prepare, possibly repent, come back and justice would take its course.

For me it has been a wonderful pastoral experience, a spiritual time. I shall always relate better now to the marginalised and desperate people on the wrong side of society. Thank you for sharing this period of detention with me.'

'Oh, we're not finished yet, sir,' said Helen. She twisted her hands, to control herself.

'Very well, sir,' said Mark. 'However, we come to the third point and this is very difficult. Your crosier, Bishop, which you carry everywhere; there is a long dark stain on it. This is the evidence which decided Chief Superintendent Smalledge to arrest you, sir. That is a blood stain, is it not, on your crosier? We hope to have the lab confirmation back this evening or tomorrow.'

Helen and Mark had no need to send each other signals. They were appalled at this pompous prelate's acting skills. The rat. He pretends to be a good bishop and friend to his priest, to protect him, then betrays his confidence, oh so reluctant, assumes the priest's guilt and hands him over. The bishop protects himself, and looks good at the same time. The problem was, the priest might be guilty. Helen and Mark felt bad: they might have to accept the bishop's methods and agree with him.

Not if they could help it. It was best to press home the advantage. The bishop was not remotely in the clear.

'Well, sir, the blood on your crosier?' asked Mark. He decided to play the ace. 'You see, sir, the victim had a severe head wound at the front of his head and also at the back. We believe it very likely you struck him with your crosier, which caused the heavy loss of blood from his forehead, staining your crosier. He was knocked by the force of your blow onto the stonework of the porch where he sustained the wound on the back of his head. What is your reply to that, sir? We will come later to the question of how he ended up in the sludge pile.'

'Oh, absolutely,' said the bishop. There was a smirk on his face. 'Well spotted. I see why she's a chief super. Super Barbara. Quite right. That really is a blood stain on my stick.'

He sat back, put his arms behind his head and grinned. 'Yes, it really is blood.'

Chapter 21

It was Tuesday morning and Maisy had not slept for excitement. At 6 a.m. she skipped down to the local mini-supermarket and looked for the papers. There it was: *The Daily Render* and she was shaking as she handed over her pound coin. The nice lady reporter had interviewed her at home in great detail and told her what a wonderful carrot cake it was, and the best cup of tea outside London. Maisy was sure she would get a mention saying how lovely the vicar was and there was no truth in any allegations of wrongdoing. Yes, it was a wicked murder, you can't go around killing journalists just because they tell lies, but the sad late-deceased really should have checked his facts, and at least he wouldn't be telling any more lies about a wonderful man. When the lady asked her if Maisy thought that Fred deserved to die, Maisy said of course not, but it's not surprising as he had made some real enemies. Perhaps it would have been punishment enough if Fred had been made to attend church for a month. The lady reporter appreciated Maisy's wit, and wrote this down in her book, in real shorthand.

She had been very impressed by Maisy's testimony and promised to do her best to quote Maisy in tomorrow's big front-page article. If the dear vicar saw the paper wherever he was that would encourage him to come home quickly and show how innocent he was. The lady journalist was very sweet and said she would do all she could to get to the bottom of this mystery. It was a pleasure to meet such a nice and interesting person and thanks again for the lovely cake.

Maisy read the paper cover to cover twice. She tore it into little strips, walked down the garden and stuffed it deep in the compost.

There was not one mention, on the front page, or page five, or anywhere in the whole paper of any bishop or any vicar or any murder. The lady journalist had seemed so nice and to be trusted. They weren't interested in helping Father John. They couldn't care less he was missing.

The *Render* editor had received a much better offer. He could not choose between a new scandal of allegations against a dead politician or financial accusations against a living banker. He decided to go with the pack and the politician. Evidence was flimsy at present but he could live with that. The story was what mattered. Accusers would emerge. He was narked that he had lost the exclusive over his rivals that morning and on an ordinary day the bishop story would have served very well, very well indeed, but this one was just too big. He soon got over his regrets and settled down to work on the dead man's life.

Plus, even his best two journalists had found little of interest. They spoke to some eccentric churchgoers, with one nice snippet of an ex-army church official swearing at them in very military language better directed at the Taliban (crusty colonel should direct his violence at a proper target), and there was the possible loss of the chief constable's daughter's wedding (cosy county coterie discomfited), all good in its own way. There was a possible angle from a silly middle-aged, middle-class group thinking they were so radical with a canine gang name (so old-fashioned, why do all these trendy groups get too boring and comfortable? Why do they think they are so dangerous when they have as much sap as a wet mattress?). There was the vicar-on-run-with-mistress story, not bad, what is the church coming to? We appeal to all our wonderful readers to find this vicar and bring him back to face justice (the best angle yet and normally a great story); so all OK if there is nothing else, but thank goodness today there was a better story. Thanks for nothing, Hillford, dull, dull, dullsville. To think he had wasted a promising young journalist by sending him down there to get killed. And only trying to help the dozy place! He might keep an eye on the story. As he said, there were several excellent spins he could use. When the bishop came to trial; now that would be good.

Helen and Mark were ready for the spread, and even Helen was conflicted that the newspaper preferred to seek the blood of the dead politician than of a living bishop. They knew all about the newspaper's plans to run this big story. It might have brought in valuable leads, but hundreds of hours too of tiresome fantasies to check. The bishop had frustrated them yet again by refusing to say another word about the blood on his stick as he called it. "I want to make quite sure that my priest has not been captured, before I say more. And, you surely wish to wait for your lab results, to confirm anything I might say?" That night he got basic cheese omelette for his supper, with Manchester tart.

Tuesday morning they began again. The bishop and

Mr Smith seemed relieved that the newspaper did not run the story. Edward – "please call me that, we've really got to know each other over the last few days" – was at ease and charming. He announced that he was ready to answer all questions.

'That is very kind of you, Edward,' murmured Helen. 'So tell us about the blood.'

'With pleasure, my dear,' he said.

Helen clenched her knuckles and her temper.

'When I was informed by the prime minister's office that I was to be Bishop of Hillford, I was at first surprised, then honoured, then delighted and then felt panic, and the need to reflect and think.'

'I do not imagine it took you long, sir, to accept the call,' smiled Helen.

'How well you know me, Helen, if I may?' he said. 'My primary feeling, it may surprise you, was panic. Was I up to the job? Was I prepared? Why did people imagine I could do it? I did in fact spend two days in contemplation before I accepted. The next week I went on pilgrimage, not to the Holy Land, but to Greece, where I felt there was peace to reflect at one of the great monasteries. I was there for five days and left pretty much to myself. We had simple food, mostly bread, olives and cheese. I went on walks and came back feeling a new man in spirit and body.

It was the last evening. I went wandering round the little town and there, would you believe, I saw some authentic shepherds' crooks for sale to the tourists. I bought one, the stick as I call it, which is my bishop's crosier. Yes, the wood is a little rough but it seemed so fitting, a real shepherd's crook for a shepherd of my spiritual flock. I then went for a little celebration meal at a local taverna.

They served a beautiful lamb dish. It seemed so fresh, and I told the owner how delicious it was. He told me the animal had been slaughtered that afternoon. We got talking and I told him who and what I was. He became very thoughtful. "Shepherd of men's souls are you?" he said. "Look, I saved some of the sheep's blood to make a special dish. Why do you not dip your crook into this blood and it will be a perpetual reminder of your spiritual time here and of the solemnity of your office?" I was horrified, but came to reflect that I had not been too squeamish to eat the meat, so why draw the line at this wonderful symbolism? My friend made sure my crosier was well and truly drenched with that lamb's blood along its length.'

'So, Bishop, you tell us that it really is blood on the crosier and it is the blood of a lamb?'

'Yes,' he whispered. 'I have often wondered if that is most suitable or highly sacrilegious.'

No one spoke for some time. Mr Smith shook his legs as if warming up for a race.

'Interview ended at ten-zero-nine,' said Mark to the recording machine. 'Sir, we will come back to you.'

Barbara was waiting for them in her office. She heard what they had to say. 'Let him stew,' she said. 'Let him think that this is still not good enough and we frankly don't believe him. But,' she added gloomily, 'we will have to if the lab comes up with something. I've called in a thousand favours for a quick result. I expect the information some time tomorrow.'

And so the Tuesday passed by. The bishop called for his

robes but his wife had sent someone to take them away and he was left to think of spiritual things. He was determined to wait for the lab results and to keep to his story.

The chief constable rang Barbara twice a day. She kept him fully informed, in particular about the bishop's tricks. By Tuesday afternoon he was more resigned. 'Had a word with Susan. Seems she doesn't care one way or the other, told me I was the one who wanted the bloody bishop, because of my status, she just wants to marry the man of her dreams if that is all right with me. What's the matter with today's youth, Barbara?'

'Don't know, sir,' she said. 'I'm not one of them.'

'Seems she likes the idea of a woman marrying her, top-ranking church female in the county apparently. It's still the cathedral. Says it will be the hit wedding of the year, pity it took a bishop on a murder charge to get it to happen. She's terribly excited. Wife agrees, dammit.'

'There you are, sir, it's an ill wind.' He was less than pleased. His chief superintendent had an irritating knack of being right, especially when she was being most awkward and way out.

'I bloody well expect a conviction after all this, chief superintendent,' he roared and would not wait for an answer. Slam. Barbara worried about the health of his poor telephone.

The three officers fidgeted around the offices of the Hillford station for the rest of the day. Bishop Edward was given lamb chops for his tea, and some chocolate ice cream.

On the Wednesday, the team came into the office expecting a resolution that day. Ten, eleven, twelve came round and the bishop was left to meditate in his cell.

Nothing happened by two o'clock. Barbara swallowed a health fruit bar for lunch, and worked on the emergency safety strategy of the county.

At two fifteen her phone rang. It was the lab and the blood was confirmed as that of a sheep. It was the oddest and most difficult set of tests the lab had done, and they had needed to think of new strategies. Sheep and human blood were so similar, though not identical. Pete thanked Barbara for this interesting challenge and yes, there was no doubt, the blood was from a sheep. Barbara for once did not know whether to be glad or sad. She called Mark and Helen at once to her office.

They agreed that the case against the bishop had collapsed. He was released within twenty minutes with an apology, without a stain on his character and without the national press spitting on his reputation. The bishop was most courteous and thanked them for helping his patience and spiritual development and for humbling his pride. He limped away with his stick.

At three o'clock a happy chief constable thanked his chief super for her incorruptible handling of the case, and for keeping him informed but out of the process, with the happy result that nobody could claim he had misused his position or placed undue pressure on his colleagues. The good bishop's innocence was proved beyond all doubt and Susan's wedding would go ahead, with the bishop in charge, whatever she said, since after all the most important thing was marrying the man of her dreams. He presumed that a full hunt was out for the missing vicar and it seemed likely that a conviction would follow in due course.

There was a rare satisfaction in his voice. For once,

he had been proved right and Barbara wrong. He was in excellent spirits. He placed the phone down as if it were made of rare Venetian glass. He was humming a little tune. He was too discreet to berate Barbara for her strange error of judgement: he didn't need to, he was certain she would feel it more keenly without any prompt from him. It was not for nothing he was chief constable; he had to work with her again, and knew how to handle his colleagues.

For the first time in twenty years Barbara doubted her inner instinct and her methods and wondered about her future. Mark and Helen thought she looked ten years older than her fifty-three. They tried to console her by complimenting her on her wonderful coffee and support. They promised to redouble their efforts to bring the funny vicar to justice.

They met in the Ramsey Room. It was Archdeacon Barbara, Polly and the major. It was one o'clock and they allowed until three, as the only time Polly could get from work and that was pushing it. The major had all the time in the world as had presumably the vicar, but he was not there. Babs convened the meeting in the light of the extraordinary events of the past few days in order to plan the way forward.

The vicar was not there. Barbara had optimistically left messages by phone and text and so had the two churchwardens. They knew he was in a fragile state and decided it best to contact him each in his or her own style. Each told him he was valued and hoped he was enjoying a restful break. He would be very much welcomed back when he was ready and in the meantime not to worry about the services. At eleven o'clock Babs gave one last call to the vicarage, and began to sense that it would be a long time before he returned. Still, the meeting that lunchtime could go ahead and if necessary the vicar would simply be informed what was happening.

And so it was that as the bishop sat in his cell over a bowl of nourishing chicken stew and chunks of bread with cheese, the triumvirate of officials sat down in St Martha's church hall to decide that church's future.

They discussed first the dramatic arrest of Bishop Edward. Amazing, he was still being held.

'They loved it. Pretended to be shocked, but look at their eyes,' said the major. 'Bishop arrested in daylight, marched off in police car with markings. They will talk of it till the next big war.'

'What do you think, Polly?' asked the archdeacon.

''Fraid Bernard's right,' said Polly. 'Maisy was so excited she nearly wet herself.'

'Oh dear, we can't have that. I wonder when the bishop last had that effect on a woman,' mused Babs. 'Sorry. You have to laugh or you'd cry. This is all so terrible. So what do we do?'

'Get ourselves a new bishop?' suggested Polly.

'Steady on, Polly,' said the major.

'Well, if he's guilty, he'll have to go to prison? Won't he?'

Bernard Blake had never seen Polly so fierce. She didn't really think it, did she?

'Let's leave all matters of the murder to the police shall we?' said Barbara in her best honey voice. 'Our job is to look after the church. We may have to live week by week until the matter is resolved.'

'Day by day, more like,' said Polly.

'You're right,' said Barbara. 'So what does everyone suggest? I have ideas but want to hear what you think first.'

The meeting dragged on till well past three. The two churchwardens took their chance to update Babs on issues which had been left to simmer for perhaps too long. Polly accepted she would be late back for work. Never mind, it was worth this long and very helpful session with the archdeacon.

Her phone rang a merry tune of "Oranges and Lemons". 'Archdeacon,' she said. She listened in silence for a whole minute. The tirade could be heard down the line. She finally said: 'No, don't do that – you can't – wouldn't recommend it – no, I can't – let's talk – yes, five at your place. I'll bring along my best twenty-year malt. You sound like you need it.' She snapped off her phone before her speaker could contradict.

'That was Edward,' she said, 'the bishop. The police released him about half an hour ago. Poor boy, he sounds rough and is hopping mad. He's talking of not doing the chief constable wedding this Saturday and asked me to do it. He thinks the CC could have stopped this nonsense about his arrest and didn't raise a finger to help, so why should he marry the man's daughter? Don't worry, I'll bring him round.'

Chapter 22

They took two hundred pounds each from the bank on the Sunday. John suggested they might delay their journey till Monday morning and take another four hundred between them from the Hillford branch. That way they would leave with eight hundred and no suspicions. John also kept hold of the three hundred pounds he had borrowed from the vestry safe and not spent. He had seen the detective series on TV. Wherever you drew money or paid money by debit or credit card that left a trail of where you were at that time. Easy for the police to find, trace your likely path and pick you up. So just pay cash.

Katie told him to think. 'We could stay for example in Brighton for a week, and pay the bill by card at the end as normal. Our whereabouts will only be known after we have long paid and gone far from the scene. You can overdo this trail business,' she said. 'So long as we don't stay just single nights, yes, then you might just as well leave them a route map, but – oh, we'll be all right. Offering cash will raise suspicions in most places, they don't like cash.'

The Monday morning plan was rejected and they were long gone by midnight on Sunday. They would get more money elsewhere.

As ever John took her word and her sunny optimism as gospel.

They swung down into Brighton by lunchtime on Monday. They wandered round the Pavilion. In The Lanes, Katie bought a silver necklace with tiny clasped hands. John was sad to find an old tabernacle church was now a tavern. It was once the scene of a minister who laboured in the vineyard for many Victorian decades. Katie thought it was sweet, and a good modern use of plant. 'Both we and they are in the enjoy-life business,' she said. John said you can overdo anything, and she told him not to be such a young pessimist.

They stayed at a small guest house that evening and paid the next morning in cash. John tucked into a full English. Katie sipped green tea and ate croissants. By ten they were on the road. They paid cash to fill the tank of the car.

They hit Bournemouth and decided that was a good place to hide. Salisbury was too obvious a choice to a cleric to visit. Wells too was off the agenda.

They bought an all-day ticket for what Katie insisted was the Dotto and John called the Bournemouth Land Train. They went east and they went west in various stages. They enjoyed every step of the way between Boscombe and Alum Chine Beach. They liked the floral displays and the bands. They ate fish and chips. They had fun fighting off some thieving seagulls with Katie's green and yellow parasol. 'We could grow old together doing this,' whispered Katie linking her arm in his. 'When we are old and have seven grandchildren.'

The next day they lunched at Hengistbury Head and wished they could stay there for ever. The wind was light and the bright sky held those high wispy clouds which children for ever associate with summer and sand and sun. Each one was quiet and they clung together. They ate ice cream and wandered round as if the world were made just for them. This week could be their final time together.

He became hyper cheerful. 'I'm getting all sorts of ideas for when I get back to St M's,' he said. This worried her much more than his sad moments.

On the Thursday they left. While there was yet time they both wanted to fulfil their ambition to see the Eden Project, so far away in Cornwall. By evening they reached Dartmouth. They were in a glorious old hotel by the harbour and lucky to find a vacancy.

They climbed into the four-poster bed. She drew the curtains.

'Darling,' she said. 'You know how every night this week we've been trying to make babies.'

'So that's what we've been doing.' He laughed, as he had rarely done for the past fortnight.

'Looks like nature's beaten us to it,' she said.

'You mean?'

'Yes, my love, you're going to be a daddy. Looks like we needn't have bothered all this week.'

His face was a picture of massed emotions fighting for primacy. 'Come here, silly dear,' she said. 'It's been wonderful and of course we'd still be doing things and a lot of things. I waited till I was quite sure before telling you but it seems likely I was already pregnant before that journalist entered your church.'

John kissed her.

'I take it you are not displeased, Father?' she said.

'Pleased, pleased, it's fantastic, it's wonderful, it's

amazing, it's marvellous, it's glorious, it's, well, I don't know what it is.'

'Now you're a real father,' she said. 'Come here, you naughty vicar. We'll have to get married now.'

He woke up at two o'clock. She asked him what was the matter.

'How can we get married?' he said. 'When the police get me, as they will, how can we have time to get married? You'll be left with a child from that disgraced vicar in jail, and I'll be in no position to support you and—'

'John, don't spoil it. You're innocent, my love, and even if they take it in their heads to get you for constructive manslaughter or whatever they call it, I'll stand by you, I'll marry you in jail, Babs will do the ceremony, you'll get out before long and we can go far away, where nobody knows us and our little boy, or girl, will be part of a normal family and we've got time to rebuild, maybe have more children. Isn't that what you are always telling people – you can always redeem and rebuild?'

'Not so easy to follow one's own doctrine, is it? When one is in real trouble?'

'Go back to sleep, John. It'll work out, you'll see. In the meantime, if this is our last week, let's at least enjoy it.'

It was no good. After half an hour she got out and made tea. They ate a digestive biscuit each and went back to bed and to sleep. The four-poster bed surrounded them with refuge and calm. They just managed to reach breakfast in time.

That morning they took the river trip to visit Greenway, home of Agatha Christie. The weather had turned and there was strong rain. It was difficult to see the creeks and corners. 'Good murder weather,' remarked Katie.

'She set some of her murders in the grounds,' said John.

'John, we know nothing of real murder, remember that, John,' she said. There was an elegiac tone in her face and voice. 'Let's just enjoy the fictional variety.'

'While we can,' said John, and Katie did not have the energy to contradict him.

They stood outside and let the spray spin round them. The rain swirled on the river and bounced from the trees. It was grey, and mist entrapped every inlet which in sunshine would have been bright adventure playgrounds. The mist and deep, fine rain crept towards them from every creek. They held hands and when it became too wet, they went inside the covered deck and tried to see out of the misted windows and failed.

They landed on the jetty and climbed the path to the house. Apologetic weak sun tried to break out. It gave up and hid away.

They paid their money and started the tour. The guides were exceptionally friendly. Instead of an attitude common to some houses – "keep your hands off my drapes, never let sun shine in my sacred seat" – here it was different. People were encouraged to see this as a living home. They were free to touch and handle.

They admired the hall and the library. Then they met the sitting room. John's eyes misted over when he saw the beautiful piano, decked with photographs, at which the famous writer so often sat and played. He must have looked longingly, because a guide asked him: 'Would you like to play, sir?' There was music on the stand; such a beautiful wrought-wood design in intricate weaving. The seat had a lovely cream base. The piano was in a corner, and a standard lamp shone light on the off-white walls. The floor was of polished dark wood and the instrument held a dark brown sheen. It cried out to be played.

'Is it really allowed?' asked John. The guide replied that not only was it allowed, the property positively wanted people to play this fine piano as surely as Mrs Christie would have wanted it. She trained as a pianist in her youth.

John looked at the piano. It was too wonderful. He sat.

He played from memory the three Gershwin preludes, music of that golden era. He was a considerable musician and he swept forward for around six minutes. It was not flawless but he covered any mistakes so well that only a professional would have spotted them. The mistakes were part of the music. He danced his way through the lyrical middle section of the second piece. He raced and swung down the crashing octaves of the third piece. Syncopated rhythms had never seemed so lovely to Katie. He played as if it were his last time on earth.

He finished and there was utter, unbelieving silence. The River Dart flowed more peacefully beneath the house. The applause erupted from a group of older tourists. They could do no more than smile and wipe secret tears and nod to each other. It was just too good to praise with words. Three guides had suddenly appeared who were not there at the start.

John gave a bow and said, 'Thank you.'

The guides said, 'No, sir, thank you. That was wonderful.'

Katie was standing nine feet in from the door. She heard a sharp rhythmical cracking noise, a dactyl followed by two spondees. It was a slow satirical clap.

She turned and saw a thin figure in the corner shadows. It was Professor Tavistock.

'Oh,' she cried. 'What are you doing here?'

'Listening to the sweet music,' he said. His tone was unfriendly. He was nothing like the eccentric logician he usually presented. 'I thought I would escape awhile from the unpleasantness at Hillford. I see Father John has also run to ground. Somehow it seemed I had a better chance of finding him in these western haunts than the police ever would.' He swept his arm round the room. 'The places where someone is not expected to be seen are the places that others must search.' He looked with disdain on the unacademic group of older than middle-aged people who were there to enjoy themselves and learn a bit more.

'Tell me,' he said, 'when is John coming home – to face the music, if I might use so imprecise a phrase?' He gave a short sarcastic wave as the ecstatic tourists crowded round John to thank him so much with their provincial endearments. John seemed overwhelmed.

There nearly was a real murder at Greenway, but Katie decided the sneering philosopher was not worth it. She would not tell John about this logical professor's sense of offence at being upstaged by something so lovely. He slid back into the corner and Katie hoped never to see him again.

John disentangled from his new admirers. They drifted by and told him what a delightful treat that had been; he had so much made their day. A woman who looked nearer eighty than sixty announced that she was inspired to start playing again. John gave the excited group a little wave, and one lady greatly daring gave John a little kiss on his hand.

He had not looked so happy since before the journalist had entered his world.

'Who was that you were talking to?' he asked Katie.

She said, 'Just someone who called your music sweet.'

The professor had disappeared. Katie expected to find him waiting for them in the tearoom. Where, after all, was the logical place for them to visit next? Professor Tavistock reminded Katie of one of those implacable obsessives who knows the exact tram-routes of Manchester in 1936 and are sure you want to know all about them. They cling like burrs and insist on turning up again place after place when you think they are safely gone away to study more transport. They want to share their love with the whole planet, and talk of nothing else, indefatigable. Katie smiled: perhaps religion and politics and hobbies were much the same. Her mum had a similar thing about Fair Isle knitting.

'That was thirsty work,' said John, glowing. 'Let's go and get some tea.'

She linked arms. 'You deserve it, love, they might even have some cakes. That was awesome. Did you see the way those women were looking at you?' She steered John past the bookshop in the courtyard and into the restaurant. He sat down and she returned with a large pot of tea and two slices of lemon drizzle. She had knives and napkins. She waited awhile and then poured their tea into fine china cups. He cut a corner of his cake.

'Hello? Well, well, what a surprise, may I join you?' It was the professor and it was not a request.

John swallowed his cake and took a sip of tea. 'The surprise is all ours,' he said slowly.

'We were so worried, Vicar,' said the professor. 'You

disappeared, and with the bishop under arrest we wondered what on earth was happening to dear St Martha's. We heard that the police have started a manhunt for you, and Maisy became so excited. I decided, and I hope you will forgive me, John, to see if I could find you out and reassure everyone. As you know my ancestors are from these parts, therefore I often visit, and I know that you are very fond of this area too. So it seemed logical to take a little holiday and help the police if I could, so to speak, with their enquiries. And here we are. Isn't it cosy?'

John ate quickly as if it were the last peaceful tea in civilised surroundings he would take for some years. Katie's eyes burned like lasers at the logician with his stratagems.

The professor tapped his mobile. 'So,' he said, in the style of one giving an elementary lecture to first year students who coming from a state academy could not be expected to have a grasp of thinking, 'I've texted people back home where you are and that you are safe. As the only person in possession of this knowledge apart from yourselves of course, who did not want to tell, there being only myself able to reassure people, then naturally this task fell to me. Where others have not the capacity but one does, then it is up to that one, to do so. People, as I say, have been so worried, and I have asked the major and Polly to tell everyone, especially Maisy, and then everyone will know what has happened.'

'And the police? You mustn't forget the police, Professor,' said John.

'Make sure you wash your hands, Professor,' said Katie angrily.

The professor was unperturbed. 'The police have

naturally been contacted. It would not be logical to exclude them. They are waiting at your hotel. They would not want to spoil your day out to this centre of fictional crime. They see no reason to take the trouble to come out on the river to interview you. Here they are more relaxed. Perhaps their logic is that technically you are not known to have done wrong, you are as yet under no arrest or search warrant, but as free citizens are merely on holiday. One admires proper process in this country, does one not?

I am fairly sure they will speak to you briefly and permit you to stay one more night. I do like that attitude, don't you? Have one last happy day and we hand you over to the right people and no trouble here in the west?' He sighed and mused. 'What it is impossible to escape, that it is better to face with good grace.' He mused again, 'The Devon police have agreed for one of their officers to accompany you back to Hillford in your own car. I call that very civil.'

Katie took the lid off the pot and gave the tea bags a good stir. She accidentally spilt the hot teapot into the professor's lap and it drenched the crotch of his shabby jeans.

The police were waiting. It was a young constable, raven-haired, his uniform impeccable and a perfect fit. His boots were black as Erebus. He was pacing outside the hotel as they arrived. He introduced himself as Constable Wright and he was charming. He asked if they were enjoying their stay. Katie loved his consoling Devon drawl. 'Very much, thank you,' they said and he seemed pleased. Katie thought the young constable was very vulnerable. John whispered to her not to be taken in.

It was agreed that there was no hurry. The constable in consultation with his sergeant allowed them one more night. 'You won't be going anywhere, will you?' They agreed to meet at the hotel next morning, Saturday. He asked if there was any chance they might be going via London and Katie said sorry but it was best to avoid the congestion charge. The young man was disappointed. 'Nine o'clock then,' he said, 'not eight fifty five, mind.'

They ate their final supper and clung to each other in the four-poster. John told Katie it might be the last civilised bed he would enjoy for at least ten years. They got up early. They said Matins together. John tried to eat a hearty breakfast but could not. He and Katie had tea and cereal. They paid the bill and left.

Wright appeared at eight fifty nine. The couple were already two counties away. The constable phoned his sergeant who informed Hillford. Sergeant Gutteridge took the call and told Barbara. She was not worried. 'Oh, they'll be back by five o'clock,' she said. Let the vicar stew with worry as he came closer to home, and he would be more likely to tell all. If they did try to run, it would be quite easy to pick them up. If he disappeared into the ether, this habitual disappearing would only indicate guilt and make it easier to secure a conviction.

Constable Wright was disappointed at losing his nice trip east and in compensation his sergeant let him have the day off. There was not much local business. 'To be frank,' his sergeant told him, 'I'm glad to be rid of 'em. It's Hillford's problem, they'll get them. Not your fault, Pete, you were there in plenty of time, as agreed.'

They travelled slowly through quiet routes. The

country had never looked so green. The flowers were gaudier than a child's colouring book. No perfumier ever assembled more lovely scents. The birds sang just for them. A honey bee flew in a window and out the other. They were like children on the last day before the dungeon door of school clanged behind them and threw away the key of summer bliss.

They stopped for coffee at a wooden motel deep in the woods of the New Forest. They sat outside and listened to the scuffling creatures of the ferns.

'We could live in a shack here,' said John. 'We could stalk game and eat acorns and burn peat or whatever they have around here.'

'And we can weave our own clothes,' she said.

'Or we could go to the Forest of Dean and grapple with wild boar,' he responded. 'Roast boar is nutritious and delicious.'

They drove on. Nothing was said for half an hour. 'Oh, it's been so lovely these past few months with you,' he said.

She was angry. 'Pull over,' she said. He did as soon as he safely could. A red tractor went by and turned into a muddy field. The farmer gave them a cheerful wave.

'What makes you think we aren't going to have many more months and many, many years together? You are innocent, John, you're innocent, and I won't have you talking or guilting your way into saying things that will get you into trouble and make them think you did do it. Look, you hated that journalist for a short time as what sane person wouldn't, but your values kicked in, then you got all guilty and you would never have hurt him in any shape or form and you offered to shake hands with him if he came to church and put things right. OK, there was that condition but you wouldn't have insisted in the end. I know you, John, you would have sooner or later shaken on it and you'd have become best friends over time, you're two of a type, two men making points and both in show business, trying to make an impression. But go on like this, with your stupid, stupid perfectionism – "oh, I contributed to his downfall by my general behaviour" – and you'll have the police believing you. They're desperate for a conviction and you will do as well as anyone, better than most, pardon my cynicism.'

He started to say something but she took second wind.

'All right, they would much rather get the right guy or girl who did it, but go on like this and they will think it really was you. You are innocent, my darling, you are innocent. Yes, we all do sometimes add to the pool of misery by the stupid things we do but that don't make us murderers. You're no more capable of murder than a seagull can compose a symphony – and, and, know this, John Newman, I will never, never leave you, not after all this effort to find each other, not if they lock you up for a hundred years, and I will still be waiting for you, and will visit you every day and, and—'

The flood subsided and she kissed him. 'Now can we go on? Stop your fantasy, John.'

He said, 'Reality it is then. We face reality together.'

'Yes, please,' she whispered. 'Now let's get on.'

He started the car. Somewhere south of Guildford he paused at a roundabout and waited for a safe moment to turn right. The car behind hooted him and trailed him aggressively for half a mile. The driver was flapping his arms like a soccer coach angry at last week's defeat.

John next tried to turn left. The man hooted him for being slow. John was an impeccable driver and was upset. 'Vladivostok,' he muttered.

Katie put her hand on his knee. 'It's not personal,' she said. 'He doesn't mean it personally.'

'The journalist didn't either,' said John, 'but he still ended up dead.'

They drove on to meet whatever awaited them in Hillford.

Chapter 23

When they arrived back at the vicarage, they got the shock of their lives. No one took the slightest notice of them. The little red car spluttered into stillness in the vicarage drive and John got out trembling as he expected to see several of Her Majesty's finest at the front entrance lined up to take him off in perpetual captivity. There was nothing. Even the hedge had not grown much and the hollyhocks were still too young to give him a nod.

John pushed the front door hard, to force his way in against the normal flood of pizza adverts, back issues of the *Church Times*, the latest copy of *The Weekly Bugle* ("We Make a Noise for the County"), adverts for hedge cutters, tree trimmers, roof repairers, paving experts, estate agents, takeaway meals, circulars saying "this is not a circular", pension management schemes, banks offering loans, holiday brochures, cruise supplementary leaflets, invitations to local events, the local theatre magazine, the remains of local election leaflets, charities asking for vital donations and some letters.

The door pushed open with no resistance and he stumbled into the hall. He recovered just in time and Katie followed him. He went back for their two suitcases, locked the car and followed Katie into the lounge. She had picked up the answerphone already.

'Well?' he asked. 'Seventy-two messages from the police ordering me to see them five minutes ago?'

'You have two messages,' said Katie, imitating the voice of the lady who lived in the phone. 'One from Maisy hoping you are all right and everyone at St Martha's knows you didn't do it. The other one is, indeed, from the police. You may as well hear it and get it over with.'

John listened. It was Constable Walker, with his voice as deep as a Yorkshire cavern. "We do hope you have had an enjoyable trip, sir. We would be grateful if you could contact us at your earliest convenience in connection with the recent unpleasant happenings. We are sure you may be able to help us and then we hope to eliminate you from our enquiries."

'I've never understood police logic,' said John. 'The police say that to everyone. It's the last thing they want. Surely they don't want to eliminate people, certainly not their chief suspect, from their enquiries. If they eliminate everyone from their enquiries, how can they enquire and get a result?'

'Sit down, John,' she said. 'We're both tired. I'll get us some tea.'

Ten miles out of town they had stopped at a supermarket and got in food. They had their tea and biscuits and discussed what to do. If the police were being so civil, then why be so uncivil as to bother them on a Saturday night and disturb their well-earned rest? Tomorrow, Sunday, was a day of leisure, at least for a lot of people it was – so Monday was plenty soon enough. Might as well enjoy their last few hours together. Yes, it was only civil not to bother the police before they had to. The police clearly were not in a hurry, said Katie.

'Like a cat who has its poor little victim helpless and plays with it before moving in for the kill,' said John.

'Think of it as a bonus,' she said.

They often shared the cooking. John made a move to the kitchen. Katie put her hand on his arm. 'Let's read it,' she said. They had been afraid to open the local paper. Would the editor while staying correctly within the law, somehow insinuate that John was the killer and the only job for the police was to find him and put him away, after due process, of course?

It was the opposite of last time. Then they had opened the paper with a spirit of optimism to see what the nice young journalist might say after their interesting conversation. They had been devastated. This time they started with a feeling of dread, and were happily surprised. The editor had taken personal charge. The front page edged in black was a tasteful *RIP Goodbye Fred We Shall Miss You* piece and on page three was an excellent factual obituary. The editorial praised Fred as a talented young journalist with a mighty future on loan from London to broaden his experience and bring the paper new ideas. It was hoped that people agreed that Fred had shaken up the paper and improved it without losing its best features.

Otherwise there was the merest factual account of time and place of the crime and ongoing police investigations, with no witness statements, and it ended with the words:

We leave the police to investigate. At present we hear that the bishop is helping police with their enquiries. It would not be proper for us to comment further.

'Very fair,' said John. 'They've been very fair. Can't complain.'

She smiled. 'For once, my love, I have to agree with you. OK, forget it, let's cook.'

They had their favourite meal of pizza and trimmings in front of the TV, watched a film and went to bed.

On Sunday morning they had egg and bacon butties and two pots of coffee. They decided not to go to church. Father John was sure that Polly and the major would have the services covered. He would apologise to them later for being out of radio contact, but was sure they would understand. Today would not make much difference anyway, if he were to remain for several years in custody from Monday. They'd have to get used to arranging the services, with help from Babs. It seemed a long time since she had teased him before restoring Katie to him.

As there was no television morning service on the main channels, they decided to give religion a miss. He expected the prison chaplain would become a friend, and maybe John might be allowed to resume his ministry, among his fellow prisoners?

They had a full beef roast lunch at two o'clock. It had all the normal ingredients and lots of vegetables and gravy. There was treacle pudding. They sat down content at three, and John thought he would have a little snooze in front of the TV cricket.

The doorbell rang. It was Maisy. 'I knew you were back,' she said. 'I saw your little red car. I've made you a nice fruit cake.'

It was enormous and Katie smiled over Maisy's head at John. He put on his best smile and thanked Maisy.

'Now I want to know all you've been doing, Vicar. Did you have a nice time? Where did you go? We were worried but I told them not to, you will come back and convince the police and they will get the right murderer, they thought it was the bishop you know, but they set him free and he did that police wedding yesterday …

… but it's only fair to tell you that the professor has been exceedin' odd, this week, as he might put it, and I think he thinks you did it, don't ask me why, as when I came out of the porch I saw the poor young man staggering away to the garden. I was too scared to follow, and the professor now thinks I'm shielding you, and I did see someone wearing a cross walk away quickly, when I put the light back on second time for the porch, but it was not you, was it, Vicar, because I can't expect you to have worn that nice cross on your chest straight away which I gave to you that night at the meeting and—'

'Stop!' said Katie. 'Maisy, please stop. Let's all sit down and have some of your lovely fruit cake, and hear what you saw and thought you saw. Tell us everything, Maisy. I'll put the kettle on.'

After such a good breakfast and a hearty lunch, the pleasure of Maisy's fruit cake seemed a penance worthy of Henry VIII, but it was a vital necessity. John had to learn the evidence against him, from this good, silly and shrewd old lady, and to work out if the police might believe it. Perhaps she would speak to them again. He had to mollify Maisy.

His liberty for the next fifteen years could depend on his eating a heavy piece of delicious fruit cake when he least wanted it, with every appearance of pleasure.

Chapter 24

As Big Ben in London was sounding the first of its booms for eight o'clock on Monday morning, the Rev John Newman went into Hillford Police Station on the ring road near Eastgate. He tapped tentatively on the reception desk. No one was there. He waited. Sergeant Gutteridge came from behind a door. 'Sorry to keep you waiting, sir. It's the cuts, short of staff these days.' He was friendly and confiding. 'How may I help you, sir?'

The vicar explained his mission. Gutteridge became serious and asked him to accompany him inside. 'We'll have someone to look after you soon, sir. Can I get you a cup of tea?'

It was the last thing that John could face but he accepted graciously, to calm his nerves. The die was cast. He had refused to let Katie come with him to reception. He waited half an hour before sufficient staff arrived to get the process going. At least the tea was strong English Breakfast, properly stewed.

And so it was that by nine of the morning, John Newman, priest in charge of St Martha's, sat where his lover and his bishop had been before him. The interviews were in the second best suite and were conducted by trainee DC Debbie Thompson, DS Helen Roper, DI Mark Ellis, in various combinations and shifts. Barbara watched it all on the link.

The vicar answered earnestly, fully and in detail. He was accompanied by the same lawyer who had been alongside Bishop Edward. Father John hoped that the church was paying.

In the late afternoon, they let John rest in the best cell. Helen, Mark and Barbara met in her office to review the evidence.

Barbara poured as usual. They all felt like tea. It was Earl Grey, with its restful citrus scent and most refreshing. There were neat tomato sandwiches and French fancy cakes, in all colours of icing. Barbara chose a green one. 'Don't talk, just rest,' she said. 'We'll enjoy our tea first. I'm paying for it, don't worry.'

Mark was amazed how green the tree was outside Barbara's top-floor office, surrounded by all that traffic. The cathedral was an island over the rooftops, and the city walls reflected hope. It would soon be August and his first holiday with Victoria for three years. The family was getting older and he was worried they were all drifting apart. He would have to end his affair with Helen. She looked over at him as if she were thinking the same. What a mess, what fools we humans are, even a vicar can't be trusted.

There was a vase of bluebells on her window shelf. Mark floated back to the beautiful Kent woodlands of his childhood and Aunt Julie who took him every year to see them. The fragrance was ravishing, the best on this earth. Perhaps if every cell in every prison, every school or war zone, office and refugee centre, every transport hub, every parliament, could be given this scent of heaven, it would soothe everyone. Footballers would never cheat; they would thank the referee for correct decisions. It was so glorious as to transform the world. Mark felt faint in its gentle grip.

'They're beautiful, aren't they?' Barbara said. 'So fragile and so strong. Such a lovely perfume, enough to send one dizzy. They're the native English variety. Nearly over now, but Albert and I picked them yesterday; from our garden, naturally.' She smiled, daring Mark to contradict. 'Mustn't pick them from the woods, of course.'

Scary how she could read him, thought Mark. It was a nudge back to the present sordid enquiries. How elegantly she had brought him back.

'All done?' asked Barbara. She cleared everything away without waiting for an answer.

'That was lovely, thank you, ma'am,' said Helen.

'Just what we needed, ma'am,' echoed Mark. Helen gave him her third-worst grimace.

'To business: I want us to review all we know. We need to go through all the suspects, reasonable or not, make the case against each one, and decide who we think most likely to have done it. This is not a vote. I want you two to clear my mind. We've had all the statements from all the possible witnesses, interviewed everyone, got all the forensic evidence we are going to get, we now have to think. Mark, summarise, please.'

'Right. We began by thinking it was one, some or all of the Wolf Gang who took away the victim and left him by their own admission in the compost heap. They know nothing, they say, of any injury, no head wound and certainly claim to have left him in a healthy, if sorry state, covered in filth, as a lesson, but otherwise none the worse.

They have clung to this line consistently and no one has contradicted it. They had no motive to kill Fred, but did admit to wanting to teach him a lesson.

The bishop was arrested, as you know, ma'am, as chief suspect, because it was felt he gave away his subconscious feeling by wearing green and had blood stains on his crosier. We all have the feeling he has not told us everything he knows and was at various times most obstructive. He gave us the impression and indeed claimed he was protecting someone else. This is either true, or is itself most suspicious, casting the blame on someone else while trying to appear noble. The witness Maisy described seeing Fred stagger to the garden and a priest wearing a pectoral cross hurry away. One of the Wolf Gang also saw a priest with a cross. The bishop adores wearing this on all occasions. We have released him but questions remain.

There are no obvious lay suspects. Many people had reason to dislike, even hate the journalist, namely the two churchwardens, various parishioners, especially Maisy who adores the vicar. The professor seems loftily above it all, making chop-logic points of philosophy. Nothing has been shown to incriminate any of them.

It brings us therefore to our chief suspect, the vicar. He had excellent reason to hate the journalist, none more so. He has run away on several occasions. We even pulled in his partner Katie at first as an accessory, but we don't think she had a hand in the killing. The vicar was undeniably seen in conversation with the victim after the meeting. He told Karen, the victim's wife, he was there. Karen gave a full detailed account of her meeting with the vicar in the garden and again, she gave us the full account in front of Katie, who confirms it was exactly the account Karen had given her. Today he told us the same and the three accounts have remarkable agreement in detail. Maisy, the chief witness, who, remember, loves the vicar has confirmed he met Fred for a long conversation after the meeting, in the porch. We now know the vicar was wearing a pectoral cross, which Maisy had recently given him, so we can't claim the man Maisy saw with the cross must be the bishop.

The vicar admits he saw the front head wound of the victim and claims he told Fred to go to hospital, even offered to take him, and Fred refused. The vicar just walks off leaving a wounded man to his fate. We do not find that a plausible scenario.

Further, the vicar admits he refused to shake hands with the victim even though Fred pleaded for this as a sign of making friends. Vicar claims he wanted Fred to show he was really making up by going to church first, then the vicar would shake hands. Like you I find this another sign of aggression. So we have passive and active aggression. If Father John had shaken hands, then Fred would have come with him to hospital and lived. Shake hands or die. The vicar admits he is now very sorry about this and will regret it for a very long time. He does say to that extent he feels responsible for Fred's death, but did not kill him directly.

It seems then, that while the bishop has been arrogant and obstructive, the evidence points to the vicar. I think he became very angry, pushed Fred against the opposite wall of the porch, where the jagged stones smashed the back of his head. Then the vicar in a panic shoved the wounded Fred back in the heap of sludge, hoping to pin the blame on the Wolf Gang, and the wounds on the front and the back of the head explained by the the general bashing he got from the gang. We know that Fred died by being smothered, and not from the wounds, but they did make him weak enough to faint and fall into the pile and not struggle up.

So, my vote, ma'am, is for the vicar. Helen was right all along. She told me several times that an innocent man does not keep running. As you have often said, ma'am, Helen has solved most of my cases for me.'

'Helen?'

Helen knew better than to gloat. 'I think Mark is right, ma'am. He's been very generous of his praise and I thank him.' She gave Mark her inscrutable look, hidden beneath a grin. Few could have spotted it but he did. He gave her a rueful smile.

They both knew it was over.

'Thank you, very much, both of you. This has been very helpful. So we think the vicar did it?'

'Yes, ma'am,' said Helen and Mark together.

'And you think it was deliberate murder?'

'Yes.'

'It could be a tragic accident. Here is another reading. Father John goes to find Fred after the meeting, to make peace. Eventually he finds Fred wandering near the porch, in a daze after his rough treatment from the Wolf Gang. They chat and Father John sees the wound. Fred is also angry and won't take Father John's advice to seek medical treatment. Father John goes away and Fred in a daze bangs his head against the porch, wanders off, falls into the slimy pile and suffocates.'

'Not likely, ma'am,' said Helen.

'Or perhaps more convincing, we go for manslaughter, not murder. Vicar gets upset, thumps Fred in chest, Fred accidentally falls against the porch wall. Vicar runs, as he often does, but he never intended Fred any harm. Fred wanders into the filthy pile and dies.'

'I think we had better allow the lawyers to argue all this in court, ma'am. I propose we go for murder, and we may get manslaughter. It might of course be seen as a horrible muddle of accidents and the vicar found innocent.' Mark said it and Helen agreed.

Barbara went over to her window and looked out. She studied the traffic, the people below hurrying home and the cars rushing to avoid the rush hour. The fire station clad with flint opposite seemed quiet. The fire engines glistened red and innocent in the bright sun. The cathedral soared ready for evening prayer above the city. She placed her hands behind her back, clasped and unclasped them. She came to a decision and turned to her colleagues.

'Right,' she said. 'We ask the prosecutor to go for a murder charge against the vicar. My instinct against the bishop was wrong. Go ahead, you two, prepare for prosecution.'

Mark and Helen went for a meal to wrap up. The long case was over and they had a result. The pair were in the Italian restaurant opposite the main cathedral gate, in Old Market. Tourists loved this cosy space, neither square nor triangular, but its own irregular shape. In the middle was the modest war memorial surrounded by little railings, stone steps and a few benches. Buskers gathered here and many were very good. In one corner was The Old Market pub, next to the Milton Arms, with attractive shops of household goods and beautiful pottery and china. You could get any souvenir in this area, including wacky trinkets and dodgy tricks which so amused the visiting schoolchildren and annoyed their elders. Many languages were spoken here.

The two were at the front-window corner with a fine view to the whole square and back into the restaurant, which was elegant and spacious. The menu was eclectic and offered enough for people who inexplicably were not fond of Italian food.

They ordered. Helen informed Mark that he had chosen the same as the first time they had dined here together, before going back to her place for the first time. 'Vesuvio pizza. I thought good, he's hot and he eats hot.'

They fiddled with the first course of bruschetta. 'You haven't noticed, have you? I've also ordered the same as our first time, my favourite, risotto primavera.'

'Just about wraps it up then, doesn't it?' said Mark. He poured their Chianti from the bottle with its little rooster logo. She put her hand on his. The huge green marble man above the cathedral gate looked down on them inscrutably. He did not seem unfriendly or in judging mood.

There were few people in at the time. It was gone half past eight, Monday night. They were not afraid of being discovered. Victoria had long expected Mark to work late and he had kept her informed as much as he could about this long and difficult murder case, so don't wait up for me, love. Helen's mum was only too happy for any chance to look after Aaron, and she was forever encouraging Helen to go out and have fun and not just work all hours.

They sipped at their wine. The main course arrived. They said very little. Helen then said: 'Thank you, Mark.'

'It's over, isn't it?' he said.

'You are referring to the case, sir, of course,' she said. She said it with her very best smile, the one that set the county alight. The tears gathered in the corner of her eyes. Mark could not speak. She squeezed his hand. 'Thank you, Mark, it's been lovely and maybe what we needed. It was never going to last, was it?'

'No,' he said. He swallowed at his pizza and half choked. He recovered with a cough.

'Was it something I said?' She was determined to be playful. 'We knew, I knew, you knew it was just a fling. We could have lost our careers.'

'Still could,' he said.

'Naw,' she said. 'Even if Barbara does know, and knowing her, who can tell, she values our case-solving abilities as a team and won't want to lose it – providing of course we are discreet and end it now.'

It was his turn to well up. 'Thank you, sweet, fiery Helen,' he said. 'I wouldn't have missed it for the world. No regrets, none at all.'

They held hands for a long time.

'One final time?' he said.

'Better not, Mark. I think we both said our goodbyes last time.' She giggled. 'It was particularly good, I seem to remember.'

'We both knew then, didn't we?' he said. 'So we made it special? Didn't we?'

'Yes.' They continued trying to eat. The waiter came over and took away the half-finished plates. They ordered an affogato and a tiramisu. They shared them in a last act of intimacy. 'Anyway,' she said, 'I'll be passing my inspector's exams soon and want to move on, and you might even get to be a chief inspector if you pull your finger out.'

'Sounds vaguely vulgar, Sergeant,' he said.

'Get on with it, Mark, get your finger out of the gun, so you can fire your bullets. Mind you, without me to chivvy you, I can't see you making the effort. It'll be fun being your superintendent one day, then your chief super, while you're still solving minor Saturday night assaults and when I'm your chief constable and get my damehood, maybe just possibly I'll invite you as my protection officer.' There was a sad mythological tone to her voice.

'At least we've got the vicar stitched up,' he said.

She brightened. 'We've got the vicar stitched up.'

'I'll get the bill. I'll pay,' he said. He waved to the waiter, who nodded.

'Thank you, kind sir,' she said, 'such decisiveness.' She turned her head away as if to hide her feelings. 'Look,' she said, 'quick, Mark, just look.' She pointed.

Opposite, two figures approached the closed great wooden gates. They had their arms wrapped round each other. One took out a key and let them into the postern gate.

It was the bishop and his archdeacon Babs. He held her hand as he helped her into the secluded cathedral precinct.

'How interesting is that?' asked Helen.

At around the time that Helen and Mark decided to end their affair, Father John's lover came to visit him in custody, as one about to lose him for life. She had spent the day back at work trying to forget their pain by helping others. It was partly effective and only twice did she get into trouble for having her mind elsewhere. Thankfully she did not, by neglect, cause any harm and she did help a lot of patients.

She hurried from her shift and was allowed to see John for twenty minutes just before nine o'clock.

They swore everlasting love to each other no matter what and she told John she believed against all the odds that he was innocent and the true killer would be found.

The call came at 9 p.m. precisely. Gutteridge took it. The reedy voice said: 'What I have to tell you, ah, let me be clearer, the information for you which I possess, and also which I am obliged to tell you, I cannot keep to myself. I have spent the week in Devon and am now able to impart it.' Gutteridge took it to be a stray Monday drunk and was about to put the phone down.

'Don't put the phone down,' said the professor. 'I assure you I am in full possession and this is a true call. I have information to assist your murder enquiry.'

Gutteridge switched on the call machine. 'We should be very interested to hear it, sir. May I take your name, and address?'

He got more than that. Gutteridge could not stop the flow of words. He asked the professor to come at once to the station and it was agreed. Gutteridge called Barbara.

'You, Bill; do you ever go off duty?'

'You know me, ma'am. Gutteridge at the gate. With all these cuts, ma'am, happy to help.'

'Useful overtime too, Bill?' Her smile came down the line. She listened to what the sergeant had to say.

'You did right to call me, Bill, even though it's Monday Music Night. This is serious. It could change everything.'

'Shall I call DS Roper and DI Ellis in, ma'am, to take the official statement? While the witness is feeling co-operative?'

'I'll come myself. Mustn't disturb their last evening together.'

'Ma'am?'

'Oh, nothing. I'll be there in twenty.'

She left Albert and was there in ten. She and DC Debbie Thompson conducted the interview and got a signed and official statement. If Maisy and the professor had separately seen not the vicar, not the bishop, but the archdeacon talking to Fred, it blew the case apart. Barbara decided to keep the vicar in overnight and trace the archdeacon's movements. She felt sorry for Helen and Mark. Just as they thought it was all over, it wasn't. Not the investigation at any rate. She wondered if they realised she knew what was happening between them. Pray they had the wit to end it, before she had to step in. Already she had put her neck out with the chief on their behalf – "leave it with me, sir, best avoid a public scandal," and the chief constable who was very keen on PR agreed.

Professor Tavistock gripped the curved arm of the chair at his writing desk and eased down onto the cushion. He adjusted the lamp with its blue shield and started to write in his journal.

Tuesday 16 May 0130 hours
It is a regrettable necessity that the daily entry one cannot

make during the evening, one must write as soon as possible the following day. We may still count the entry as pertaining to the day of reference, in this case Monday 15 May. I was quite unable to write yesterday evening and being now returned from the police station will write now, while events are fresh in the mind.

I was ushered into the custody suite, and was assured that this was not by way of personal custody, but because it was the best place to receive my testimony which was of great value. The room was spartan as befits the methodical taking of evidence and I approved. It is good to see no unnecessary expense on the public purse. I had the honour of being questioned by a very young lady detective constable and the very senior superintendent, a woman who appeared quite maternal but one must not be deceived by this. One does not reach such a high position without considerable qualities of detection. Thus, though without personal guilt or blame I was circumspect in offering my evidence.

That whereof one has a duty that one must not shirk.

I told them of my strong belief that the person responsible for the regrettable murder was none other than the female cleric, Archdeacon Barbara. This is the evidence I gave.

"I left the church meeting early as I had to go and teach a group of keen young students at The Thane Centre. I am so pleased to find an appetite for philosophy in the most unlikely of places. We have good debates on ethics, such as, what is the difference between the government and the state, and what does each owe to us and we to them? I was returning after a particularly satisfactory session at around ten fifteen, and as it was on my way I passed near to the church and the garden. There I observed a clerical figure in animated conversation with the late young journalist. I did not want to intrude but I saw what transpired. I am sure it was the archdeacon − she was wearing a long skirt, similar to clerical garb, a cross around her neck and hair which was short for a woman perhaps and long perhaps for a man. I say this to give an accurate description.

You may tell me that from a distance it is easy to confuse the archdeacon with the vicar. They are both of similar height, similar build and when wearing clerical garb or long skirts may happen to present a similar appearance. The hair length may indeed appear similar.

I am sure it was the archdeacon. She and the journalist appeared to be in angry exchange of views and I am glad that I left before she attacked him − for I have no doubt it was she who became provoked and angry. It is entirely possible that violence, which I am sure she regrets, was offered after I left.

You may think I am merely trying to shield a much loved parish priest, and I have heard that you hold him in custody. It was I who in Devon last week encouraged him to hand himself in for interview, so that he might definitively answer all your concerns and that the police would become convinced of his innocence. It was only on my return a few hours ago that I was resolved to offer this further testimony, in order to help his case. He did not commit this crime; I hope you will be convinced of *this. Please direct all your enquiries to the archdeacon. I believe that the bishop held out so long in your custody, not to shield his priest but his archdeacon."*

We held detailed discussion and the two officers treated me with that kind of disdained politeness that indicated that they did not believe a word of my testimony. I am sure that they believe they have the true killer in the priest. Nothing I said would shake them. They were civil but one could sense, one could surmise, the irritation these two officers felt about my calling them out so late in the day with my evidence. They asked why I had not spoken earlier. I did apologise but begged them not thereby to discount what I said. They replied that they would indeed give my evidence the weight it deserved.

They thanked me and I left. On reflection I think the police were indeed grateful for my intervention. I am deeply afraid that my intervention has perfected the case against the vicar. Alas, I sensed the hostility of the vicar's partner towards me in Devon. She thinks that I am against him. Nothing can be further from the truth. Alas, I might as well have been against him. Foolish man, I seem to have made things far worse for the father and I await the police proceedings with trepidation. I fear nothing can save him now.

Alas, I had a telephone call from the police some thirty minutes ago. The young woman officer thanked me but said that the superintendent has now made some discreet enquiries without alerting the archdeacon. It is proven that she was away all this time at an archdeacons' conference in Durham. Alas, I had so thought it was she that I saw talking to the journalist. While thinking I was describing the archdeacon, I was describing the vicar perfectly. Hence the police gratitude to me. In trying to save the vicar I have made certain the evidence which damns him. I have unwittingly betrayed him. No wonder his partner knew by her instinct that I would prove to be the enemy of my friend.

Great philosophers warn us not to speak beyond the capabilities of language, and thus distort the case. Alas, by my prattlings I have worsened beyond repair the vicar's case.

Chapter 25

The great cathedral gate was shut. The postern door was shut, and shut tight were the two other entrances cut in the great wall around the precinct. An army would have needed reinforcements to get inside. The door to the bishop's enclosure was shut. Behind its high walls the garden slept. The door to the bishop's porch was shut, and the front door was shut and the door inside that was shut. He sat in his cosy lounge with Archdeacon Babs. Under the glow of a warm standard lamp they nestled a hefty glass of whisky each. On the table by the sofa where they rested together stood a pot of coffee, once refreshed.

'When's Georgina coming home?' said Babs.

'Wednesday morning. You and I have got two evenings together.'

'But not the nights, Edward.'

'But not the nights,' said the bishop. He was sad.

'She knows all about it, Edward. You do realise?'

'Of course she does. But we haven't done anything. She's glad I've got you to lean on. What else is there to know about?' He put his arm round her and she couched her head on his shoulder.

'This,' she said.

'We're too emotionally close even though we haven't—?'

'Exactly that,' she said. 'She thinks you're being emotionally unfaithful.'

'You don't understand,' said Edward. 'It's not that at all, it really isn't.'

''Fraid so,' said Babs. She kissed him on the cheek and then stood. 'Coffee?' she asked. 'And I mean just coffee.'

'I'll take your coffee any time.'

They sat and supped their drinks. They swallowed their last slurp of coffee. Each one cradled their round glass of whisky. The wind started to rattle the old window. The bishop looked at it in irritation, and became lost in thought. He struggled and then came to a decision. He took a large pull on his drink.

'We're human, even if we are religious, we're human and anyway religion is supposed to set us free,' he said. 'Babs, would you like an affair with me? Let's run away together, far away from this.'

'It's been a long time since my last offer,' she smiled. There was the ache of lost youth in her eyes. 'Yes, I would. It would be lovely.'

It was the way she said it. 'But you're not going to, are you?' he said. 'We're not going to.'

'No, dear man, no. We can't, Edward, we just can't. It wouldn't be right. Not with Georgina so sick.'

'Thought not.'

'But thank you so much for asking. You've no idea how much it means. Makes this girl feel good.'

'Regard it as a pastoral offering.' He went across and swept the red curtain across the rattling window.

'Don't be sad, my love. This is all we can have. It's good enough. It's just within the rules. Enjoy. While it lasts.'

'Within the rules.' He snorted. 'Do you think when we get to heaven we shall be allowed to love each other as much as we all want without any harm?'

She kissed him on his cheek. 'Yes, love, it says there's no marriage in heaven – it can't mean there's less love, so there's more, much more, and there's new arrangements.'

'There *are* new arrangements.'

'Edward, stop correcting my grammar when we're talking serious.'

'It's my defence mechanism. *Seriously*. Will we always be friends?'

'Yes, we'll always be that.' She kissed him again, on the forehead. 'And, Edward, thank you, thank you so much for wanting me. Sexy man, you don't know how much it means. Georgina's so lucky to have you.'

'She's given me permission, you know. To satisfy my needs, as she calls it. She said she was sorry she couldn't make me comfortable now, and she didn't mind if some other woman could.'

'She must really love you. How is she? You've nursed her so wonderfully, if only people knew how devoted you've been.'

'I'm afraid she has weeks not months. I wish there was more I could do. At least she's not in pain. The hospice people are wonderful and they encourage her to come home when she can.'

She paced round the room. 'I shall always love you, Ed. If only it were possible.'

'That does not sound very logical. Even to a thick rugby-playing Low-Church bishop like me.'

'Don't, Ed. You are as you are and I can't help—'

'Do you love me enough so I can tell you anything?'

'Yes.'

'You will stand by me, whatever – within the rules, of course?'

'Bugger the rules. What is it, Ed?'

He clasped her and started to cry. 'I've done a terrible, terrible thing. I've been in denial, Babs, but I must tell someone, and it had better be you. Promise me, you will stay with me? Babs?'

She sat, quiet. 'Tell me.'

'It's only because of you I can admit it to myself and only to you can I confess. Not as a priest but as a woman. When I've told you, then you tell me what to do.'

'Edward.' She held his hand and waited. Nothing happened. The window had stopped rattling. She went across and opened the curtain. 'Oh look,' she said, 'how beautiful.'

The cathedral was covered in moonlight like an angel's robe. It was enough to make an atheist weep, that the world was so beautiful without a God, or because this indicated enough of the divine as to make it irresistible. The bishop and the archdeacon stood there by the window hand in hand. It was impossible to detect if this was as man and woman or as priest and priest united in praise.

'Quite, quite lovely, yes,' he said. 'I am so glad to have seen this, one last time. So, so pleased.' He seemed exhausted, and slumped back on the sofa.

She sat with him and waited.

He turned to her. 'What I tell you now is to my friend I trust and love, not to you as a priest. This is full confession, if you like, but you are not bound by the seal of secrecy.

You may advise and do as you wish with what I tell you. Do you understand and are you willing for this burden?'

'I am ready, Edward.'

'When I insisted to the police that I was guilty of no murder either alleged or actual, I was telling the strict truth.' He went back and shut the curtains and returned to her. 'I did not set out to kill that young man and when I met him I did not kill him with intent. However, kill him I did and it was a wicked thing.'

She looked at him as if she had known all along.

'As if that is not enough, I committed a deeper sin. I allowed the police to become convinced that the foolish but somehow wonderful priest, Father John, of St Martha's, one of the best in my diocese, did the murder. I was willing to implicate him by my sly silences, by my half revelations to the police, yes by direct lies, by my innuendo that I was shielding Father John. I was so clever that the police fell for it and the poor man is at this very moment in custody, the police are sure they have got their man, and he will be tried for a murder he did not do and it will be easy to get a jury to convict. He will be in jail for many years.'

'Wicked indeed, if it is as you say.'

'I told myself I was doing it for her. If only I could hold off the disgrace before she dies. I can't afford a trial and be locked away when she needs me so much.'

'Ed, you've been under so much pressure – maybe it's stopped you thinking straight. She can take it, you know. You can't do right by her in doing wrong by John.'

'Full disclosure time now, Babs, my confessor. Remember, I have bared myself to you in this and seek no escape from the results that will flow. First, the release and full restoration of that poor priest John to his rightful place and reputation.'

'Ed, are you sure? Are you quite sure you leave me free to advise you and then do as I think best?'

'Why do you think I like you so much, Babs? I can count on you to do the right thing.'

'Tell me everything, Edward.' Outside the wind had disappeared as if it had never been there. It blows where it wishes and no one can tell where it has gone. There was the stillness of centuries in the close. The cathedral stones heard everything and said nothing.

'That evening after the church meeting, I decided not to stay long but go to the estate where the Wolf Gang live and see if I could seek them out and rescue the poor young man they had taken off in triumph. I wanted to tell them how wrong they were and to have a conversation with the journalist and ask him to treat my priests with respect. I like journalists; they do a good job even if they are self-righteous and judgemental from time to time.

I was delayed by Maisy who wanted to know if I fancied some patterns knitted for my Easter robes and the professor engaged with me on a point of logic for a full eight minutes. He wanted to know if I was convinced by his answer to the old why-does-God-allow-suffering conundrum. I only got away by saying I would think and pray about it, and get back to him.

As I left there were only the two churchwardens and Father John left with the council officials anxious to set up their stalls. I said goodbye and went in search of the gang. I did not manage to find them after much searching and there was no sign of young Fred. I gave up and drove back via the church premises to check if there were any clues there.

Imagine my surprise when I did find Fred in the church porch. He was in a weak state and had a head wound on his forehead. He explained to me how the gang had dumped him in the pile of filth and as they did so he hit his head on a rock hidden in it. They rolled him about in the muck for a while, then left. He was feeling dizzy but came back to sit in the porch a bit, recover, then go home. He told me that he had just had a conversation with Father John who tried to help him, but Fred wanted to stay a bit. He thought that Father John had gone off either to get his wife, who is a nurse, or to phone for an ambulance to come and get him.

We got in conversation, and I must say for a man who had just been through all he had, he was impressive. He was lucid and we had a good talk. We might have become friends if alas my old impetuous rugby ways had not come over me. I'll tell you the conversation as best I can remember it and then tell you what happened next.'

She sat as still as the elements outside. She did not flick away the bit of blue wool she had noticed on her red woolly sweater.

'We had a big debate. I won't quote it all. The journalist, poor thing, seemed to be very tired. "Look, Bishop," he said, "I've already had this discussion with your colleague earlier this evening. He said there were three forces fighting it out, the government, church and the press with social media. I said only the media protect us."

I said, "But they can cut people's lives in shreds, the media set howling mobs at people. No one dares protest against media orthodox thinking, and protect the victims."

"Oh stop exaggerating, Bishop. Truth at all costs, Bishop, and it comes at a price."

"You really think I am a fool, don't you? You think the church doesn't care about the truth as much as you, silly little man?"

I was surprised at Fred's reaction. He smiled. "Let's just agree to differ, Bishop. We're both as you say in the business of telling stories, to give a shape to life – only my pretensions are not as high as yours, the press merely revels in other people's sins, you claim to cure people and take them to heaven."

"And," he said, "all these gimmicks or lack of them are irrelevant. What people need is to feel loved in church, get a warm welcome. As long as you get grumpy people in church scolding others or showing resentment at them disturbing your cosy club, or making them believe things they can't, or making impossible demands, you'll never get people coming in."

I was weary. It was enough preaching from him. "So be it. Come, let's shake hands and make up."

He surprised me again. I was offering him the branch of friendship, well it seemed like a whole olive grove, but his mood seemed to shift. Maybe it was his head wound. "No, Bishop, not just yet. I offered to be friends with the vicar, no conditions, simple handshake. He refused, so now it's my turn. Your priest says he won't shake hands till I surrender and go to church, then he will. So if you don't mind, Bishop, I won't shake hands with you, not till your priest and I shake hands in a way that doesn't mean my surrender. I must stay free. Only an independent press keeps us free, tells the truth, and guides our life."

I poked Fred in his chest. "You pompous little idiot. Who do you think you are? Shake hands now, you silly man. You're not right, you're not thinking straight."

"No, Bishop, no handshake till I make proper friends with your priest. Then you get your turn." He yawned in my face.

He was insufferable. Who was he to refuse my handshake of goodwill? I am afraid I took action; one I shall regret all my life. I lost it. I think, Babs, after all my years of sucking up to the press, I'd finally had enough of those reptiles. I yelled, "What to you is an amusing little story is someone else's career or loss of marriage or relationship or their children, and feelings and work and happiness and mental health and reputation. Who are you to play with people's lives, you smug, self-righteous rat?"

Thank God I had left my crosier in the car.

The old rugby aggression swung in, the violence I controlled in my playing days and in my church career. I pushed him hard in the chest. Alas, I forgot how tall and strong I still am. My cross swung as I laid into him. I pushed Fred across the porch. I flung him against the wall. There was a sickening crash as Fred lost his balance, and staggered. He fell and cracked his head against the jagged stonework. He slid down and was silent.

I came to my senses. "Oh, my dear chap," I said, "I am so sorry. I lost it, I am so sorry. I can usually control my strength. Let me help you. We'll get you to the palace and patch you up."

Fred said nothing. He was limp as a garden sack. I must have panicked at this stage. "Don't move," I said, "I'll go and get help." Fred lay there then stirred. I decided to stay and phone for help, but he saw me and told me to go away. He staggered into the garden. It was the last I saw him. I think he must have fallen into the manure pile again.

I am a coward. He was in trouble and I let him shoo me away. I should have insisted and should have helped. I decided to avoid trouble and not phone. I walked away. I was afraid of getting the blame. No. I'm deluding myself. I was angry and didn't care.

I didn't kill him directly, but I did by accident and gross neglect and I hereby confess and am willing to face whatever I have to. Oh, if only he had shaken my hand he would not have died.'

He broke down and wept in her lap. 'Oh, Babs, what shall I do? What have I done?'

She stroked his hair, and let his tears fall. 'My dear boy,' she said. 'Do you really need me to tell you? Do you really?'

They remained for some time as his sobs subsided. 'No, love,' he said. 'All is clear. Thank you for listening to me, Babs, thank you for being a true friend. My life is ruined. At least I still have one, while that poor young man – oh, what have I done?'

'What you did, you did in defence of the church – but Ed, what a dreadful method. These last two years of faithful devotion to Georgina were wonderful. Ed, you're under so much strain and nobody knew, you hid it, and you haven't been right for some time now. I should have helped you more. I didn't want to get too involved with you and it's so sad, here we are.'

'Pray for me, Babs, pray for me, I need strength for what I must do. I don't think I could have faced this without your help. As usual, you've helped me face things and to do the right thing. Finally.' He put his head in her lap. 'Thank you, Babs, thank you. You understand.'

She smiled like a sad Madonna. 'It's our last evening. Come, Edward, and may the Lord forgive me, let's go and say prayers together in my bedroom.'

He roared with laughter. 'So that's what Christian girls call it these days.'

Chapter 26

The next morning, the bishop woke at 6 a.m. He and Babs read Morning Prayer in the old version together, spoke a little and had a light breakfast. They each had a private conversation with the bishop's chaplain, and no one else will ever know what was said. The three took Communion. At 8 a.m. he walked by himself into the police station and asked to see his previous interrogators. For once it was not Gutteridge at the desk.

By nine, the formalities began. The bishop was dressed in a lounge suit, with his purple vest, clerical collar and his pectoral cross. Gone was the pompous prelate. Here was the purple of penitence, of a man who had besmirched his office, though not by design. His zeal and his fear had led him into wickedness and he was truly sorry. He meant the contrast between his clothing and his sin to be painful.

The original cast was there, and this time, the bishop told the plain unvarnished truth, with no inward or outward reservations, using language in its normal meaning. He confessed the whole thing and by eleven o'clock the police had a watertight case against him. Helen found herself in tears. Oh, what a pity, a good man gone so wrong.

Barbara was harder. She set her face as flint. The killing might, just might, be seen as a dreadful accident, but then not to get help which might have saved the young man; that she felt was a mixture of lack of self-control and negligence worthy of prosecution. And then to hide what he knew, and then, then, to blame his priest! She would talk to the prosecutor on whether that amounted to perversion of the course of justice. He should not have tried so wickedly to pin the blame on his innocent subordinate. Barbara decided to ask the prosecutor for a murder charge.

The bishop remained in custody and did not ask for bail. He was placed in a regulation cell, and allowed his Bible to read. Mr Smith advised him and left.

The police team worked hard on the paperwork and the station was unusually quiet that day. By late afternoon Barbara had had enough. She stormed into the open-plan floor where Mark and Helen had their half-offices and swept them away.

'Come,' she said, 'we're going to the park. We'll get a cup of tea at the Caff.'

They left the station and went over the new pedestrian crossing provided for the mass of new students at the nearby new students' hostel. This led them to the front of the fire station, a source of irritation to Barbara, who thought it had a nicer face with proper flint stones. They took the underpass and emerged near the bus station, crossed over another zebra crossing and were in the park. They walked under the glowing May trees, green and innocent. The flowers gave them a good afternoon. Some parents had collected their children, who were playing as if they would never grow old.

Mark bought plastic mugs of tea and some crisps. They sat near the wooden maze where children played with dinosaurs that lurked behind the next wall.

'Congratulations, ma'am,' said Helen. 'You were right about the bishop. Mark and I were sure it was the vicar, and we were wrong.' She sipped her tea. 'Your instinct was better than our considered judgement.'

'Well thank you, kind lady,' said Barbara. 'Even an old-timer like me has doubts and likes to turn out right.' Helen hoped she said it with a twinkle. One took one's life in one's hands when offering praise to Ma'am. 'No, seriously, Helen,' she continued, 'I thought this time, Barbara, you've blown it. What must those kids think of my hunch, no real evidence, just a feeling? Just what they warn us against at college. Get a grip, girl, I told myself. Otherwise the chief constable will get me at last and I'll be leaving my colleagues such a poor example.'

Helen and Mark glanced at each other. It was rare to hear confessional from Barbara. So even she had self-doubt.

'Ma'am, I still think the vicar bears some blame.'

'Make your case, Mark. I'm listening. It doesn't do for me to gloat.'

If Helen could have done so safely, she would have squeezed Mark's hand.

'The vicar was the first who met and saw that Fred was injured. If he had not been so weak, he would have insisted Fred got taken away for treatment and the death would not have occurred. He should have used his mobile phone to summon help, or if he didn't have it on him, run back to the hall to phone or do anything, anything to make sure Fred was looked after. He was weak and wet, that vicar. I still hold him responsible. It's no good only blaming the bishop for not getting help when the vicar did just the same.'

'No Good Samaritan there then, eh, Mark? Two priests walked on by.'

The reference was lost on Mark. He barged on. 'So really, ma'am, Helen and I are right – the vicar bears some responsibility for the death. If he'd done his duty, there would have been no Fred there for the bishop to meet and cause the death of.'

Helen waited for the explosion.

Barbara placed her plastic mug gently on the warm grass. The children played on, with only dinosaurs to fear. Fond single mums, dads with custody, two-parent units, groups of friends, au pair girls watched their children carefully from a distance.

'You are quite right, Mark,' said Barbara. 'You do well to rebuke me. I'm sorry. I did think of that. Alas, we are only legal agents, thank goodness. We have legally nothing to charge the vicar with. How far back do you go in the chain of blame? I don't like blame. What makes the vicar so weak and yet so wacky and successful? Leave it, Mark, leave it to moral philosophers.' She laughed. 'That's one for the resident philosopher of that church.' Her laugh was heavy. 'Oh, what a world, Mark. We just have to plod on best as we can. When all is said – it was the bishop who lost his temper and struck the fatal push which smashed Fred's head. He did not get help when he saw the damage he had done. The vicar merely left thinking he could do no more, we can't always interfere. Come on, the wind's starting to make me feel cold. Back to the dull paperwork.'

Helen could not resist. 'I don't think the vicar was at all weak. He saw it was only a graze to Fred's forehead, there was no need to fuss and he left Fred in peace.'

'Thank you for your support, Helen.' This time Barbara's laugh was light-hearted. 'Still, better leave it now. Poor Mark'll think the women are ganging up against him. Thanks for the tea and crisps.' It was all she could do not to give her colleagues a hug.

It was a juicy scandal. Hillford down the centuries had had five bishops executed, killed or murdered in unsavoury circumstances. Never had Hillford enjoyed – as *The Daily Render* called it – a bishop who had done the killing. The editor of that newspaper had his story. He congratulated himself for his wise waiting for the real deal. He personally wrote a long article in praise of his wonderful young journalist who paid the ultimate price in defence of press freedom.

The main broadsheets' sniffle left the story alone beyond the basic facts. One had a long feature asking whether it was not now time to reconsider disestablishing the Church of England. The tabloids wrote along the lines of "well, this is just the latest in a long list of scandals we have sadly come to expect in the church, but don't forget it does some good work."

The BBC gave a brief and strictly correct account of events and made it deliberately dull. The local independent television showed the police briefing and were given a bland résumé. Few local people were willing to give an interview. The weatherworn reporter who did the outside broadcasts gave a potted two-minute description of the church and city. His voice ended on a falling cadence: "In its long history Hillford has seen worse and no doubt will see worse again."

It was a two-day wonder for *The Daily Render*. On the third day, the paper dropped the story in favour of a famous actress who married a Nobel Prize winner three times her age.

The local editor produced a superb edition. He repeated the fine obituary of Fred Vestal, the best young journalist of a generation. The editor praised the police and featured a long article on St Martha's and its valuable work for the community. They respected the wish of Father John not to give an interview. They wrote a lyrical article on Hillford, this lovely old city which has seen so much in its famous history and is still unbeaten.

It was the editor's swansong. He took early redundancy and thereafter wrote freelance articles and became a respected tutor on the media studies course of a local university.

That morning, as the bishop and Babs made their separate confession to the chaplain, Father John woke with a feeling of dread. He was facing a charge of murder. In a sense he agreed. He felt more guilt than he could express over leaving the poor young man with his head wound and not getting help. He held himself to blame for Fred's death. Doubtless what had happened after he had left Fred to his own devices, was Fred had become ill and dizzy, wandered around, maybe suffered a little stroke and fallen into the sludge pile never to wake as he died by suffocation. That must be it.

He had failed his parish, he had failed Katie and he had failed his bishop. He had failed his calling. This was a just punishment.

He seemed to hear Katie's voice. "Don't be so daft,

John, stop being self-indulgent. Don't give up. I told you I'll stand by you and I will."

He said his prayers and pulled the thin blanket over him. The next thing he knew was a young policewoman at his side. She was not unsympathetic. 'Drink it while it's hot. Best brew for ten forces around,' she said cheerfully. 'Toast, too, with jam, lucky man! Sorry I can't pull the curtains.'

She didn't sound sarcastic. She looked as young as a girl in Year 10. 'Thanks,' he murmured. 'What time is it?'

'Half eight; we let you sleep in.'

She hovered as if wanting conversation. Though he was not accustomed to wake in custody, John felt that this was an unusual procedure. She sat on the chair as he enjoyed his frugal breakfast. She seemed ill at ease.

'Just to let you know, your bishop appeared just now. He told my colleague he had something important to tell us.' She put her hand on her face. 'I shouldn't have told you that. Just thought you'd, sort of, like to know. Maybe he wants to give you some advice. Hope he helps you.' She felt sorry for the vicar, and a little disturbed that someone who should be on the good side was in this state.

She took away the mug and the plate, and left John wondering. It was kind of the bishop to visit him in trouble, but why was he taking so long to appear?

No one came near Father John all morning, apart from a beaming Gutteridge who brought him a steaming mug of coffee, and a chocolate biscuit in a red wrapper. John made some joke about the service being good in this hotel and they leave you alone in peace.

'Maybe you won't be staying here for long,' said

Gutteridge gnomically. He winked and said, 'Bear up, lad, things are looking up.'

John knew better than to give in to false hope. They were clearly a nice bunch who were doing their best to be kind within the strict limits of their duty.

At noon, Chief Superintendent Barbara herself appeared like an angel of deliverance. She beamed. 'You're free, Vicar,' she said. 'Sorry I can't provide an earthquake. This place could do with a shake-up.'

John was too fraught to believe her. This was too much of a miracle. He saw Barbara nodding in encouragement. He smiled.

Helen and Mark observed. Barbara and the vicar seemed to be singing private songs to each other.

Barbara gently put her arm on his shoulder. 'It's true, John,' she said. 'This morning your bishop came in early and we spent the morning interviewing him. He has confessed to the crime and we have charged him. You're in the clear, Father John, and you may go.'

John slumped on his bed. 'Get Katie,' he said. 'I want Katie.'

He was lucky. It was her half day. She flew like a bullet out of the hospital to her car then drove as a careful actuary to collect him. The police team who had grown to like the vicar gave him a friendly wave and asked him to say one for them. By mid-afternoon Katie and John were sipping tea at home.

They sat easily in each other's company. They did not say much; that time would come later, floods and floods of conversation and absorbing all that had happened. Today it was enough to be together, together without any storm to tear them apart. It was enough.

Katie went into the kitchen to make a pot of coffee, for a change. She found some old birthday cake wrapped in foil, which was still fresh. She put it on her best dish, the one with flowers twined round an old cottage. She placed the coffee pot, two matching mugs, milk, spoons, two forks, two knives, plates, napkins and the cake on a tray and brought it into the main room. She planned later to get proper pastries. She opened a bottle of prosecco and a carton of apple juice.

The doorbell went. It was as welcome as the ninth cold sales phone call of the day which began by asking her who she was; and if she was in good health.

'Damn,' said John. He sprang up with unexpected vigour. 'I'll get rid of them.'

Half a minute later he ushered Archdeacon Babs into the room.

She took off her coat without invitation. 'How are you, how are you both? Isn't it lovely news for you? I felt I had to come and tell you how pleased I am. John, I never thought for a minute you did it and I'm so glad it's over. Look, I've brought four Danish pastries, one each and one spare. I hope you don't mind.' She saw Katie looking at her. 'I hope you don't mind? Felt I just had to come. Actually, I need the company.'

'I'll get us another plate,' said Katie.

'Oh, what a shame about Edward, such a shame. He didn't mean to do it, you know, he's a good man, he's not a killer.' Babs collapsed in a chair.

Katie put her arms round Babs and gave her a tissue. 'I'm sure they'll sort it all out.'

'What do you think will happen to him?' asked Babs.

John barged in. 'What would have happened to me, if the bishop had not owned up; maybe a bit less. He'll plead guilty, get credit for that and I imagine will get five or six years, serve half of that for good behaviour.'

Katie added, 'If he's lucky enough to get an atheist judge, it'll be less.'

'What difference does that make?' In spite of her upset, Babs was curious. 'How can that possibly make any difference?'

'Don't you see, Babs?' said John. 'An atheist judge thinks religion's all nonsense, so he'll go out of his way to show he's not biased when he sentences a bishop. He probably quite likes the heritage Olde England side of the dear old C of E as well, so he won't want to rock the boat too much.'

'Whereas a Christian judge will feel it keenly that a bishop has let the side down and want to make an example, in order to purge things a bit.'

'You school me well,' said Babs, in a humble spirit they had not seen before.

Katie poured two glasses of bubbly wine and said, 'Cheers.' She filled a wine glass with apple juice for herself. She got more plates and cutlery. She shared out the pastries. She and John wolfed down half of their share before noticing that Babs was not eating. She had not touched her glass.

'What do you really think will happen to him?' she asked. She flicked back her hair, as she did in the days of her youth.

Katie saw. It was sudden light on a midnight moor. 'Oh, Babs, I see. Do you love him very much?'

The archdeacon wept as she had not done since she lost her first love in her third year. 'He's a good man,' she said. 'He looks rough and so strong he doesn't need help, and he gives out so much looking after others but he needs someone, and he's lovely and – well, he didn't mean to do such a dreadful, terrible thing, and he's suffering terribly, no matter he won't say. How is he going to cope?'

Katie wrapped her arms around Babs. 'Shush, there, darling, shush, we'll work something out.'

Babs disentangled and took her glass of bubbly wine. She downed it in one swallow. 'Sorry, so sorry,' she said, 'I came here to share your joy and to say how wonderful it is that John is cleared and life goes on as normal and the nightmare's over. And here I go acting stupid. Sorry.' She took the bottle and refilled their glasses.

'I shall visit him round the prisons, you know. Do you think they'll let him stay in a nice open prison? He's not a violent man and he won't ever do such a thing again. Maybe he can be a sort of chaplain to the prisoners.'

'Babs, I think that is more than likely.'

'I'll have to leave. I can find a nice country parish in the Dales or somewhere. I'll visit Edward every month, or when I can. Georgina is sure to divorce him now, and one day—'

John said gently, 'Georgina will not, you know. She loves him and even if she didn't need him so much – think, Barbara, think. Marriage through thick and thin, Babs.'

The arrow pierced to her bone. She sipped her wine and thought. The old strength reasserted itself. 'Yes, yes. She'll stick by him. Strange, you know, it might even make her more determined to survive a bit longer. Oh, what am

I saying? We move on. Maybe he can be a college lecturer one day. I can't see him becoming a monk.' She laughed. 'Not our Edward.' She gripped her glass, in meditation. 'As for you, John, it's quite clear what you must do.'

'I know,' said John sadly. 'I will resign and seek another place. I can't stay here. I suppose I give my resignation to you, Babs. Ironic. I might get somewhere nice in the West Country. People won't know me and won't remember what has happened here. Yes, nice clean start.'

'Not for that unlucky young man, eh?' said Babs.

'Not that poor young man. The least I owe to him is to give up this church.'

'Don't be wet, John. He couldn't destroy you in life. Don't let him destroy you in death.'

'I haven't the heart to carry on. As for what he called my stunts, and so did the bishop, well, let him win. I'll be straight as a bat in future. Sound as an old church bell, and no gimmicks.'

Barbara flared up. 'You good man, that's just what he wouldn't want. You owe him nothing. He tried to damage your ministry with his stupid articles and now you let him walk all over you. Don't do it.'

Katie decided to get involved. Babs was not going to steal her man, even if she wanted Georgina's. 'Quite right, John, no option, got to continue.'

'See, John, Katie thinks so too. You must carry on. Gimmicks, family friendly, fun as usual. Don't let the press destroy you. John, you really mustn't, mustn't, give up. Not after all this pain and sacrifice.'

'Face it,' said John, 'he's won. He's won and I have no heart to carry on.'

'Talk to him, Katie,' said Babs. 'For once I can't think what to do. Tell him take his time, get better, then just do it.'

Katie spoke as if John was not there. 'It was you, wasn't it, Barbara, who persuaded the bishop to hand himself over? Without you he would not have done it and my man would have taken Edward's punishment. You sacrificed your love – for us?'

Babs savagely poured another glass of prosecco. Her hand shook and wine spilt on the carpet.

'You could have got away with it. You could have persuaded Edward to stay silent and go away with you as part of the deal? You didn't. Oh Babs, Babs, what a wonderful woman you are.'

Babs fiercely stabbed her pastry and rammed it into her mouth.

'You brought us together, Babs, now you've kept John and me together. And you gave up your chance of happiness for our sakes. Babs, Babs, how can we ever, how can we ever thank—' She gave a passionate hug to the passive archdeacon.

'I could have had him, you know, I could have kept him, you know. But I had to – I do love him, you know.'

And the raven-haired Barbara wept once more as she had not done for anyone since her third year, she who could have had a new boyfriend every term and was still a beautiful woman and so faithfully clung on to the lost love of her dreams, she wept until she fell limp in Katie's arms and was cried out. She accepted half a box of tissues. 'Oh so unseemly, such a scene,' she said, 'not quite what one expects of an archdeacon.'

'Thank you, dear,' said Katie, 'thank you. John and I will bear you gratitude till the day we die.'

'Well, in that case, tell John to show it by sticking to his ministry in this place and staying true to his vision.'

'I can't say how grateful we are, Barbara,' said John. 'We can't thank you enough. I still don't see how I can carry on. Fred was right, my methods don't look good. I can't forget I had some hand in his death. I owe it to him to make up in some small way. If he didn't like my church and my methods, maybe he was right, maybe—'

'Oh, stick it, John. Just do as I say for once.' Barbara shook her raven hair at him and it was not in flirtation. 'Tell him, Katie. Why won't he listen? We've both got more sense in our little toe than he has in his whole body.'

There was a thundering knock on the front door. 'Just what we need,' said John and went to see who it was. He was shaken as he brought her into the lounge.

It was Karen. She was carrying a large bouquet. It contained a glorious mix of roses, forget-me-not, hazel flower and syringa.

'For you,' she said. 'I'm pleased for you. I had to come round and see you.' She and Katie embraced. 'The vicar turned out to be genuine when he was so kind to me in the garden. Not a crazy man at all.'

Katie bustled about looking for a vase. If she had not, she would have dissolved.

'Doesn't take long for word to get round,' said John in wonder at the ways of a small city. He had no idea what else to say.

Katie placed the full vase on the window ledge. 'Thank

you, Karen, they're lovely, it's such a pleasure to see you. This must be really hard. It's lovely of you to visit us.'

'It's nothing,' said Karen, 'you were kind to me when I really needed it. I am so glad it wasn't John.' She was twisting her hands as she spoke.

'Hello, I'm Babs, John's archdeacon, his sort of church boss, though we don't think of it like that. You must be—'

'Karen, widow of the murdered man; nice to meet you. I hear the bishop did it.'

Babs winced. 'Nice to meet you, Karen. I can't say how sorry we are over this awful thing. Yes, well, yes, Bishop Edward is accused. We'll see what the trial says.'

Karen looked. She understood. 'He's your boss, I see. It must be very hard for you.'

'My boss, colleague and friend.' She flicked back her hair, black as Bess.

In that moment Karen read the whole thing. What a wicked bishop. She fought back the rage. How dare this woman love him?

'Forgive me,' said Babs. 'One day, if it is possible, forgive him too his moment's lapse.'

Karen glared at her. 'Perhaps. One day. Maybe we are both victims.'

'Your loss is infinitely worse,' said Babs. 'I wish I could help.' She hesitated, and held out her hand.

'OK, not your fault. Sorry, mustn't blame you.' Karen embraced Babs.

Babs whispered to her. 'He stood up even to the bishop.' She took Karen into the kitchen and told her more of Fred's last conversation.

Karen's face was shining as they rejoined the others.

'Look,' said Katie. 'Babs must have known. She brought four pastries, so there's still one left for you, Karen. Let's have a feast!'

'It's a *Danish* pastry,' said John, helpfully. 'How suitable is that?'

The three women burst into merriment. The ways of man could still make them laugh.

'What?' said John.

They made more coffee and found more cakes. They chatted as if their biggest worry was where to go on holiday.

It could not last. 'So what now, John?' asked Babs. 'You still won't persist in this nonsense of leaving us? Just when things are going so well?'

'Were going so well, were, Archdeacon. Don't try to stop me. I don't see how I can stay any longer. He's won, with apologies to Karen, apologies, but Fred has succeeded, he's ended my ministry here. How can I stay after all this? People will always say there's no smoke without fire.'

Karen slowly put her plate on the table. She wiped crumbs from her mouth and gathered the crumbs from her dress. She swept them on the carpet and made no attempt to hide this. Oh dear, thought Katie, she's very angry. John, what have you done? Oh Lord, she's going to let fly. Well, he deserves it.

Karen turned her face with its long blonde fringe towards John. 'I understand, dear John,' she said, 'how guilty you must feel. I do, even though we all know you did not cause my poor husband's death. My wonderful Fred died for his principles. I understand, believe me, none better, how much his criticisms of you must have hurt and made you want to run away. Believe me, I'm his wife, I know how he could be.'

Katie waited. She waited for the "but". Babs gripped the arms of her seat.

'Let me tell you this, Father John. If you are talking of letting Fred win, or somehow making up to him with the little power you have still to help him, let me tell you this. The best way you can honour Fred and make it up to him is to stay just where you are, make your church flourish, and give the likes of Fred something big to really bite their teeth into.

Stay strong; don't you get it? Fred only bothered to write about people and things he deep down admired. He didn't bother with things he thought were pointless. Father John, take it as a huge compliment, he liked you and if only he'd lived to tell the tale – well, you and he would have become great friends and he would have written nice things about you – from time to time, as well of course as teasing you without mercy. I know. I was his wife.'

'Oh,' said John. 'Oh.'

'Well?' she asked.

'Well?' asked Babs.

'I'll have to think about it. If you put it like that.'

'He'll stay,' said Katie.

Faced with the combined might of Babs, Katie and Karen, he had no choice. He was staying.

'Thank you,' said Karen. 'That means a lot. I couldn't bear it if I thought that Fred's legacy was to destroy your church, or you. I can go away in peace.' She gave John a shrewd look. 'By the way, I'm so proud to hear that Fred refused the bishop's handshake, out of principle. It was kind of you to say the same of yours. I choose to believe you, Vicar. Thousands wouldn't.'

John choked on some pastry.

'It was a kindness, Vicar,' repeated Karen. She laughed. 'And I am glad to be kind to you.'

'What are your plans, dear?' asked Babs.

'I'll go back home and stay with my parents till the baby is born, and a bit beyond. I'll finish my qualifications and get a good job. Maybe Tobias and I will get back together again – we had a thing going at school, and sadly, he and his girlfriend broke up some months ago. Who knows?' She did not seem sorry about Tobias's romantic break-up.

Dark shadows flitted past the window and were gone before anyone had the chance to see what this was. It grew dark outside, as if the sun was hiding its modesty behind the clouds.

A loud whispering sounded from outside. 'They won't want to see us. It's not logical, why would they want to see us at this stage? Let's come back tomorrow.'

A loud voice pierced the old oak door. 'I'm going in. Come or not as you wish.' There was a huge banging on the door.

'I think I know who this is.' John smiled and went to see. It was Maisy, the professor and the major. Maisy held the biggest cake yet presented at the vicarage. It had cream and strawberries falling from every angle. 'I thought we might celebrate with this,' she said.

'Come in, come in,' said John. 'Let's have a party.'

Chapter 27

The trial took place at the end of July. The streets outside Hillford Crown Court were littered with TV cameras from several countries, excited commentators talking to their studio newsreader, journalists, photographers. They liked this little city and were hoping to enjoy a nice long stay. The restaurants were known to be superb and the accommodation really not bad at all. The famous cathedral was a delight and how exciting that its bishop was on trial for murder. With a bit of luck it would drag on and a pleasant time be had by all.

The bishop was unlucky. He had the fiercest judge on the circuit, a lapsed believer who held the clergy to the stratospheric standards which he had abandoned. Bishop Edward had recovered enough to accept the advice of his barrister, the best for seven counties round. He pleaded not guilty to murder, with a clear conscience.

The prosecution had decided to go all out for a charge of murder. They were punting on a manslaughter verdict and hoped for voluntary not involuntary to be awarded. Either way it looked like an easy win. It would help the statistics.

To everyone's astonishment, the bishop was found not guilty of murder, not guilty of any form of manslaughter, not guilty of anything. The jury were merciful, as they understood how easily anyone could fail so horribly under such a terrible concatenation of circumstances. They did not regard the bishop's shove or his undoubted failure to get medical help for Fred as amounting to culpable homicide. They were deeply swayed by the deep devotion of the bishop to his dying wife, and her need for him in these last days. The judge scowled at the defence barrister for so artfully introducing this as highly relevant to the defence – the bishop was understandably and so lovingly under such stress he could not think straight, this good man meant no harm – and was powerless to silence these pleas. The judge harrumphed. In his final words to the court he muttered something about British justice moving in a mysterious way its wonders to perform.

The judge wished Bishop Edward 'Godspeed', and not everyone thought he was being satirical. Later, the judge told his mistress, a human rights lawyer, that he was looking forward to giving the bishop seven years, one each for the seven sins. That meant, in effect, forty months, with parole less two months for time served on remand, very symbolic also, did she not think? His mistress told the judge he was an ass, and the jury had more sense in their little digit than he in all his body and she should know.

'Plus,' she added, 'legal is not the only form of punishment. That man will have regrets all his life.'

The press quickly dropped the whole matter. *The Daily Render* muttered something about how right it was that they had brought this matter to the nation's attention, and the freedom of the press being the freedom of England and how glad they were to see justice prevail and this good, poor suffering man so correctly acquitted, and able now to say farewell to his dear wife in peace. And yes, in spite of appearances, the church was doing a fine job.

It was all over, of course. Edward had no heart to remain as local bishop even if it could be thought advisable. Supporters who emerged in droves said they always knew he was innocent. They argued that he was guilty of nothing, so what possible case was there for him to leave his see? Indeed he had shown such devotion to his poor, sick wife, and had not told anyone. Indeed he had suffered so much and learnt so much in these final days that he was well on the path to a saintly ministry.

It cut no ice with him. He wanted to leave and find a quiet parish somewhere calm where he could look after peaceful parishioners and become a sort of Parson Woodforde. In the meantime he had to stay to look after Georgina. They were together a few more months. One lovely day in October when the trees were showing ravishing reds and golden greens, she died in total peace in his arms.

Bishop Edward retired to a parish near the Lake District. He lectured occasionally in Manchester and became well-loved for his deep understanding of ordinary life. He enjoyed and was well versed in the television soap operas and from time to time argued with people in the pub. He lived in a sort of healing purgatory of calm. From time to time he would have lunch with Babs in London. She remained exactly where she was in Hillford.

Two years later they were married in Hillford Cathedral crypt by Father John. Two years after that she became Bishop of Barrington. He adored being her chaplain and consort at the small cathedral. It became a famous partnership and they never changed nor wished to change their place.

Inspector Mark Ellis was given a severe lecture by William. 'I hope you've ended that foolish affair, Brother.'

'How do you know that?' said Mark. They were sitting in the restaurant at County Hall. No one would take any notice of them there.

William grumbled about the lunch. 'Really,' he said, 'they do quite a fair roast on Wednesdays and this is not entirely ruined. But you'd have thought they could provide a decent Carménère. You can't get anything remotely like a proper drink here.'

'I should think not, William,' said Mark. 'We can't have councillors rolling drunk around County Hall.'

'Why not, little puritan?' said William. 'Has no one ever told you of the Persians, who got drunk to make a decision? If they still felt the same way when they became sober, then they knew it was a good one.'

'Some of the decisions from County Hall feel drunk enough already, Big William.'

'Precisely, dear boy – just like your little fling. I can't keep it from Victoria much longer, you know. It spoils my dinner when I'm with you both. It's not for me to tell her, but it makes me feel mean. Stop it now, little brother, I beg. Do not adultery commit; advantage rarely comes of it.'

'Who's being the puritan now? It does some people good.'

'Go and sort your marriage, Mark.' He attacked his dinner and spilt some gravy on the table. He placed a huge lump of roast potato in his mouth. 'I say, this is not at all unbearable.'

There was a sad edge to the banter. They munched on in gloomy solitude.

'All right,' said Mark. 'We ended it last month.'

'Delighted, dear fellow, delighted. Never should have started it. Still as that good bishop of yours would have said, joy over one sinner that repenteth or is it better to have loved and lost or what do they say these days?'

Mark knew he was thinking of Clare.

'Sorry,' said Mark. 'Do you think Vicky knows, and do you think we can mend everything?'

'Know nothing of these things, little brother. People write vast books about them. Stick with her, dear boy, she's the best. Where will I go for my roast dinner if you separate?' He considered. 'OK, Brother, only piece of advice. Take her for a nice long holiday, soon; get to know each other again. When did you last have a holiday, just the two of you?'

Mark wondered how he was going to manage the whole matter. Solving murders might turn out to be easier.

Life resumed as normal at St Martha's. There were just as many gimmicks, and the people never knew when they might occur, so they came along most Sundays in the hope. He made sure the services were warm and friendly. He took to heart the words of Fred: people want warmth and love much more than gimmicks; that's why they will come, for warmth and love and stories with meaning.

The church flourished. He and Katie were married there in the September. Babs conducted the service. The place was packed and the happy pair went to Devon for their honeymoon. A few months later they had a little girl and called her Barbara Karen.

John had a warm handshake for everyone. He overdid it slightly and did not care. He shook hands at the start of the service as people came in, he shook hands during the Peace, he shook hands in the vestry after the service, he rushed out and shook hands with everyone as they left, he shook hands with people who stayed for coffee and he shook hands with casual visitors to the church.

Most of his work was done among people who never came to church. Most people never knew.

He continued the annual washing of feet. People adored it and the crowds were larger every year. There was no need for gimmicks. Maisy was always first in the queue. She loved even more his warm, manly handshake, which after all she could enjoy several times each week.